D1439086

90710 000 484 134

WITH TEETH

ALSO BY KRISTEN ARNETT

Mostly Dead Things

WITH
TEETH

Kristen Arnett

corsair

CORSAIR

First published in the US in 2021 by Riverhead
First published in the UK in 2021 by Corsair

13 5 7 9 10 8 6 4 2

Copyright © 2021 by Kristen Arnett

The moral right of the author has been asserted.

A CIP catalogue record for this book
is available from the British Library.

HB ISBN: 978-1-4721-5649-5
TPB ISBN: 978-1-4721-5650-1

Printed and bound in Great Britain by Clays Ltd, Elcograf S.p.A.

Papers used by Corsair are from well-managed forests
and other responsible sources.

Corsair
An imprint of
Little, Brown Book Group
Carmelite House
50 Victoria Embankment
London EC4Y 0DZ

An Hachette UK Company
www.hachette.co.uk

www.littlebrown.co.uk

For Willie & Vivian

teeth

TEETH

And for Mattie, again

The truth does not change according to
our ability to stomach it.

—FLANNERY O'CONNOR

Winter

The man took her son's hand and walked casually toward the playground exit.

Sammie had left him on the swing set. He'd just learned to work the
swing himself without her pushing, which was a relief, so she let him
stay on for a few more minutes while she cleaned up and gathered their
things. She'd said,

I'll be right back

and

Keep pumping your legs, you're doing great,

and then she'd walked down to the gate that led to the main exit, passing
a woman with a double stroller bogged down in diaper bags and a kid
so big that their legs hung down either side. It was stiflingly hot outside,
even though it was already December, and the woman was huffing and
puffing her way through the silty dirt with all that weight. She had on
a pink visor with a palm tree and the word *Orlando* embroidered in

cursive script. She was muttering something Sammie couldn't make out—"Many, many," it sounded like, or maybe "Money, money." It sounded like crazy-person gibberish. Sammie hurried past so she wouldn't end up getting involved.

There was a garbage can near her car, but it was rancid and overflowing already, so she wadded her son's half-eaten lunch up tight in its paper bag and dropped it onto the front seat. It was so scorching inside the car that she opened all the doors and stood outside for a minute to let the heat roil out, because Samson would start crying if he felt "sticky," and she was too tired to deal with it. A cloud of gnats circled her head, thirsty for the sweat beading on her neck, and she swatted at them absentmindedly. She picked up her son's bottle of overheated lemonade from the floor, grimacing at the chunks of backwash before dumping it out on the sun-soft asphalt and tossing it back onto the seat. But it bounced and rolled off onto the floor, and her back hurt too much to pick it up, so she didn't. Her back hurt because she'd spent the last three months picking up Samson and taking him to the bathroom every night after he wet himself. Four years old and still wetting the bed—but then every child was different, that's what the doctor said. Sammie wasn't sure she believed it.

So she left the bottle there and turned back around.

There was the man, walking away with her son.

"Hey," she said, because no other words would come. "Hey!"

The man and Samson didn't stop. They didn't walk any faster, either. Just kept strolling toward the exit on the far side of the playground. Her son was holding the man's hand as if he'd known him his whole life. The guy was medium height, in his forties maybe, with thinning dark blond hair and a scruff of beard, wearing a gray polo tucked into dark blue jeans. White sneakers. Her son had on khaki shorts and his yellow T-shirt with Ruff and Tumble, the cartoon dalmatians, on the front. His hair was a real cloud of curls from the humidity; it was well past time for a haircut, but Samson had thrown a fit when she tried to take him.

Sammie jumped the fence. She didn't know she was going to until she did—didn't even know she even *could*, really; she wasn't particularly athletic, and her body was small—but she vaulted it and landed directly on the other side. And then she ran. She kicked up a storm of mulch, and one of her sandals fell off, but she kept going.

"Hey!" she kept yelling, louder and louder, but neither the man nor her son looked back. Her son never listened when she called him, never responded to his name or to her commands. The man had led her son through the gate, and now they were walking through the parking lot, headed toward a big red truck.

She stopped yelling and ran faster.

He opened the passenger door. Samson just stood there beside him. She could see the man's lips moving, but she couldn't make out any of the words. Her son, quiet all day every day, looked up at the man and smiled. Actually smiled. Full-on toothy grin.

Sammie started screaming. Not just a scream—a prolonged siren shriek, rising at the end like the wail of an ambulance. Still nothing from the man. Nothing from her son. Could *anyone* hear her?

When she finally reached them, the man was buckling Samson into the front seat.

She pushed past him and yanked her son out. Then her back, already strained from running, seized up altogether. She crumpled and almost dropped him onto the asphalt, catching him by the arm just in time. She was wheezing. Out of breath. Her foot was bleeding, she saw now, and so was her left thigh from when she'd scratched it hurtling the chain-link.

"You!" she said. Took a breath. Took another breath. "You. My son. *You.*"

The man put up his hands, as if to ward her off. Ward *her* off!

Unreal. He was about to abscond with her kid in the middle of the afternoon and he was acting like she was the crazy one.

Then again, she probably looked crazy. She *felt* crazy. He didn't look scared at all; in fact, he looked concerned. She studied his face, tanned and wrinkled around his deep-set eyes. He looked like the kind of guy who smiled a lot. He looked like someone's nice neighbor.

"I was just showing him my truck," he said. "Kid said he liked trucks."

Samson was yanking at her hand to get away, and she gripped harder.

"Your truck. Your *truck*?"

"I swear." The man smiled at her, revealing a line of very large bright teeth. Super white teeth, all even. Maybe not even real teeth. Too perfect for that face, with its crooked nose and scratchy beard and smile wrinkles.

"I am calling the police," Sammie said. But where was her phone? Back in her car, along with her keys, along with all her stuff. Where was her other shoe? Halfway across the playground.

"Mom." Samson tugged her hand again, sweaty fingers wriggling. "It's got a CB radio."

She looked down at her kid, and he looked back at her with that same indifferent look he always had. No grin for Mom, even though she'd saved him from imminent danger. No thought at all to how her heart was hammering inside her chest. She could have a heart attack right there in the parking lot, and he'd just climb up into the truck over her downed corpse.

She looked down again at her bleeding foot. One of her toenails had ripped half off, the littlest one on her right foot, and she was standing in a small puddle of her own blood.

"I am calling the cops," she repeated. "I am calling them right now."

The man closed the passenger door. Then he skirted around the front of the truck and opened the driver's side door.

"Don't you get in that truck!" Sammie yelled.

Samson was squirming, and she could barely keep a grip on him. She stepped back, dragging her son out of the truck's path.

"Don't you dare get in that truck! I am calling the cops, and you are going to stay right here!"

The man didn't listen, didn't even look at her, just climbed in and started the engine. He was going to leave; he was going to drive away from this, and there was nothing she could do to stop him.

"Help!" she yelled.

Samson wriggled and nearly escaped, so she caught his T-shirt by the neck and gripped him there, too hard, she knew, because he made a squeak and then stopped moving.

"Someone help me! Child abduction!"

There wasn't anybody else in the parking lot. She looked around frantically and saw that the woman who'd been pushing the stroller with the kid too big for it was setting out a picnic lunch. Only fifty feet away, maybe less, and still the woman didn't acknowledge her screams for help.

She pulled Samson a few feet farther back, worried the man might plow the truck straight into them. But he just eased the truck around Sammie and her son and pulled out of the lot.

It was a Dodge, a bright, glossy red Dodge. She strained to see the license plate and started repeating the numbers aloud: "GN5 8V6, GN5 8V6, GN5 8V6."

Samson was on his feet but hanging limp, dragging like he weighed a thousand pounds, the way he always did when he was being forced to do something he didn't want to do. She kept repeating the plate number as she struggled back to the playground, steering him in front of her with one hand clamped around his neck and a fistful of his T-shirt. There was something in the sole of her foot, glass, maybe, and her toe was throbbing, and her back hurt so bad she couldn't breathe. It felt like the truck had run her over.

Throughout all this, the mother with the stroller had been sitting calmly nearby, at a picnic table under the park's solitary oak tree. When they reached the fence, she called out to the woman to call 911. Then she sat down right where she stood and wept.

"Ants," Samson said, rubbing at his neck. It had a wild red mark where Sammie had grabbed him, and his collar was all yanked out. His face was dirty. He could use a wet wipe.

The woman came over and handed her a cell phone. "I didn't know what to tell them," she whispered, as if the situation were some kind of embarrassing secret. Her own kid was still sitting in the stroller, Velcro shoes kicking so hard the bags on top nearly fell off.

Sammie wondered if the kid had some kind of problem that required them to be in a stroller well past the usual age.

But what did that matter? She needed to focus. Sammie took the phone and spat out the license plate number to the dispatcher before she forgot it. Then she backed up and tried to explain what had happened, calling it an "attempted abduction." She described what the man looked like, what he'd been wearing. She told them about his too-perfect teeth. How his truck had a CB radio. She ran through everything she remembered, which wasn't much. She could barely remember her own name. It had all happened so fast, sped by in a blur. Then, in a fit of embarrassment, she hung up—only to realize she hadn't taken down any information. She didn't know the dispatcher's name; all she knew was that it was a woman. Or she *thought* it was a woman, anyway, with that high-pitched voice. And Sammie had hung up before giving them a number to contact her. How would they reach her? Was the callback number logged automatically? It was the stranger's cell phone, not Sammie's. Would she need to call back and start all over with someone new? Already the license plate number had flown from her brain.

She looked down at her son leaning against the fence.

"Ants," he said again, and he kept saying it: "ants," "ants," "ants."

And then she felt them crawling up her legs.

Sammie leaped to her feet and dusted them off, then moved the both of them around the corner to sit in a spot without any bugs. There were hundreds of dandelions peppering the grass, wild, fluffy things that stirred in the breeze, but her child picked up an abandoned straw from a fast-food cup and started playing with it. She was going into shock, she could feel it. Her entire body was shutting down. She knew she should call her wife, tell her what happened, but all she had was this borrowed phone, and she couldn't remember the number.

Why don't I know my wife's phone number by heart? she wondered. *What if there was an emergency?*

Samson dug the straw into the ground and scooped some up, then blew into the other end. Dirt rained down onto Sammie's head, sprinkled down her top. Then he did it again. Sammie just sat there, too exhausted to stop him. Finally, the other woman came over to get her phone. When she saw what Samson was doing, she took the straw away herself and tucked it in her pants pocket.

"Don't put things from the ground in your mouth," she said. "That's not nice."

As she walked away, Samson picked up a fistful of dirt. He held it over his mother's head, slowly opened his fingers, and let the dirt land where it wanted.

Spring

1

The doll looked like total shit. Sammie was about five seconds away from throwing it in the garbage.

It was a school project, which meant her son was supposed to be the one working on it, but Sammie had done nearly all of it herself. It wasn't her fault; it was the teacher's fault for giving the fourth graders a project so massive they couldn't do it alone, and it was the school's fault for going along with it. Of course she'd complained, but there was no getting out of it. The project was a requirement for every single fourth grader. Samson would complete it or take a zero for the project, which meant that his average—already a C—would tank to a fail. He might even have to repeat the grade over.

Samson, going through fourth grade again? No, thank you.

Sammie sat at the dining room table, surrounded by pieces of Styrofoam and craft glue, attempting to assemble a quarter-scale approximation of her son. Her son, who was supposed to be sitting at the table beside her, who'd said he had to go to the bathroom twenty minutes ago.

She'd bet her entire salary (much less, she grudgingly admitted, now that she was working part-time from home) that he was back in front of the television.

"You better have diarrhea," she yelled. "You better have the worst stomachache of your life."

She'd gone to the craft supply store after she'd finished her work for the day to pick out some things they could use. Sammie was not a crafts kind of person. Sure, she'd had to do all this stuff growing up, but once she was an adult she would have been happy if she'd never seen a bottle of glue again. That was one thing about having a kid: all the stuff you thought you'd never have to think about—math, art, PE clothes that smell like dead feet—all came rushing back like nostalgic reruns.

Monika could have picked up some of the supplies, but she was out of town for the next two days. She traveled a lot for work, which had been fun before they'd had Samson, but increasingly it meant that Sammie was shouldering most of the mom duties on her own. Over the phone, Monika said Sammie should let Samson do it himself, as if that were an option.

"He'll never do it himself," Sammie said.

Monika told her it wouldn't hurt to let him try. What Sammie wanted to say was *You have no clue who your son is*, but she'd tried that before and all it got her was Monika sleeping on the couch and Sammie sitting up in bed all night, furious. At least this way only one of them would be mad.

"Samson, if you don't get your butt back in here by the count of three, I'm gonna chuck this whole thing in the trash," Sammie yelled.

She loudly counted to three and waited for her son to appear. Waited three more seconds. Four more seconds. Two minutes later, he slunk back into the dining room wearing one of Monika's oversize sleep shirts. Sammie could see his red Superman underwear through the thin white shirt.

"Were you watching television?" she asked.

He just shrugged. Samson never spoke unless he absolutely had to, at least not to Sammie. He didn't really like talking to Monika, either, but that never seemed like a problem. If anything, Monika preferred it when he was quiet. She brought it up all the time when they went to dinner parties or hung out with friends: *Our son is so well-behaved*, she'd say. *He never talks back to us!* But the subject didn't come up that much these days, now that Monika was traveling all the time and Samson was having problems at school.

Sammie could have added that he never talked back because he was too busy doing just exactly the thing you'd asked him not to do, but that would have ruined the image Monika wanted them to promote: a happy, well-adjusted little family of three, gay, but otherwise just like anyone else.

That was a big thing for her wife. She wanted them to be normal. On their living room wall, she'd hung a framed photo of the three of them at a fancy birthday dinner for Sammie. They were all dressed up: Sammie in a new lace dress and her hair done up in a twist, Monika wearing her best blazer over a crisp white shirt, their son sandwiched between them in a navy suit with a paisley clip-on bow tie. On the table in front of them was a giant birthday cake, candles aglow, and everyone was sporting toothy grins for the camera. What you couldn't see was Monika's hand clenched around Samson's leg under the table, because he kept jabbing Sammie with the toe of his loafer. You couldn't smell his stinky little foot, open to the air after he'd kicked off the other shoe. Anyone who came to the house—especially Monika's coworkers, whom she was always eager to impress with their "normalcy"—commented on the sweetness of the picture. Two perfect gay moms and their handsome, grinning son. Monika would smile and tell them what a great time they'd had that night, but all Sammie could do was wince and recall, silently, that things weren't always as idyllic as they seemed.

Sammie looked out the far kitchen window and watched the sun sink behind the neighbor's house. Birds called to one another, heading to bed for the night. Her son yawned and scratched at his neck.

According to everyone they'd consulted, their son was a problem only because he chose to be. He was a perfectly capable, fully functioning fourth grader who just needed an attitude adjustment. To Monika, that was a problem that would work itself out in time. To Sammie, it meant that her days were spent waiting for that magical shift to finally happen.

"Here you go," Sammie said, pushing a mess of irregular-looking limbs across the table. They squealed as they scraped over the wood. "Paint these."

Samson put his hands over his ears and made a face. "I don't like it."

The paint had dripped all over the place, even though she'd put down newspapers everywhere, especially on Monika's grandmother's antique dining table. Sammie ran another paper towel under the tap and tried to do some spot cleaning while her son half-heartedly glopped gold paint onto his brush. He dunked it over and over on the paper plate, stirring it around before dragging it down something that should have been a thigh but looked more like an oversize turkey leg. Three stripes later, he huffed miserably and dropped the brush directly onto the plate, sending a big splat of gold paint directly onto the wall behind his head.

"Fuck!" she yelled. Samson just sat there, staring at her. There was paint on the table, paint on Monika's sleep shirt, paint everywhere. Big drops of gold, glimmering like coins.

She walked into the kitchen and filled a glass with water from the sink. She drank it all, took a breath, then refilled the glass and drank that, too. The water tasted bad, kind of metallic. It was the pipes and the Florida aquifer—they had one of those filtration pitchers, but no one ever bothered to refill it, so it just sat in the fridge with a useless half inch of clean water in it. She ran both hands through her hair and then realized she had gold paint on her fingers.

This had all seemed easy enough when she'd been in the craft store. She was embarrassed to admit it, but the project seemed childish. The whole thing was way too easy for her, a former manager now reduced to running a household. And if she was being honest with herself, not even running it all that well. She'd never gone back to work full-time after quitting her job to stay home with Samson, and the job she took on after he started school was only part-time work and full-time brain-numbing. She could do it all—copyediting, client emailing—in her sleep, and sometimes that's exactly how she felt: like she was sleepwalking through her work and her life. So when the craft store employee came over and asked if she needed help, she'd turned them away, and she wasn't all that nice about it, either.

How hard could it be? Styrofoam ball for a head, Styrofoam block for a torso, four foam dowels for legs and arms, two small blocks for hands and two for feet. She bought felt to make little clothes to match Samson's own T-shirt and shorts, and yarn for his mop of curly dirty-blond hair. For his eyes, googly-eye stickers! Easy enough.

It was not easy.

She'd already cut her hand trying to carve the legs into shapes. She hadn't thought to buy craft knives—why spend extra for something they'd never use again?—so she was using a kitchen knife, and it wasn't as sharp as she expected, so she had to keep pushing till it slipped and stabbed dully into her palm.

When she'd measured Samson, to get a sense of his proportions, he'd wriggled so much that she'd struggled not to yell at him. These days her voice sounded like someone else's, like someone she'd hate to have to listen to. It sounded a lot like her mother's, which is something Monika had pointed out once when Sammie got mad at Samson for spilling a drink in a restaurant. Sammie didn't bother replying to that, just went out to the parking lot and cried. Monika never said it again, but she didn't have to. Sammie knew exactly who she sounded like: Her mother, the woman who'd never understood her. Her mother, the least maternal being on the planet.

So she downed her second glass of water, tied back her paint-streaked hair, then opened the freezer and got out the makings of two sundaes— ice cream with chocolate syrup and rainbow sprinkles and three maraschino cherries in each dish. She took another deep breath, then carried the sundaes into the dining room.

She was greeted by a gold-coated nightmare.

Sammie had bought four oversize bottles of gold paint, because she wasn't sure how much the Styrofoam would absorb and she didn't want to have to go back to the craft place for more. Samson had emptied all but one. It was dripping off the edge of the table, coating the chairs. It fell to the floor in flat, drippy splats. The newspapers she'd used to line the tabletop were crumpled into a big, slimy ball and tossed onto Monika's favorite chair. The china cabinet, a wedding gift from another of Monika's relatives, was covered with wild gold handprints. The rest was streaked everywhere, slicked over every surface in the room. It was as if King Midas had come to life in her dining room and touched everything to golden shit.

The only thing the paint hadn't touched was the doll, which was sitting in the corner, dismantled, and still a pristine Styrofoam white.

Samson had disappeared, but his footprints led from the dining room into the hallway. Sammie followed them down the hall to the living room, shaking so much she worried she might have a stroke. There sat her son, perched on the couch, absolutely coated in gold paint. It coated his hair and dripped down his face, soaking through his nightshirt and leaving slick bands of gold along his neck.

"Samson," she whispered.

He turned to look at her, and his eyes were shockingly bright in his face. The blue of them was almost electric. It looked like something, but at first her frazzled brain couldn't place it, until finally it leaped from her mouth: "Carrie."

That was it—the scene from *Carrie* when Sissy Spacek got the bucket of pig's blood dumped on her head. Except this was molten gold, as if her son had been transformed into a golden statue.

"You little shit," she said, wheezing out a giggle. There he sat, her monster. Ruiner of furniture and good moods. Able to wreck an entire evening with three containers of paint. And with that, the laughter just rolled out of her. It was uncontrollable, the kind that nearly bent her in half. Tears leaked from her eyes. Even her cheeks hurt. Samson just sat there, drops of paint landing in growing puddles on the hardwood floor, leaching into the rug under the coffee table.

She laughed until she thought she might throw up; even after she got herself under control enough to walk him upstairs to the guest bathroom, she was still suppressing it. She had him hop in the shower with his nightshirt on and pulled the shower curtain closed as the spray dripped liquid gold all over everything. She sat down on the toilet lid, held her face in her hands, and waited for the paint to slick off her boy's face and body. *What a weird thing, to love another human*, she thought. Her stomach trembled, still quaking from the giggles; even thinking about the mess she'd have to clean downstairs didn't make her mad. It made her want to start laughing all over again. She bit her lip as she struggled to pull herself together.

"Almost done?" she asked, but of course there was no response from Samson.

She got him out and dried, then bustled him off to his room at the end of the hall. Luckily, the paint seemed to come off easy enough. It was water-soluble, so it would probably wash off the walls, too. Worst case, she'd have to paint. And, anyway, she hated the color of their walls; Monika had picked it without even asking her, just came home one day with a giant bucket of the stuff. *It's nicer than the brand you mentioned,* she'd told Sammie, which was basically her way of saying, *I make the money in this house, so I'll be making the decisions.* This way, Sammie had an excuse to choose something new. She could thank Samson for that.

Sammie went downstairs and opened a bottle of chilled white wine. Then she got to work cleaning up the mess. It took several rolls of paper towels and a couple gallons of hot water, and by the time she was done she was exhausted and well on her way to drunk.

The doll still sat in scattered pieces. She looked again at the measurements she'd taken of her son: Height, average for a fourth grader. Weight, average. He looked nothing like her, though she was the one who'd given birth to him. Their skin tones were wildly different: his was pink and rosy, while hers tended toward sallow. Her hair was brown and frizzy, hanging stick-straight to her mid-back, nothing like his mop of curls. She and Monika had chosen an anonymous donor, so they had only a few basic facts about his biological father, but when Sammie looked at their son, all she saw was a tiny stranger who'd been dropped into their home.

Kids were aliens anyway, Sammie thought. No way to know what they were thinking, when their thoughts were the product of an unfinished brain still training itself to act human.

Sammie and Samson's one similarity was in the eyes. Hers were dark brown and his were blue, but they both were set in their faces in a way that made them look eternally surprised, as if someone had come up behind them and shrieked.

The googly eyes felt appropriate. Maybe her one good idea at the craft store.

Sammie sawed away at the arms and legs, trying to approximate something human. She jabbed toothpicks into the ends, dabbing them with glue, and miraculously they held. Careful of her hands, she cut out pieces of Styrofoam and made a nose and some ears. Whittled out a neck. She jabbed all these together, too. Then she took the last container of paint and shellacked the whole mess.

It didn't look terrible. She found herself enjoying the work, actually, finishing off the wine while she cut some clothes out of felt and glued them onto the body.

The hair, she realized, was going to be the biggest challenge. There was a current school photo of Samson on top of the china cabinet. He wasn't smiling in the picture, of course—he hardly ever smiled—but the photo gave her a chance to look at his face long enough to see how his hair was supposed to look. She glued a mop of curly yellow yarn to the top of the doll's head, brushed a few strands into place, and then sat back to look at the finished product.

Unlike her messy painted son, who resembled a horror film reject, the replica looked almost like an object of worship. It reminded her of the Bible story of Baal, which she'd read a million times as a child—the one about the Israelites who decided to make their own golden calf when Moses was up in Mount Sinai getting the Ten Commandments from God. Sammie hadn't been to church in years—she barely spoke to her parents, who used their Christianity to shield themselves from acknowledging her queerness or her marriage—but somehow the golden idol in front of her had emerged from the swampy interior of her memory. Now she found herself recoiling at how sacrilegious it was. Strange that she'd even care about such a thing, but she often found herself responding to certain things as though her parents might still walk in and chastise her, even though she was a full-grown adult with a family of her own. Old habits were hard to break.

I can't let him take this to school, she thought, but she knew she'd have to. Everyone had to turn in their work the next day, and Sammie had already raised such a fuss about the project that there was no way the teacher would give Samson an extension.

That teacher, Miranda Hastings, was the kind of woman Sammie really disliked. On the first day of class, Samson had come home with his things all labeled with cartoon-apple stickers—but the name tags all read TOMMY. At first she thought he'd grabbed the wrong binders, but when she realized someone had plastered the TOMMY name tags all over the binders she'd bought him, Sammie was furious. The next morning, she called and arranged a meeting. The teacher greeted her at the classroom door and ushered her to one of the small tables. It was frankly ludicrous, the two of them smashed together like they were crowding themselves into a dollhouse, but somehow the woman seemed totally in her element. With her blond hair perfectly coiffed, legs bent elegantly to the side, she reminded Sammie of Alice in Wonderland, curled up serenely on the green manicured lawn.

"This isn't my son's name," she'd told the woman, brandishing one of the binders.

"It's his middle name, isn't it?" she replied, smiling in a way that Sammie felt was condescending. She explained that she invited the kids to call themselves whatever they liked, including nicknames. It was a little bit of freedom of expression, a way of letting the kids feel they had some say in a world that never let them decide anything for themselves.

"After all, is it really a bother if he goes by his middle name?" Miranda asked, and then excused herself to go pick up the class from PE, even though nothing had really been resolved.

The thing was, it *did* bother Sammie that her son's teacher felt she had the right to make that decision. Sammie was the one who'd named him, after all. Her wife had given him her last name, Carlisle, which was fine, and she'd also given him the middle name Thomas, after her own grandfather. But it was Sammie who got to choose his first name, and she'd named him after herself. She didn't really understand her son, even though she'd carried him in her body, even though she'd barfed up every single breakfast for four months straight, even though she'd spent two full days in labor before they finally carved him free of her stomach, leaving behind a scar that still bothered her, no matter how often Monika told her it was a symbol of their love for their child. But she had that one thing—his name, Samson, the one thing they shared. Her son was Samson Thomas Carlisle, and that was hers to protect, as long as he belonged to her.

Back in their living room, Sammie looked over at the miniature Samson on their freshly washed table, glaring at her with its big googly eyes. She felt creeped out by it—the gold gave it a lifelike quality, as if it were almost sentient—and for one drunken moment she thought she might smash it to pieces. Instead she turned off the lights in the dining room and the living room, drank another glass of water to stave off the hangover, and climbed upstairs to her lonely bed.

She fell asleep around one in the morning and woke again a few hours later, groggy and unsure why she was awake. It was dark in the room except for a shaft of light from the hall, though she'd thought she'd turned that off before crawling under the covers. She rolled over to check the clock on Monika's side—and saw someone lying on the pillow beside her.

Sammie screamed.

Scrambling out of the bed, she fell onto the hardwood floor, banging her elbow so hard it lost all feeling. Still muddled with sleep and wine, she stumbled over to the door and switched on the overhead light.

There on Monika's pillow lay the golden miniature of her son.

"Oh my God," she whispered. "Oh *God*."

It was 3:02 A.M., and the thing was under the covers.

She picked it up with shaky hands, carried it to the master bathroom, and closed the door.

Then she went down the hallway to check on Samson. His door was cracked, as always, and he was turned on his side, facing her. A stripe of light from the hall fell across his face, bisecting it neatly. His lips were puckered into a kiss—the way he always slept, as sweet as some porcelain doll from a catalog—and his hair was swept back over his forehead.

It was quiet in the room, and he was breathing regularly. And yet—

She walked in and dug his hand out from under the sheets. There sat the evidence: though he'd washed it clean in the shower, the skin of his palm was now spattered with gold, fingers coated and tacky with paint.

"Samson," she said. "Samson."

He didn't move. Kept breathing regularly, chest lifting and falling, lifting and falling.

"Tommy," she whispered miserably, and he opened his eyes.

Miranda Hastings decided to become an elementary school teacher because her mother always said that was the perfect job for landing a husband. "It shows you're good with kids," Dottie Hastings advised when her daughter was picking a college major. "And it's the kind of job you won't mind giving up once you get pregnant."

The thing was, she'd fallen in love with it. She wasn't even going out on dates anymore because she was so focused on her cozy classroom and all the sweet faces she got to see every day. Even the stubborn ones came around when she smiled and gave them time to come out of their shells. Like Tommy. Cutest curly hair and the nicest helper, at least once she let him choose his own name. Samson was a terrible name to put on a child, especially around other kids, who teased and mocked over the tiniest of differences. So what if his mother didn't like it? She was so uptight—seemed like she needed a night off, like most mothers whose only job was child-rearing. When she showed up in a tizzy over the name change, Miranda just listened. No big deal. Nothing she couldn't handle. Miranda didn't blame the woman. She just needed to be handled, like the kids in her class.

2

After all that hard work, at least Samson had gotten a good grade on the doll.

I got a good grade, Sammie thought, still feeling petty about it.

But even though he hadn't wanted anything to do with building the thing in the first place, overnight he'd suddenly become obsessed with it. His creepy miniature.

Monika didn't think there was anything wrong with their son's attachment to the doll. In fact, she encouraged it.

"It's weird," Sammie said, but Monika just laughed.

"It's not. Really. It's totally normal." She smiled, showing off her twin dimples, and took Sammie's hand. Sammie had always loved those dimples. Alongside her Cupid's-bow mouth, they made her wife's baby face look unbearably sweet.

Monika had asked a friend from work to watch Samson so they could have a night away—dinner, just the two of them, and then a stay at a fancy hotel in downtown Tampa, next to the university where all the

arts events always happened. She'd seen a play in the gilt-embossed the-
ater seven years ago. Sammie hadn't really liked the play itself, but the
place had been pretty, with all those red velvet seats.

That felt like forever ago. This was the first time they'd been out in
at least six months, but Sammie could barely focus on having a good
time. All she wanted to talk about was her son's bizarre fixation on
the doll.

"He carries it around *everywhere*," she said, pushing the mashed
potatoes around her plate. They didn't taste right. The restaurant was
an upscale place recommended by one of Monika's coworkers, and all
the portions were too small, with ingredients that didn't seem necessary.
Raisins in the gravy? *Really?* And potatoes studded with parsley that
felt like shredded grocery bags.

"It's okay for him to like a doll, though," Monika said. "Even though
he's a boy."

Sammie stabbed at her tough, microscopic pork chop to keep herself
from saying something she'd regret. Her knife screeched across the
plate, making a long pterodactyl shriek. A couple nearby turned to
stare.

"I didn't say it was a gender thing. You always do that."

"Do what?"

Sammie spat a piece of parsley into her napkin. *Classy*, she thought.
"Tell me what I'm thinking, when it has absolutely nothing to do with
what I'm talking about."

Monika chewed her pasta. It looked marginally better than the pork,
and Sammie wished she'd gotten it instead, but she was putting on
weight around her hips and thighs and was trying to cut back on carbs.

"Why don't you explain it to me, then."

Fuck it, Sammie thought, grabbing a roll from the basket. It was so
hard and crusty that she could barely break it open to smear the cold
butter on it. "I hate this restaurant," she said, and Monika shushed her.

"We can go get burgers or something afterward," she said, smiling again. "Something we both like."

She's trying to change the subject, Sammie thought, and almost let her wife get away with it. Monika looked terrific—her short, peppery hair was curled up from the humidity, and the emerald of her shirt made her look like she'd just come in from a day at the beach—and that made it easier for her to get away with skirting issues. It was easier to kiss and make up, let things slide, especially when Sammie didn't really want to fight. But this issue with Samson felt important.

"He uses it to do his talking for him, though. Have you noticed? It's the only way he interacts with us anymore. It's not normal."

Monika took the roll away and spread the butter for her. "He likes it because it's something you two did together. It reminds him of the good time you had that night."

A "good time" that consisted of Samson coating the entire house with gold paint and then scaring her shitless in the middle of the night. When she first told Monika about it, her wife had laughed. Monika had a great sense of humor—it was one of the things that first attracted Sammie to her—but she also had trouble taking things seriously. Sammie didn't think any of it was very funny. The doll made her extremely uncomfortable.

"He keeps talking to it."

Monika handed her back the bread, and Sammie took a bite. It was softer inside, and the butter tasted good, anyway.

"Thank you," she said, and Monika reached over and cupped her chin in her palm. It was nice. Sammie leaned into the warmth.

"What would make you feel better about this?"

Sammie wasn't sure anything would. The doll was creepy and ill-made, so it was coming apart in chunks. Samson carried it with him to the dinner table, took it out to the backyard to play, and slept with it on the shelf by his bed at night. When Sammie asked him questions, only the doll would answer. And the doll answered to Samson, while her son answered only to Tommy.

Sammie took another bite of mashed potatoes and immediately spit the whole wad of it back onto her fork. Her wife laughed and pushed the bowl of pasta toward her.

"Let's just switch," she said, and Sammie was grateful.

The pasta was good. Full of very fatty cream sauce and shrimp and diced peppers and tomatoes. Samson would never eat something like that. Too many flavors.

Sammie frowned. She hated that every time she thought about something for herself it had to come couched in what her son thought. There were times now when she didn't feel like her life was her own—that she'd become like a service bureau for what her son might want: his needs, his preferences.

"I want another baby" is what Sammie said, and right away she knew that was the exact wrong thing and absolutely not what she wanted.

"I don't think that's a good idea." Monika held up her empty wineglass and waggled it at the waiter, a thing Sammie found tacky and a little bit rude. Her wife had grown up with money, but she still did things like that sometimes. Cleaned her nose at the dinner table. Took off her shoes on flights. They'd been together a long time, and Sammie knew that sometimes the behaviors that irritated her about Monika were things she'd once found endearing. She tried to focus on Monika's face in the candlelight, taking in her dark, deep-set eyes, the friendly smile lines radiating from their corners.

Remember what you love, she told herself, and she felt better.

"You don't want another kid?"

The waiter came and refilled the glass. Monika pushed her hair back behind her ears, then shook it out again. Her hair was very short, but it was growing out a little. Wisps of it curled cutely over her ears. Sammie could have said, *You need a haircut*, and kissed her wife's sweet face, but instead she'd asked for another baby, and she didn't even want one.

"I want us to be able to spend more time together, though, and a baby would put an end to that," Monika finally said, and it was exactly the right thing to say.

Sammie missed the romantic vacations they used to take, missed having quality time together beyond a few stray moments on the couch at night before they fell asleep. She relaxed back in her seat and finished her drink before they shared a piece of dark chocolate cheesecake (too rich) and more wine. Then Monika paid the bill, as she always did, and they pulled on their light coats (thanks to the chilly Florida rain) and walked out without taking the leftovers.

On the way out, Monika took her hand. It felt strange holding hands, Sammie thought, and that made her unbearably sad. Back when they started dating, they used to hold hands all the time. Touching each other's palms in movie theaters, beneath tables at diners, even just sitting on a couch together—it was like some part of them had to be touching at all times. Sammie missed the hunger of that. When she'd first come out, it had felt thrilling to hold a woman's hand in public. Finally, a sign of outward affection. It showed the world how much they loved each other, even though it meant they sometimes got dirty looks—like the time when a woman standing outside a department store hissed that there were *children present*, to *be decent*. It became one of their little inside jokes—*Do you wanna go somewhere quiet and be indecent to each other?*

All the way back to the hotel they held hands. Their palms were sweaty from the chilly humidity, and Monika kept having to use her other hand to keep her curls out of her eyes, but it was the principle of the thing.

I am going to hold my wife's hand, and I am going like it, Sammie told herself. On the way back it started to rain, just a light drizzle, but enough to make Sammie wish she'd worn shoes with better soles. At the restaurant, slightly buzzed and aroused, she'd been thinking about how much she wanted quality time with her wife. But now, wet from the rain and bloated from the pasta, in a dress one size too tight, she felt done with the evening. She wanted to be home, in her nightgown, having some tea and watching some show she'd already seen a hundred times while her wife rubbed her shoulders.

They walked past overpriced clothing stores and a juice bar, ducked a waterfall of rain from an awning, skirted a stand of palms in front of a bank.

The rain makes everything smell better, Sammie thought. *Less car exhaust and more damp earth.*

They were close enough to the bay that the air had turned salty sweet. She missed the beach. She was always forgetting how close it was, and when she did remember, it was never the right time to go.

"Here we are," Monika said. "C'mon, Grace Kelly." Her wife waltzed her around a big puddle, then spun her gently through the revolving doors.

Sammie laughed, that big cackling one that always burst from her when her wife cracked her up.

The hotel was nice—another perk of Monika's job. She accrued points whenever she traveled, which meant she usually had enough left over that they could stay at good places, which was hardly ever now that they had Samson. Sammie watched their reflections morph in the warbly gloss of the golden elevators, like fun-house mirror versions of themselves.

"Shit. I was going to buy champagne."

"We can order some from room service," Sammie said.

Monika used their conjoined fingers to punch the up button. Across the lobby, Sammie heard sounds from the hotel bar, a mahogany-paneled place called the Rusty Fork—a tinkle of glass, talking, muted laughter.

The kind of place you take your mistress, Sammie thought. The kind of place someone went because they wanted somebody badly enough that they were willing to go to a place called the Rusty Fork.

They stepped into the elevator with another couple, who'd just come from the bar. The woman had her arm wedged in the crease of the man's deep-blue suit-jacketed elbow, and they were leaning into each other with the sloppy confidence that came from late-night drinking in a hotel bar. They smelled like alcohol, too, and cigarette smoke. The man was balding, with a paunch that hung over his belted slacks, and his date looked much younger. She wore heels so tall they must have been killing her. Monika punched the button for five; the man pushed seven.

"I like your top," the woman said to Monika, smiling.

Monika thanked her, said she'd found it at a boutique that just opened in downtown Orlando. The woman put a finger in her thick blond hair and scooped a hank of it behind her ear. She had on very red shiny lipstick and very particularly sculpted eyeshadow. She said she'd kill to be able to wear that shade of green, that her skin was too splotchy for it, and Monika said she thought the woman could wear any color she liked.

Monika never had trouble meeting women. She could find them in airports, at restaurants, anywhere; when Samson was in first grade, a woman had solicited her right in front of Sammie at a school function. It had been a point of contention in their relationship—Monika's natural charm made her a magnet to most women, while Sammie's body had changed so much after having Samson that she'd developed a slew of insecurities.

When they came to their floor, Sammie took Monika's hand and led her from the elevator, but not before she could see the look the woman was giving her wife. That look that femmes always gave her, a kind of helpless flirtation that said, *I might be straight but maybe not when I'm two drinks in, maybe not always, maybe I'm a little bit like spaghetti sometimes, just get me wet and I'll loosen up.*

"What?" Monika asked, and Sammie told her she knew exactly what.

That made Monika laugh, and then she pulled out her key card to open their door. It was a nice suite, with a big king bed and a comfy area with a couch set up to watch television. Sammie loved the way the city lights were reflected in the waters of Tampa Bay. It made her think of glitter, as if everything were covered in gemstones—but then that reminded her of her son and his weird golden doll, and suddenly all she wanted was to crawl into bed and go to sleep.

Monika snuggled her face into the back of Sammie's neck, and Sammie tried to relax. It took so little these days to set her on edge, but she hadn't always been that way. When she and Monika first met, she'd been extremely chill. Easygoing, able to go with the flow, smiling more often than not. Fine with a bag of chips for any meal, even multiple times a week. Would day drink on a Monday, call in sick just to go to the movies with Monika. Now that they had Samson, though, she'd slipped entirely into the role of caretaker. And caretakers had to be rule followers. Had to have discipline.

She didn't like the way other women looked at her wife, didn't like the fact that no one looked at her that way anymore. Part of it, she knew, was that with Samson's arrival she had just really stopped trying. She hadn't cared what she looked like, because her body had stopped feeling like her own. Why even take care of a thing that no one else wanted to look at?

When Sammie was younger, she was the femme eyeing her wife in the elevator. In old pictures with friends, she was the one wearing the short skirts and low-cut tops and too much eyeliner. She was the fun one, the one who loved going out, who ordered two drinks at once and then got someone cute to buy her another. She'd dab on sexy, musky perfume that women huffed off her sweaty neck in the middle of a crowded bar. She wore underwear that rode up the crack of her ass, and her bras were all wildly uncomfortable but made her tits look great. But now? The dress she was wearing was one she'd bought before her son was born. Her shoes were so worn out that the insides were half removed. Her hair was brushed, and she'd put on makeup, but in the mirror before they left home, all she'd seen was someone who looked tired. Her face didn't look like hers anymore, or what she remembered as hers. Now when she looked in the mirror, all she saw was a body that didn't belong to her.

Her wife undressed her, and they got into bed together. That was something they'd always been good at, knowing exactly how to touch each other. They didn't have sex as often as they used to, but there'd been no lesbian bed death with them, no lack of sexual chemistry. Monika rolled her over. Palmed a breast and sucked at her neck, tugged her hair.

All the things I want without having to ask, Sammie thought. She let herself be stroked and positioned. Left her anxieties behind and focused on what felt good.

Afterward, Monika wiped the shine from her mouth, and they snuggled together in the still-bright room and talked about what they wanted for breakfast.

Sammie felt postorgasm happy, that kind of fuzziness that always left her feeling loose and out of her body, but then Monika leaned against her sweaty back and started talking about how if they left early enough they'd have time to take Samson to the park for a couple of hours.

"Could we not right now?" Sammie asked, and Monika sighed against her skin and rolled away.

"You're always so freaked out about taking him to the park. It's like you think that man is going to come back and get him."

"You don't know what it was like."

It was true: Monika had been scared by what almost happened to Samson, but she hadn't been there. She didn't know the feeling of complete panic, the loss of control. The insistent worry that it might happen again.

There was that other quiet feeling, too, the one she didn't voice: that she'd felt as though her own son were trying to escape from her.

"You don't even know if he really wanted to take Samson," Monika said. "Maybe it was a misunderstanding."

"I'm gonna take a shower," Sammie replied, getting up and padding across the room. Monika walked over and opened the balcony doors, letting in a burst of damp evening air. The sound of palms in the breeze, mingled with the waves down below, should have been soothing, but even postorgasm, Sammie felt like a big ball of stress.

The bathroom had a fancy vanity where Sammie had stashed her toiletries bag. She sat down, naked, and forced herself to look directly into the mirror as she brushed out the knots from her long, tangled hair. Her body felt like a map of everything she'd eaten in the past few years, stretched and contorted by pregnancy into a completely new shape. Her skin felt loose, especially around her stomach, where Samson had kicked and pressed at her. No matter how much cocoa butter she rubbed into herself, her belly still felt like an emptied vessel.

She picked up her breasts, then let them drop, grimacing as they smacked against her body. Her tits had always been one of her best features, that's what the women she'd slept with continually told her. At least before Samson. She hadn't even been able to breastfeed him. Not really. She'd tried for the first couple of days, committed to making her child as nutritionally sound as possible, but he was lackluster at feeding, and, honestly, it hurt. No one seemed to care when she switched over to formula; her son was still blasé about eating, but at least she didn't have to deal with being his only available food source, like a penned-up milk cow.

She washed her hair with the lemony hotel shampoo and wished she'd thought to shave her legs. She would try harder, she thought. She would start eating healthier, would make them all better meals. She'd go to a nice salon and get a better haircut, one that shaped her face—maybe even color her hair, why the hell not? She'd buy new face cream, too, something to help with the crow's-feet around her eyes. She'd clean up the house when she got home. She might not be the same woman who lived off bar drinks and hangover food at 4:00 A.M., but she could be fun again. Hang out with friends. Feel productive. If she felt a little better about herself, she'd feel better about being a mom. She'd feel better about everything.

The room was freezing, and she crawled into bed beside her sleeping wife. Monika had turned off all the lights except the one on Sammie's side, and had left out a bottle of cold water for her. It was sweet, one of those nice things Monika always remembered to do. Sammie used to give herself a hard time for not doing those kinds of things, but Monika kept reassuring her that she was sweet in different ways. *You think of the big picture, and I think of the smaller one*, Monika said. It was those little things, the unthinking sweetness of a bottle of water, that reminded Sammie how lucky she was.

She watched a show about forensics and sipped at her water until she fell asleep. Until around 2:00 A.M., when she was awakened by the sound of Monika whispering into her phone.

She's cheating on me was Sammie's first thought. It was always her first thought. She looked at her wife's naked back, hunched over the side of the bed as she murmured into the phone. Her hair was mussed from sleep, the right side cresting like a wave.

Who else is getting to see this? she wondered. Her wife was attractive. Even as she got older, she'd somehow become only more virile. It wasn't that Monika was aging gracefully, it was more like she was maturing. She was like one of those handsome actors who got called a silver fox and dated women a fraction of their own age. She smiled easy. She stood tall. She walked with her hips slung forward. She looked like a woman who knew how to fuck properly. It drove Sammie crazy to think of her with anyone else.

"Who is it?" she asked. "Who are you talking to at two in the goddamn morning?"

Monika flapped her arm behind her, motioning her to silence.

Sammie got up and shrugged on the hotel robe. She turned on all the lights and got a glass of water. She felt hungover and furious. Monika told whoever was on the other end of the line that they'd be there as soon as they could, and then she set down the phone and told Sammie they needed to pack their stuff right away. It was her friend who'd called, the one watching their son. It was something to do with Samson.

"What happened to Samson?" Sammie asked, terrified.

"We have to go," Monika told her. "I'm going downstairs to call for the car. Meet me in the lobby in five minutes."

Sammie collected her things in a rush. She couldn't stop shivering. Her hair was still wet from her earlier shower, and her teeth were chattering from the hotel air-conditioning. When she got downstairs, Monika was already out by the curbside valet stand. When she stepped outside, the humidity was like a slap in the face.

"Are you going to tell me what this is about?" Sammie asked.

"Let's just wait till we're in the car," Monika replied. "Don't worry about it yet."

That was something they argued about: Monika was always the one who got to disseminate information, at the time of her choosing. It made Sammie feel like a child in their relationship, which led to her nagging

Monika about it, which led to Monika telling her to lower her voice, that it was too shrill, that they could discuss it when Sammie was ready to speak like an adult.

The driver pulled around with Monika's company car—black, always black, Sammie tried to suggest a lighter color because the Florida heat cooks dark paint, but Monika said black cars looked more expensive—and loaded their bags in the trunk as Monika climbed behind the wheel.

They pulled away in silence. Traffic was sparse. The lights from downtown Tampa petered out until there was just the long, dark stretch of highway that led back to Orlando. When they passed Dinosaur World, Monika whispered "Dino-mite" like she always did, but Sammie didn't laugh. She just sat silently, tucked a sweater under her chin, and started to drift off until Monika said, quietly, "Samson bit a kid tonight."

"*Bit?* What do you mean bit?"

Their son was ten years old, not a toddler who needed to be told not to bite. He hadn't exhibited that kind of behavior even when he was very young—never cared enough to get into it with another kid, fight or pull hair, and certainly not dig his teeth into anyone's flesh.

"Are they sure it was him?" Sammie asked, and then realized the real question was something bigger and much worse. "How bad is it?"

"Very bad," Monika said. "We're meeting them at the hospital."

Sammie didn't bother asking what "very bad" might mean. She sat back in the seat and shivered under her sweater. After a few minutes Monika turned on some podcast she'd been listening to, and Sammie just sat staring out the window, watching the fields and cows and trees blur together in a dark watercolor nightmare.

It was true—her son did sometimes let his anger get the best of him. How often had she looked at Samson's blank stare and wondered if something worse was lurking underneath? But Monika refused to see it, so Sammie was left to wonder alone about the way her son's eyes seemed to roll over black with internal rage, like a shark's.

That wasn't fair, and she knew it. Her son wasn't some feral animal. He was just a boy. Boys got into trouble. She didn't understand boys. All she knew was her son, and he confused her.

She didn't think she could possibly fall asleep under the circumstances, but then Monika was shaking her awake in the hospital parking lot. She shrugged on the sweater, realizing she'd neglected to put on a bra in her rush, and wiped a crust of drool from the corner of her mouth. Then she blindly followed Monika inside, down crisscrossing, dizzying corridors until they found their son sitting on the floor of a waiting room, in front of a mounted television playing a looped infomercial for nonstick cookware. Gina's other two kids were slumped against each other on a couple of padded chairs. Her oldest, a teenager—John, maybe?—was scrolling away on his phone.

"Hey," Monika said. "Where's your mom?"

"Back with Paul." He didn't look up. The littler one, a girl, maybe eight, was half asleep. Her name was Claudia. That one Sammie remembered, because she'd wondered more than once what it would be like to have a little girl with a sweet name like Claudia instead of what she wound up with instead. What it would have been like if that other baby had lived.

Samson shifted around and flapped his free arm at Monika. He was sitting cross-legged (*crisscross applesauce*, the teachers always called it, which Sammie found revolting), and the other arm was wrapped around his golden doll. Sammie tamped down her immediate impulse, which was to snatch it from him, and sat on the floor beside him as Monika ruffled his hair and kept talking to Maybe-John.

"Are you tired?" Sammie asked. "Do you wanna lie down in my lap?"

Samson shook his head. He was still in his pajamas, the gray ones with red fire trucks printed on them. Definitely too young for someone his age, but Samson never cared what he wore, and they'd been on sale. He was staring at the television, eyes glued to the man on-screen, who was scraping burnt cheese effortlessly from the nonstick pan. The doll in Samson's lap had a chunk missing, a startling white pit gouged from the gold of its cheek. Something had scraped across it in even rows. She was reminded of the way it might look if she bit down into a fresh apple.

Samson shifted and set the doll down beside him so they watched the television side by side. There was something dark on her son's chin, so she dug around in her purse for a napkin.

I am going to be that mom, she thought as she spit into it and used the damp corner to scrub at his face. It came off on the napkin kind of brown, but also a little ruddy. She stared at it, then tipped his chin up to look some more. Her son, in his fire-truck pajamas, with dried blood crusting his neck. Someone else's blood.

Sammie hurriedly stuffed the napkin into the bottom of her purse.

3

They took Samson to see a therapist. He'd been before, when he wasn't talking and Sammie worried he had developmental issues, but this was different. This time he'd actually hurt someone. It was one thing to imagine that her son had a terrible inner secret life; it was another thing entirely to watch it lash out, with actual teeth, and draw blood from another child.

The boy, Paul, was healing up nicely. That's what Monika said after she'd spoken to his mom on the phone. He'd gotten stitches, dark ones that lined his cheek in the shape of her son's mouth. Monika's friend had texted pictures. They looked bad, but it could have been worse. This is what her wife kept repeating—*it could have been worse*—and Sammie wanted to ask how that could possibly be true. How? How could it be any worse than this?

Samson's therapist was recommended by Ms. Hastings, which immediately put Sammie on edge. She'd once considered a complete makeover after Monika said she thought she looked like the teacher. Miranda

Hastings was a blonde, the kind of blonde who seemed like she still had a sorority sticker in her car window. How could they possibly be anything alike?

Monika and Sammie went together to take Samson to his first appointment. He piled into the car with his doll, behind Sammie, sneakers thumping out a steady rhythm on the back of her seat. She closed her eyes and willed herself not to say anything. It was a weird day for everyone.

"Should I put on some music?" Sammie asked, attempting to lighten the mood.

"Whatever is fine." Monika had had to blow off a client call and was unhappy about it.

Monika had gotten a haircut that reminded Sammie of a wedge of cheese. The stylist had cut against the natural shape of the curls, so it resembled a cartoonish hunk of cheddar. Samson hated it so much he wouldn't even look at Monika directly, which made her feel terrible. They were miserable, all three of them, and there was nothing anyone could do to fix it.

Sammie found a station playing stuff she'd liked in high school, so she left it there. When the commercials came on, a chipper voice identified the station as Sunny 1059, playing the Classic Hits of Yesterday. Sammie thought back to an insurance commercial she'd seen the other day, where one of her favorite bands had shown up in an inglorious cameo. *I guess that's how you know you're really getting old*, she thought, *when your favorite songs are selling you life insurance.*

They drove down the stretch of Semoran near the mall, past the pediatrician's office, the park where Samson liked to play and dump mulch over the plastic slide, the veterinarian's office where they'd seen a man walking a peacock on a leash through the parking lot, the Old Navy where her son once threw an entire bag of Cheez-Its all over the floor. About half a mile before the therapist's office, Sammie knew, was the ice cream shop. Samson loved it there because the walls outside were covered with a gigantic mural of the ocean floor, complete with an octopus and several toothy sharks, and inside, the piped-in soundtrack featured tuba music that he claimed sounded like farts. He liked hanging out there, even though he'd never really been wild about ice cream, and as they approached it, he started making the low gargling sound he sometimes made when he wanted to get someone's attention but didn't want to actually speak.

"Not right now, pal," Monika said. "Maybe on the way back."

"Now!" he yelled. "Right now!" He banged on the window, and then Sammie heard the click of a seat belt unbuckling. She turned around, and he was yanking at the door handle.

Of course, Sammie thought. Of course her son would choose a trip to the therapist to throw a dangerous fit. That was one thing she could say for Samson: he had impeccable timing.

She turned in her seat, belt cutting across her neck, and stuck her finger in his face. "Stop that right now," she said.

"No! I want to go to ice cream!"

"Samson! Quit it!"

But he wouldn't quit it. Monika had flipped the child lock on the door, so he couldn't get it open, but now he was trying to roll down the window. Could he make it through an open window? Would he try to fling himself free of the car and launch himself directly into traffic? Sammie didn't know, but she wasn't going to wait to find out. She unbuckled her own belt and turned around to kneel on the passenger seat.

As Monika tried to find a place to pull over, Sammie squeezed her shoulders between the seats and grabbed her son's wrist, and that's when he turned around and bit her.

"Motherfucker," she hissed. His teeth were digging deep into the meat of her forearm. She could already tell it was going to be a heinous bite, stripping flesh from her like she was a chicken leg.

The look on his face while he did it was something else. Like he was enjoying his little moment of rage. Monika was swerving through traffic, jostling them around in the back seat as she tried to find a place to pull over. Sammie slipped, banging her knee on the center console, and her son looked up and smiled at her around a mouthful of her flesh. Before she realized what she was doing, she leaned down and took a bite of his own arm—sank her teeth into the meaty place directly behind his wrist. She wedged them in, deep, and then they were both looking at each other, engaged in some terrible battle to see who'd be the first to let go. Then Monika finally managed to sneak between two cars to reach the exit lane, barely avoiding a collision, and her quick turn jounced them enough that Sammie's teeth slid in even further, and that's when Samson made a wounded animal sound and finally released her.

Monika pulled into a parking space behind the Best Buy, and they all sat there, almost gasping for breath.

"What happened?" Monika asked, and Sammie realized she hadn't seen the two of them, locked together like a couple of enraged tigers. Sammie pulled her sleeve down so it covered the purplish circle of flesh on her arm.

"Samson bit himself," she said, and she locked eyes with her son and dared him to contradict her. *Tell her*, she thought. *Tell her you did it. Tell her this is your fault.*

"Bit *himself*? Is he okay?"

"He's fine. I'm gonna sit in the back with him. Let's go ahead and head back to the ice cream shop, maybe. We can reschedule the appointment for another day."

Instead of opening the door, Sammie squeezed all the way through the two seats and sat on the middle hump, next to her son. He didn't look at her, but he didn't make any other noises or try to stop her from holding his hand. That was something, anyway. Her son was never very affectionate, but then neither was she. But in that moment, it felt like she'd managed to wear him down. Like she'd succeeded in something—something awful, maybe, but potentially something great. Her adrenaline was rocketing through her body. It was going to take a few days to actually unpack what it was she'd won from him. His respect? Not likely. Maybe a grudging kind of submission.

Monika drove them back out the way they came, carefully, and they found their way back to the ice cream shop, parking alongside the watery mural. Monika went in and came back with a hot fudge sundae for herself, a dish of strawberry shortcake for Sammie, and a plain vanilla cone for Samson. They sat in the car together, with all the doors and windows open to catch a breeze, and slurped their melting ice cream. Crows flew overhead, perched in a long dark row on a power line by a massive oak tree, and got into a loud, prolonged fight with a squirrel. Samson was fascinated, imitating their squawking as ice cream from the melting cone dripped down his arm. Monika called the therapist's office and rescheduled the appointment. Sammie offered her son a bite of strawberry and smiled when he didn't spit it out. When a song came on the radio that Sammie knew, she sang along and realized she felt better than she had in weeks. She didn't even mind that the golden doll was there in the back seat with them, staring forward into nothing.

Over time, both sets of bruises faded. They'd each bitten deeply enough to leave lasting marks on each other's flesh. Sammie found herself running her fingers along the silvery scars, her son's little teeth—half baby, half adult—and whenever Samson sat down for dinner or hunched over his homework or lunch, she'd see the flash of her own marks imprinted on him, the tattoo of it branding him as her own. It was as if their teeth had done the hard work for them: here was the proof that they owned each other after all.

Monika didn't know that Sammie had bitten their son, and it didn't seem like Samson would ever say anything about it. Though there was a moment when she'd been worried. At his rescheduled therapy appointment, the therapist had asked if she could speak to Samson alone.

"Of course," Monika replied, and Sammie started to sweat. Her eyes darted to her son, who sat quietly in the overlarge flowered easy chair in the corner, still holding his golden doll. His hair fell down and shadowed his face. What was he thinking? What would he do once he was alone with the therapist, a tiny severe-looking woman whose quiet nature left a lot of room for her son to do all the talking for once? Monika had been hinting lately that Sammie talked over their son, that the reason he never spoke was that she did all the talking for him, and maybe she was right. She'd never shown much interest in Sammie's parenting strategies, but now suddenly she seemed to be dialing in on things she thought Sammie was doing wrong.

Monika set her large hand on their son's head. "You good?" she asked, and Samson nodded, then looked up at Sammie and smiled.

Oh, and there it was, after all! That feeling she'd had—of being in control again, of finally having the upper hand—suddenly vanished, wisped away like vapor, replaced by a scrabbling knowing, a gnawing under her breastbone. He hadn't let her win, no, not her smart boy. He'd made it so she could never do anything to cross him. He'd always wear the wound she'd given him, and he knew it for what it was: ammunition.

They left him there with the therapist, Dr. Kim, with her soft, soft voice and her cap of sleek black hair, and went back to the waiting room. Monika started scrolling through her phone while Sammie reopened a novel she'd been trying to finish for months.

She bit at her thumbnail and tasted blood.

"Stop that," Monika said, but Sammie couldn't make herself quit.

Maybe Samson would tell Dr. Kim about the bite. Maybe he wouldn't; maybe they'd both sit silently in that soft, pastel room and enjoy each other's quiet company. Maybe her son would tell the therapist about the time she'd screamed at him in a convenience store bathroom until her voice gave out. Maybe he'd tell her that he loved Monika more than her, that Monika was the much better mother. That was her greatest fear, that she'd be found out. A sham as a mother. A fake parent.

On the waiting room TV, a bunch of morning-show hosts sat at a round table with coffee mugs, acting like they liked one another. They were discussing some celebrity marriage. It was boring, but it was better than the book. She'd read the line "Sometimes we breathe fire and think it's oxygen" fifteen times and still didn't know what it meant and didn't care to find out.

She set the book down on her knee and rubbed at her eyes.

"You have a headache?" Monika asked. She was still tapping at her screen. Monika loved texting, did it all hours of the day and night. Sammie never knew how her wife managed to keep up with it all. And it wasn't just work stuff. There were friends she yapped with, acquaintances, people from law school she hadn't seen in forever. High school buddies. Her family: cousins, second cousins, aunts, and uncles. Facebook discussion groups about TV shows that had been off the air for years. Even now, with Sammie sitting right there beside her, all she could do was scroll.

Sammie had tried bringing it up, but it didn't do any good. All that happened was that Monika felt bad and said she'd try to stay off the screen, and she did for a little while, but then the phone started coming out during TV shows again, then in the middle of meals, and then there it was as they lay in bed next to each other. Close enough she could touch her wife's arm, the soft skin of her biceps, but her wife was a million miles away.

And wasn't that the point of the knife that jabbed at her? Wondering if Monika wished she were somewhere else? Far away from Sammie, with people who weren't her?

She got up and stamped her feet to try and get her blood circulating.

Her calves were full of pinpricks and tingles. "It's cold in here," she said stupidly, and Monika hummed a response—agreement, maybe, or maybe just the sound she made when she was acknowledging Sammie without actually hearing a thing she was saying.

Sammie walked around the waiting area, browsing through the dusty knickknacks on end tables and counters. In one corner there was a play area for kids, kind of like the one at Samson's pediatrician's office, except these toys were all stuffed animals, whereas the pediatrician had washable stuff, like blocks and stackable cups that could be disinfected. There were shelves of self-help books and a horde of plants crowding a solitary window. It was a small space, what felt to Sammie like a repurposed house, with nothing clinical looking on display, nothing to make anybody nervous.

Her heart was racing, thumping in her chest. She stuck her hand up the sleeve of her cardigan and felt for the raised ridges of her scar. For a moment she wondered if he could feel her touch on his own arm when she touched hers. *Do you feel that, feel me thinking of you? Listen to me. Our things are just ours. Mine and yours. Keep it that way.* She pushed the thought as hard as she could through the closed office door.

"Could you please sit down?" Monika said. "You're making me nervous."

"Maybe get off your phone for a minute."

Monika sighed and stuffed the phone into her purse. "What do you wanna talk about?" she asked, and Sammie realized she didn't want to talk at all.

"What should we get for lunch?" she finally asked. Monika said maybe they could stop by the grocery on the way home and get one of those rotisserie chickens—Samson seemed okay with eating them—and they'd have some leftovers to make sandwiches for lunch the next day.

"We could get wine," Sammie said, and Monika nodded.

Twenty minutes later, the door opened and the therapist asked them back inside. Samson hadn't left his spot on the overstuffed chair, but he had set down the doll on the floor. Sammie didn't know if she should be worried or relieved.

They all sat silently for several moments, until Sammie couldn't take it any longer.

"Is there something we should be doing?" She smoothed her sweaty hands over her lap, then folded them together. That felt weird, so she took them apart again and clutched the arms of the chair. "Like, something specific? To help Samson adjust? Get through . . . whatever this is?"

Dr. Kim didn't answer right away. Her son flipped through a picture book he'd unearthed from a wicker basket beside the chair. The soft flipping of pages was the only sound in the room, and it was driving Sammie crazy. Did her son even like books? Why did she know so little about him as a person?

"Is there anything we can do?" she repeated. "I'm really feeling helpless."

Monika took her hand and squeezed her fingers, once, then twice more, and Sammie calmed down. It was a thing her wife always did when she wanted to communicate something important: *It's okay*, it meant, *I'm here, I love you, we're together, and we'll carry each other through*. It softened Sammie, brought her back to herself.

"I don't think you have to worry," Dr. Kim said. "I think you're doing everything you need to."

They talked for a while about Samson—his attachment issues, trust issues, feelings of safety and security—and how to address them. "He needs greater stability when it comes to his life," the doctor said. "Routine."

"But he has stability," Monika replied. "We have a routine. School and home. Both of us are there for him."

She looked tense; Sammie could see the frown line forming between her eyes. She took her wife's hand again, and the frown line faded for a moment.

"He's a smart kid. Very bright, but sometimes that can mean bored and in need of stimulation. He needs something to soothe his busy brain."

"You mean an activity?" Monika asked. "Like Cub Scouts?"

"Something like that. Maybe a sport. Anything that can happen consistently throughout the week. Something that engages his body and his mind."

"We can work on it," Sammie said. "We'll look into it."

They left the appointment with another scheduled for the following week.

Outside the front door, lizards were basking on the pavement, tiny bodies soaking up the afternoon sunshine.

Miniature dinosaurs in a land of giant humans, Sammie thought.

Samson chased after them as Monika and Sammie walked across the parking lot toward the car.

"Let it go," Sammie called after her son, who'd managed to catch one of the bigger ones and was attempting to attach it to his ear. It dangled there for a moment, biting onto the lobe, then dropped to the pavement and scrambled away into the azalea bushes.

"God, I feel so much better," Monika said. "Don't you feel better?" She looked like she felt better, too. Smiling again now that they had a plan in place.

"Sure," Sammie said. "Lots better."

Sammie and Samson looked at each other as they got into the car, and Sammie knew that nothing was better at all.

4

Swim practice happened every Tuesday and Thursday afternoon, directly after school. That gave Sammie just enough time to pick up her son, stuff a snack into him, and get over to the YMCA pool across town before practice began.

Samson sat in the back seat, eating his crackers and cheese while Sammie navigated traffic. According to his coach, Samson was a natural swimmer, with a lot of power and great form for someone his age. Sammie had no clue if that was true; she didn't know much of anything about swimming, but she did know it was the first activity her son had ever actually seemed to enjoy. And she'd pushed him for other things, too. He was smart. When he worked hard enough, he could do anything he wanted. And she told him that, repeatedly. Especially on the rare occasion when he seemed even a tiny bit interested in something. So Sammie was willing to brave the chlorine-scented room, watching him swim for hours on end. The noise was deafening sometimes—all the splashing, the shrill sound of the whistle, all of it echoing off the tile walls, the kids' shouts magnified to shrieks. But none of that mattered. Samson was flourishing there; that was reason enough.

He still carted his doll around with him occasionally but mostly kept it in his room. Sometimes, when Sammie was cleaning up, she thought she could hear her son whispering to it, like they were having private conversations about something. She didn't like it, but she'd tried to reconcile herself to the fact that the doll was a permanent fixture in their lives. At least it wasn't going with him to school anymore.

"Hungry?" Sammie asked. Through the rearview mirror, she saw him stacking up his snacks, cheese in one pile, crackers in the other, then eating them methodically: one cheese, one cracker, one sip of juice. One cheese, one cracker, one sip of juice.

He didn't answer, but that was fine. Sammie could see he was okay with the cheese today. Sometimes it was trial and error. He did not like cheese that was orange. He did not like cheese that had holes in it. He did not like crackers with seeds or flavorings on them. He did not like orange juice. That was a weird one, not liking orange juice. All kids liked orange juice, didn't they? They lived in *Florida*, for God's sake. But then Sammie was pickier about food than anyone she knew, so she didn't really have any business questioning her son's preferences.

They pulled into the Y parking lot with fifteen minutes to spare. It had rained earlier that afternoon, and the sun was sparking diamond bright in the puddles still dotting the pavement. A blue jay sat washing itself in one, flicking water off its wings every few seconds. Sammie rolled down her window to smell the fresh air and watched a procession of moms pull their kids from their cars, carting them into the building. One mom Sammie had gotten friendly with—as friendly as she was used to being with other moms, anyway—was Lenore, who had a little girl Samson's age. The two kids didn't really hit it off, but Samson didn't really hit it off with anybody. Sammie knew that feeling; it was hard for her to make friends, too. She missed the queer people she'd hung around with when she was single, back before she'd turned into a Gay Mom. She always thought about it that way, in capital letters, because that's what happened: you turned from a Queer Woman into a Queer Mother, and suddenly your old life and friends didn't fit the vibe of your new life. There were no gay mommy groups in Orlando, hardly any gay people in her everyday interactions besides her wife.

Lenore had two kids; Serena was the younger, but the other was already in high school, a son who played basketball. Lenore was divorced. Lenore had long blond hair she pulled back on either side with tortoise-shell barrettes. Lenore had short teeth and a dimple in one cheek and wore bright lipstick that sometimes stained those little teeth like she'd been drinking wine. Sammie thought about those teeth a lot. Too much, probably.

Sammie liked the way Lenore talked. She was blunt and aggressive, and she didn't put up with the other moms' attempts at fake chitchat. The first time they'd talked had been an accident. Lenore was sitting up at the top of the bleachers, waving in Sammie's direction with a big cardboard fan, and she had automatically waved back.

"No, not you," Lenore yelled. "My kid. She's got her fucking suit on inside out again."

Normally Sammie would have been embarrassed—waving at a woman she didn't even know, like a total idiot—but instead she was impressed at the woman, swearing openly in front of a room full of fourth and fifth graders, and, more impressively, their stuck-up mothers.

"Come up," Lenore told her. "Not my kid. You, I mean. The new kid's mom."

Sammie had climbed up to sit with Lenore, who handed her what looked like a water bottle full of Coke to share—or so she thought until she took a sip and found out it was really just a bottle of rum with a splash of soda for color. It felt illicit and kind of sexy, to drink with all those kids around them, and to not care. Lenore wore so much lipstick that it rubbed off around the screw top, and every time Sammie took a drink she tasted that lipstick and, she thought, the woman wearing it—this woman she didn't know, who kept leaning in to whisper loudly about all the other moms. There was something nice about it, something unusual, an extra moment that was hers alone. It all felt strangely important, somehow, and she wished the moment could have lasted.

"Finish your cheese," Sammie said now, watching her son methodically chew every bite. That's how he ate. Though her son's brain was still a mystery, there were things about him that she did know: He was whip smart and a fast learner. He was graceful, with catlike reflexes; she and Monika both felt he could have been a dancer, could have done gymnastics. He could catch a ball, skip rope for hours, clap on beat. He walked with confidence, more so than most children his age, regardless of gender. He was neat and tidy, for the most part. More than most boys that age, she knew. Or at least she thought she knew.

Okay, he wasn't *always* neat. And he wasn't always graceful or well-behaved. He shouted sometimes, threw fits, shut down altogether. He was normal . . . until he wasn't. Maybe that's how it was with every child. Often there were days Sammie had to remind herself that just because her son acted a certain way—withdrawn, or sullen, or hostile—didn't mean he'd act that way forever. It was hard to raise a kid. Different from what she'd expected when she was pregnant. When she had two bodies to feed.

"Could I have a bite?" Sammie asked.

Samson passed a sweaty square of cheese up to her in the front seat. She nibbled at it until it resembled a misshapen heart, then wiggled it at him. "Check it out. That's nacho cheese, Samson. It's mine."

He didn't smile back at her, but his face softened. That was something.

"Let's get you suited up," she said, and they both got out of the car. The breeze that had been sweeping through the palm fronds while they sat in the car had tapered off, and the heat was rolling off the pavement, cooking Sammie's legs. She let him carry his own bag, because it seemed good for him to learn early how to take care of things for himself. She didn't want him to grow into the kind of man who expected women to do everything for him—wash his clothes, make his meals, clean, do the shopping. She wanted him to be self-sufficient, sure, but she also wanted him to be an equal partner in a household.

Monika never washed his clothes. In fact, Monika hardly ever went to the store. It was Sammie who picked up the milk and cereal, bags of apples and tangerines and chips and ice cream, even the sports drinks Samson plowed through like he was constantly on the cusp of total dehydration. Sammie and Monika did share a bank account; it was a necessary household arrangement, and Sammie was on all of Monika's credit cards. But what this often meant was that, since Monika brought home the money, Sammie got stuck doing the rest of the work—cooking, cleaning, chauffeuring, and anything else that happened to come up.

Monika didn't always say this outright, but she didn't listen when Sammie complained about it, either. She said the real reason Sammie was unhappy wasn't that Monika didn't help around the house but that Sammie just didn't like doing housework. But what did Monika know about it? She wasn't the one who cooked every meal for a super-picky son who threw out most of what she made, or cleaned the sheets when he wet the bed, or washed his hair when he puked after getting the flu. Monika got to be the dad-mom, the fun one who came home from long trips with presents and got him all riled up before bed, then sat on the couch with a drink while Sammie dealt with the aftermath.

Which was one reason Sammie looked forward to swim day—it got her out of the house.

Lenore was already inside, hastily stuffing Serena's long blond hair under her swim cap. *That must hurt*, Sammie thought.

"Will you hold still, goddamn it?" Lenore said, pinching Serena's shoulder until she quit squirming. "Just be still and we can be done with this."

Serena frowned up at her mother with her sweet little cookie-dough face, but she didn't complain. Serena didn't complain about much. Sammie wasn't sure if that was a daughter thing, or if it was because Lenore wasn't someone you wanted to mess with. Samson put his swim cap on by himself while Sammie dug out his goggles. Serena pulled hers on, bigger blue circles over her big blue eyes, and then the two of them were off around the lip of the huge loud pool while Lenore and Sammie climbed to their spot at the top of the risers.

"Cold in here today," Sammie said, and Lenore shrugged. She was always shrugging, as if she wasn't very interested in what Sammie had to say; somehow this made Sammie want to work even harder to impress her.

Lenore had brought her usual large water bottle, but this time it was full of vodka and orange juice for screwdrivers. She only ever brought the one bottle to split between them, but it was definitely enough to share, because Lenore was so heavy-handed with the liquor. Today the orange barely bled into the bite of the vodka. All Sammie could taste was something sharp, like teeth digging into her own tongue.

She took careful, slow sips. She still had to drive her son home, and even though she always felt a little looser after she drank—like maybe she actually drove better that way?—she still felt a nagging undercurrent of guilt reminding her that it wouldn't be so great if she got pulled over, or wound up with a DUI, or worse.

"Look at that girl! What a piglet." Lenore pointed one painted fingernail down the slope of risers toward a knot of kids. It was Maisie she was talking about, a girl with short dark hair and a body built like a miniature version of her mother's, a figure that a nice person might describe as pear-shaped. Not Lenore. Lenore never sugarcoated anything.

"Her suit is too small," Sammie replied, always nervous to take things as far as Lenore. "Her mother should get her a new one."

"Her mother should get a lock for the fucking cookie jar." Lenore snorted, taking a heaving gulp from the bottle. "She should lay off the cookies herself, too."

Sammie frowned a bit at this. What did it matter what they ate? People's bodies were all different, and differences weren't a bad thing—that's what she always told Samson. But she didn't dare say that to Lenore. She just nodded in agreement and took a nervous swig from the bottle.

They were sitting close together, closer than they'd ever sat before, in part because Lenore seemed intensely drunk, like maybe she'd shown up to practice already tipsy. She was talking louder than normal, and Sammie worried that the other mothers might hear her if they weren't more careful. But she wasn't going to say anything to Lenore, unwilling to shatter their little bubble.

Sammie's phone buzzed on the riser in front of her and displayed a close-up image of Monika's smiling face, dimpled cheeks and all. The phone jittered along the wood and nearly slid off the bench. Lenore caught it with her foot.

"Is that your wife?" Lenore asked as she handed Sammie the phone. "She looks butch."

"Yeah, I guess she is."

Lenore laughed, too loud. A big puff of vodka breath fanned Sammie's cheek, and her heart galloped. "You guess she's your wife or you guess she's butch?"

"Both," Sammie replied, and took a huge pull from the bottle.

"You should bring Samson over after practice. The kids can play and we'll make drinks."

Sammie had groceries to buy and a mountain of dirty laundry waiting for her back home, along with a long list of errands she'd failed to finish before Monika got home from her last trip. "Sure," she said. "That sounds great."

When they were done, Sammie followed Lenore and her daughter through the parking lot, feeling the fuzzy climb of the vodka working its way into her muscles. Samson trailed behind, his curls slicked flat to the sides of his face. Even though he always wore goggles in the pool, water still managed to seep inside and irritate his eyes, which were bloodshot from the chlorine. Serena galloped ahead to her mother's Honda. Her blond hair was usually tinged green from so much time in the pool; Lenore probably didn't wash it out right away after practice.

"I'll follow you," Sammie called. Lenore just flapped a hand at her as she boosted her daughter into the back of the van.

Worried that she'd suddenly change her mind, Sammie hustled Samson over to their car and urged him into the back seat.

"Tired," he said. "Wanna sleep."

"I know, buddy." She buckled him in, careful not to burn him with the seat belt. "But this'll be fun, I promise."

Lenore backed out of her spot so fast she nearly rammed into a family walking to their car. The man gave her the finger, and Lenore honked at him until he moved out of the way. Sammie backed up quickly, too, and followed her out. They drove on through the neighborhood and then out into the city proper, near Mills and the Milk District, past the Publix and all the bread and eggs and dish detergent she still needed to buy there.

Samson leaned his head against the window and closed his eyes. Anxious to keep him awake, Sammie dug around on the floor when they reached a stoplight and unearthed a Coke, left over from a two-for-one deal she'd picked up one morning after a hangover.

"How about this?" she asked, handing it back. Samson sat up and grabbed it. They hardly ever let him have soda—one thing she and

Monika agreed on was that caffeine and sugar just weren't a good idea for him—but for once, Sammie didn't care about any of that. She put her foot on the gas and sped up, trying not to lose Lenore's minivan, which was dirty and covered in bumper stickers that all seemed to promote divergent causes. MY KID CAN BEAT UP YOUR HONOR ROLL STUDENT *next to a* PTA *sticker?* Sammie wondered. *What the hell was that about?*

They pulled into a run-down apartment complex about half an hour from Sammie's house. It looked like it was going to rain again any second, but there were kids running around outside in the gray humidity, and none of them looked very happy. Sammie drove past a stagnant pool, a solitary loop of yellow pool noodle floating there like a limp piece of macaroni. Lenore pulled into an empty slot, and Sammie parked directly beside her. Samson had finished the Coke, and there was a brown mustache of liquid over his lip. Sammie brushed it off with the back of her hand and wiped the residue on her pants.

They walked together up the path to Lenore's unit, Samson burping repeatedly as they trudged up the stairs. Sammie's phone rang—Monika again—so she switched it to silent and dropped it back in her pocket.

I'll call her back later, she thought, *after we've all had a nice time.* Her wife could find something to keep herself busy. Let her be the one waiting for once.

Lenore unlocked the door and let them inside. The living room was spacious, with a big overstuffed sectional sofa and a black leather La-Z-Boy recliner, but the place smelled funky. A large gray cat wound its way around Sammie's ankles, and she recognized the odor: a litter box that desperately needed cleaning.

Serena picked up the cat and squeezed it so hard it grunted. "Jasper," she crooned, and stuffed the cat up under her chin, where it sat lodged, fat and unhappy, before showing it off to Samson.

He didn't look interested. He'd never asked for a pet. No puppies, nothing. Not even a fish. When Sammie was young she'd begged for a kitten—a tiny calico ball of fluff that she'd found under a neighbor's house—but her parents hadn't wanted to deal with it.

"Go show Samson your room," Lenore commanded, shooing the kids down the hall.

Serena took the cat with her, and Samson followed, dragging his feet. That was the thing: she might not always know what her son was thinking, but she always understood his body language. The way he was scuffing down the hall, she knew he was this close to acting up. Sammie just hoped he'd wait to throw a fit until after they left.

Lenore led Sammie into the galley kitchen. The sink was full of dishes clotted with food, a crusty dish towel spread over the top as if to hide the mess. Lenore grabbed a gigantic bottle of vodka from the freezer, nearly the size of a toddler, and poured the booze into two water glasses. She plopped two green olives apiece inside, splashing the counter.

They carried their drinks onto a concrete balcony that overlooked a parking lot. Even though it felt like rain, the sky hadn't broken open yet. It was hot outside, but the drinks were cold, and the clouds swept past quickly, racing one another as the wind picked up and speared fingers through the fronds of the palm trees that surrounded the complex. There was a café table and a set of two matching chairs, so that's where they sat, next to each other, balancing their glasses on the rickety top.

"How long you been married?" Lenore asked. She was taking long sips of her drink. Not hurried, necessarily, but with a look that said she was already thinking about her next glass.

"Just a couple of years. We've been together a lot longer, though."

"I'm divorced."

Sammie nodded. "Right, yeah."

"Let me tell you, it's better than I ever thought it could be." Lenore laughed, and Sammie could see into the way back of her mouth where her molars sat, rooted and dark. One tooth was missing completely, a demolished house in a small, crowded neighborhood of teeth.

"Marriage is . . . hard," Sammie finally replied, and Lenore laughed again.

"Probably not as hard for you, right? Gotta be easier with another woman."

Sammie smiled like she always did when someone had something dumb and off base to say about lesbians. A smile that said, *Sure, think what you like, women who fuck women never have relationship problems.* But inside her pants pocket her phone sat *ringing ringing ringing,* and she didn't want to go home or have to deal with any of it, so she'd come here with this woman she barely knew, on the off chance that she'd . . . what? Show her some attention?

They both sat quietly and drank some more. Sammie waited to experience what she liked about being with Lenore, that not-feeling feeling that happened at swim practice, but instead she felt the wrongness of it settling in the pit of her stomach. Lenore casually placed her arm on the back of Sammie's chair, like that was a normal way to sit, when both of them knew exactly what came next. Hadn't Sammie been building toward it for weeks? Hadn't she engineered things to wind up precisely this way, making choices that could wreck everything she'd worked her whole life to build?

Lenore scooted closer, chair screeching as it slid across the concrete of the balcony. Her hot vodka breath forced Sammie to remember the cool mintiness of her wife's mouth—Monika who chewed wintergreen gum so her kisses felt icy. That was the first memory she had of that tongue, a taste of something like winter in Florida. Then Lenore put her hand on Sammie's knee and her mouth over Sammie's mouth, and it was happening, just like Sammie knew it would, and it wasn't even fun, because she was still thinking about her wife. She pictured Monika waiting at home, sitting on the couch worried and hungry.

Lenore and Sammie were both making the kind of sounds you were supposed to make to show that the kissing was good. Maybe Lenore was enjoying it, Sammie wasn't sure, but to her the kiss just felt like lips rubbing against lips. She could have been making out with anyone. It made her want to dissociate. She imagined herself outside her body, grabbing her son, walking them downstairs and getting into their car, driving the whole way home, and then she was back in her own living room, sitting on her couch with Monika, arguing about what they'd have for dinner and who'd take charge of making sure Samson got dressed for bed on time.

"You taste good," Lenore mumbled against her mouth, and Sammie moaned, but she thought she couldn't taste anything. Maybe that's what vodka did, just wiped a person's taste away completely. What did it matter? She'd made the decision weeks ago; she'd chosen it herself. She brought up her hand, pressed it lightly against Lenore's breast, and the woman huffed into Sammie's open mouth.

I wonder if I could get drunk from her breath alone, Sammie wondered, and the sliding glass door squeaked open behind them.

They scrambled apart. Sammie's knees knocked the table as she shoved back into her chair, overturning her glass, which splashed the ground and dripped onto her legs.

"Shit," Lenore muttered, uselessly attempting to catch the spill with her hands. Her face was red with embarrassment and booze. She wondered how her own face looked.

"What do you guys need?" Sammie asked without turning around, breathing heavily. Her voice sounded wild, like she'd just finished a strenuous workout.

"That cat scratched me," Samson yelled. "I hate this stupid cat!"

Then it was the cat that screamed—a high-pitched wail like a baby— and suddenly a gray-and-white blur flew by overhead and vanished over the side of the balcony. Sammie jumped up belatedly, as if she might be able to prevent what had already happened, but the cat was long gone.

Serena was screaming now, too. Lenore called over the balcony rail and then yelled at her daughter, telling her to shut up. Only Samson stayed silent. He stared at Sammie from the safety of the apartment, then turned and vanished back inside.

5

They sat in the car with the doors cracked while Sammie pulled herself together. The evening sky was coming on purple dark over the apartment building, and the heat, though fading with the sun, still roasted the interior of the car. Sweat broke out on Sammie's neck and chest.

She tapped the code to open her phone. *You have seventeen missed calls from Monika*, it read. There were dozens of unread texts:

Where are you

are you okay

where's Samson

did you get in an accident

Sammie, where are you

I'm getting worried now

where are you

where are you???

She couldn't decide what to do first. Should she drive straight home? Call now, or maybe just text back? Pull into another parking lot and call her wife from there? Her hands were shaking. She tried to stick the key in the ignition, but she dropped the ring on the floor and had to feel around blindly for it.

"Why?" she whispered. "*Why?*"

She didn't know if she was asking Samson or herself, or even what she was asking, really. The eternal *why* of her son, the eternal why of herself—forever the same open-ended question, but never any satisfactory answers.

Luckily the cat seemed fine. It had landed in a large clump of palm, which had mercifully broken its fall. But Serena was hysterical. She was sure the cat, still trapped and yowling in the top of the scrub, had leaped to its death. Lenore had finally slapped her face to get her to stop screaming. Then they'd all stood there like they'd been hit: Sammie, still out on the balcony; Lenore, hulking over her daughter; Serena, red-faced and mouth agape, like she wanted to start screaming all over again. But not Samson. He just stood there nonchalantly, playing with the hem of his gym shorts, as if he hadn't just chased a live animal over the side of a second-floor balcony.

They'd left right after the slap, hardly any conversation between them. Lenore went out with a box of Friskies to try to coax down the cat and left them in the parking lot without another glance. Sammie didn't think they'd be sitting together anymore at swim practice, and that felt fine. Kind of a relief, actually, to know that she'd somehow managed to extricate herself from something that would have gone worse, given more time and her own self-destructive tendencies. She had Samson to thank for that small grace.

The realization that she could still fix things finally shook her out of her stupor. She started the car and turned on the headlights, navigating out of the complex and away from that gray, peeling place. When they hit the road outside she felt even better. It was as if everything that had happened that afternoon had all been a bad dream. None of it was really her.

"We don't have to talk about any of this," Sammie said, looking back in the rearview at her son. "We can just . . . pretend it never happened. Right? We don't have to tell your mom."

Samson stared at her and rubbed at his wrist. Saying nothing.

"Right. Just like that."

She and her son could have their secrets, too. They could do that for each other, at least. And wasn't that love?

Where the hell have you been? I thought you both were dead!"

Sammie carried the groceries into the house—four plastic Publix bags, looped around her wrist and cutting into the skin—and tossed them onto the counter. "Don't be dramatic," she said. "It's only been a couple of hours." She'd stopped at the store and picked up a frozen lasagna, a chocolate cake, and a twelve-pack of beer. Before she did anything else, she popped open a bottle and chugged a third of it. She didn't want her wife smelling the vodka on her breath.

Monika glared at her. "It's late," she said, and Sammie rolled her eyes good-naturedly. Or at least she hoped it looked good-natured. It might have looked like really lousy improv. She was incredibly bad at faking her feelings.

"Here." She opened another beer and handed it to her wife. It was the kind Monika liked, that dark, heavy stuff that Sammie thought tasted like burnt coffee. Sammie was more of a white wine person—sometimes she joked that she was like one of the Real Housewives, that's how much she liked it—but she knew the beer would help chill Monika out. When her wife drank, she was always in a great mood. Sammie loved that about her. Such a happy drunk.

"You're not going to tell me where you've been? That's it? No explanation?"

Sammie peeled open the cardboard box that surrounded the lasagna and stuck the tray inside the cold oven. "We went over to another kid's house for a playdate. It was fun, no harm."

"So why didn't you call?" Monika asked, taking the lasagna back out and setting it on the counter. She turned on the oven, waiting for the preheat light to pop on.

"I forgot my phone in the car," Sammie replied. "Then we were driving back, and I figured it would be faster to tell you in person, so we could all eat before it got too late."

Monika still hadn't had any of her beer. Once she had some, everything would be fine. Sammie put all her energy into wishing her wife would take one good swig.

"Samson," Monika called. He was in the living room watching an episode of *Nature* about hyenas. Every time one of the hyenas howled, he laughed. From the kitchen, Sammie could see him lying on the couch with his shoes still on. Normally she would have yelled at him for that, but not today.

Samson sat up, but he didn't come into the kitchen.

"You had a playdate?" Monika asked. "With a swim buddy?"

Here it was, the moment when he could tell Monika anything, say whatever he liked, bring the whole thing tumbling down. Sammie took another sip of beer to fortify herself. Samson shrugged and lay back down, putting his sneakers directly on one of the white velvet throw pillows.

"I just wish you'd called," Monika whispered. "I was worried about you."

She was drinking her beer. Finally. Sammie sagged against the counter and finished her own, then put her arms around her wife and kissed her neck, right in the soft place behind her ear. She smelled so good, like clean laundry. It was a relief to be home with her family, her son safe and sound, knowing her wife had genuinely missed her. Worried over her because she cared. Sammie squeezed her again, tighter, and promised herself that she'd try harder.

"I'm sorry," she said. "I won't do it again."

She and Samson looked at each other. He took his shoe and swiped it directly across the top of the cushion. Later, Sammie would have to scrub for twenty minutes to remove the stain.

The lasagna took a long time to cook. She should've thought of that when she'd bought it, but she was in a hurry. She'd left Samson in the car because she didn't want to argue with him about taking too long in the store, not when he was so tired and upset after what happened at Lenore's. Or was he? It was hard to tell, with her son. If anything, he seemed upset that his routine had been disrupted. As a person who thrived with a set schedule, she could understand the feeling. Probably not to a chasing-a-cat-over-a-balcony degree, but she definitely understood the stress behind Samson's freak-out. Anxiety felt like a falling cat. Flailing. Yowling. A miserable, all-consuming thing that shadowed much of her life.

Yes, that she understood.

They ate standing around the kitchen island, except for Samson, who sat on one of the barstools, his head hanging so low that his hair grazed the meat and cheese in his bowl. Sammie had dug some Italian bread out of the freezer and slathered on garlic butter, but it still tasted freezer-burned; the only one who didn't mind eating it was her son, who would eat a rock if it were coated in flavored grease.

"Off to bed," Monika said once Samson's head finally caught the edge of the table. He didn't argue, just left his stuff right there and trudged upstairs.

Sammie and Monika had another beer apiece, then one more— normally enough to get Sammie a little drunk, but she was too wired and on edge to feel it. Monika, however, definitely seemed buzzed. Her eyes were glassy, and her voice had softened, and they kissed for a while in the kitchen as they cleaned up before migrating over to the couch.

"You look so pretty," Monika said, proof positive that she was tipsy. Monika never gave out compliments unless she was under the influence. The worst part was that Sammie was starved for them, those compliments that spilled so easy off her honey tongue after a couple of beers. All those *pretty*s and *beautiful*s and *sweetheart*s and *angel*s she never heard when her wife was sober. For that matter, Sammie didn't think to sweet-talk her wife that often anymore. It was easy to take each other for granted when they'd been together so long.

Jesus, why was it so hard to be nice to each other? Sammie wondered, and then thought of Lenore's vodka kisses and made herself focus on her wife.

They pulled off each other's clothes, neither of them worrying that Samson might trot back downstairs asking for a glass of water or wanting to watch something on TV.

"That feels good," Sammie said, because it absolutely did— everything felt good, finally—and when she came it felt like coming three different times, as if she'd banked all the orgasms she'd been missing out on.

Afterward, they sat together on the couch and let their sweat dry. The TV was showing an ad for a food dehydrator. Monika had shine all around her mouth, and for once Sammie didn't nag at her to wipe it off.

"Did you have fun today?" Monika asked, snuggling under Sammie's arm.

Sammie could feel the wet heat radiating from herself, that fetid funk that accompanied sweat. She knew it would get on her wife, and then she'd smell her own stink in bed, because Monika wouldn't wash, would think it was sweet or nice to have their smells tacked to each other, as if they could carry their lovemaking with them wherever they went.

"It was nice," Sammie said, remembering that vodka mouth again, that mouth that wasn't her wife's, the one that tasted like nothing but that was something different. She didn't want Lenore again. It wasn't that. But she did want something different. She wanted it with her wife, wanted it for her family. Mostly, though, she wanted it for herself. She wondered if that would mean destroying everything they'd created so they could build something new in its place.

The cat needed five stitches, and Lenore was goddamn furious over it. Spending money she didn't have, on a cat she detested, all because she'd gotten too drunk and decided to have a good time. She could barely remember the night, she'd had so much vodka, but she thought that she might have been . . . um, kissing . . . Sammie Lucas. It was just friendly, not anything gay. Not serious, really. It was just that she'd wanted to try it out. Sammie was pretty, and funny, and Lenore hadn't had a friend like that in a while. Just someone to shoot the shit with. Those swim practices were brain-numbingly boring, and the other moms were so stuck-up, with their fancy cars and clothes. And they all seemed to know one another already—PTA and shit. There was no way to infiltrate unless you were wealthy like them. Sammie had some money—she wasn't poor like Lenore—but she didn't act so stuck-up. Anyway, it didn't matter. Lenore had gone and ruined it by getting so drunk, just like she ruined everything these days. She was so mortified, she stopped taking Serena to practices. Not sure she could bear it if Sammie ignored her there, too, like those other snotty moms. Sometimes it was just better not to know.

6

Back at swim practice, Sammie was wishing she were home with a cold glass of chardonnay. Maybe even a cheap beer. She wasn't feeling all that picky.

Lenóre had stopped showing up. She wasn't up at the top of the bleachers with Sammie fucking around, sipping booze, and shit-talking the other moms. There was no sign of her. Of course, now Sammie knew where she lived. She could stop by to visit her anytime she wanted, in theory. Just in case she ever wanted to, she absolutely could. Not that she would. She wouldn't do that. She wouldn't need to. Why would she need to do such a thing?

It was just enough to know it was there.

Now she sat alone and watched her son move cleanly through the pool, his young body razor-sharp, cutting through the water like a saw, the water having to work to suture everything back up in his wake.

She wasn't the type of mother who yelled for her son from the bleachers. That wasn't in her. Her love stayed caught inside her body like a crab trapped in a net. Sometimes she wished she were the kind of mom who could cheer for her son—when she heard other moms screeching gleefully, as if their children's accolades were their own—but all she felt when she watched Samson knife his way through the water was a kind of relief. *Of course he can do this*, is what she thought. Of course he knows how to make himself a dagger and stab his way through.

After all, isn't that what she'd tried to teach her boy? That he could get anything he wanted, just by throwing himself hard enough at the challenge?

There he was, speeding through the wake. Brute force, all arms and jutting torso. He was the first to arrive and the first to land, always. Her son was the best swimmer on the team. The coach repeatedly told her how good he was, often suggested that he'd benefit from private lessons, but that seemed like more work than she could possibly bear. Why was it that adding more to her son's life made her feel like she was taking away from herself?

A lot of the moms sat huddled together on the benches a few rows below her. When she first started bringing Samson to practice, she'd had the opportunity to get to know those women, to sit with them and be part of their circle, but she'd chosen to lodge herself in the upper deck with Lenore, like a couple of vultures. Now that it was just her again, the power dynamic had shifted. She could feel the smiles the women gave one another when she climbed past them to sit alone in the back, heard their whispers and laughter as they snuck glances at her. Sammie brought books with her, messed around on her phone, tried everything she could think of to seem busy. She really missed the alcohol.

Weirdly enough, it made things worse that her kid was better than everyone else on the team. If he weren't leagues beyond all of them, maybe the moms would've accepted her, let her cram into that huddle with them, their benches littered with Snack Packs and damp suits and towels with names hand-lettered across one end in bold black Sharpie.

But, no, her son was absolutely the best. Embarrassingly better than his teammates. And he wasn't nice about it—wasn't humble, anyway, which is sometimes fine for boys though never for girls. When Samson won a race, he didn't shake hands with any of the other kids, or accept compliments graciously. He didn't say thank you. He just stood there at the edge of the pool, looking like he was waiting for them to finish talking, like he couldn't wait to get away, which maybe he couldn't. The swimmers were all loud and boring and basic. Sammie didn't blame him. She wouldn't have wanted to be friends with them, either.

Her boy completed another lap, still yards ahead of the closest swimmer: a girl named Delia, who wore a violently purple swim cap with her name emblazoned in a bright pink bubble font. Samson stroked quickly down to the wall, tapped, turned, and emerged sleek as a seal to double back past everyone, churning up wake. When he landed at the other side, he'd outdistanced even Delia by nearly the entire length of the pool.

The coach helped Samson out of the water, then congratulated him loudly, holding up his hand for a high five. Samson's arms stayed by his sides. He was never going to be easy, her kid. He just couldn't be *normal*.

More laughter from the moms below. They weren't looking at her, not yet, but soon enough one of them would dart their eyes back at her and smirk. She stared down at the open book on her lap, willing the words to swim into focus. Her son was making a fool of her, and she wasn't willing to engage with any of it.

Fuck it, she thought. It occurred to her that she could always bring her own alcohol with her to practice. Couldn't she just pour some vodka into a water bottle for herself? And she immediately felt better, almost as good as if Lenore were back with her in the top row again, like two girls at the back of the bus.

• • •

That night, she made chicken from a recipe that a friend of a friend had posted on Facebook. The woman who posted it was someone she'd slept with years ago, well before meeting Monika, so borrowing their homestyle family recipe felt extremely lesbian. The sex with that woman had been subpar, too much tongue in her ear and not enough in her pussy, but the breakfasts the morning after had been excellent: chef-quality eggs Benedict and waffles topped with fresh fruit and home-made whipped cream. It turned out that Monika had slept with the same woman, which they'd discovered by accident because they both called her "the Ear Girl."

Queers really are part of one big flow chart after all, Sammie thought as she diced carrots into wildly uneven chunks. *We're all part of the extended cast of* The L Word.

It seemed like a nice idea, to make her family something home-cooked from scratch, even though she wasn't exactly the world's best chef. Most days she only halfway cooked dinner, meaning she'd buy a rotisserie chicken and broil a couple potatoes and toss some dressing onto a bagged salad before calling it a day. But today she was excited to try something new. She imagined herself like a gay Martha Stewart, dressed in a crisp white button-down, perfectly preparing something delicious for her delighted family. She chopped some celery into strips but then jabbed herself with the knife, dripping blood onto one of the chicken cutlets. Her slicing got less precise after that, as she worked around her bandaged finger. A few of the potatoes rocketed off the counter under her blade, skidding under the kitchen table. Sammie left them there, the blood pooling in her fingertip, pulse pounding.

Everything went into one casserole dish, which was supposed to save time but still allow the food to look Instagram-worthy. A bunch of fresh herbs on top. Lemon slices layered over the chicken, very chic. Sammie was looking forward to setting it down on the table between Monika and Samson—napkins on their laps, and a bundle of fresh daisies in a vase she'd dug out from beneath the counter—and snapping a photo.

But then the chicken came out of the oven, smoking and nearly inedible. The interior was bone-dry and gristly, and the skin—which she'd spent almost an hour basting with herbs and garlic and lime—had an unfortunate bitter flavor, as if the entire thing had been doused with kitchen cleanser. They sat at the dining room table and pushed the food around their plates until Monika suggested that maybe they should order a pizza.

Sammie got up, picked up her plate, and threw it directly into the garbage. Utensils and all.

"Well, that was mature," Monika said. She collected the rest of the dishes and the full pan of chicken and took it to the sink. Samson had already left the table, wandered back to the TV. *Wheel of Fortune* was on, and Pat Sajak was asking a woman in a spangly teal tank top if she'd like to buy a vowel. Samson yelled at her to choose an *A*, but instead she picked an *E* and lost her turn. Her son shook his head in disgust.

"I'm sick to death of cooking," Sammie replied, and realized she absolutely meant it. "I'm not cooking anymore," she declared, and that felt even better. "I mean it. Not another damn thing, as long as I live!"

"Don't swear in front of Samson," Monika said.

"Damn, damn, damn," Sammie muttered, pulling a big jug of chardonnay out of the fridge. It wasn't very good, according to Monika, but Sammie couldn't tell the difference. She poured wine directly into the glass of water she'd been drinking from, even though there was still a half inch left at the bottom. "I think he's heard worse."

"I can't talk to you when you're like this," her wife said, and left the room.

I can't talk to anyone, Sammie thought, and that made her feel extremely sorry for herself, so she downed the rest of her wine and immediately poured herself another glass. Monika was right, it didn't taste good—it had a flavor like maple syrup, which was disturbing. But there was no other alcohol in the house, and she was in the mood to get lost in a glass of something boozy.

And wasn't that what Monika had always said about her? *You like to feel bad. You like feeling miserable.* Sammie would push back, half-heartedly, but there was something to be said for that achy bad feeling that came with truly wallowing in misery. Either too much good or too much bad, that's what Sammie always longed for. When it came to feelings, there was no such thing as a satisfying middle ground.

Give me all or nothing, Sammie thought. *Give me pain or pleasure.*

She drank her wine, grimacing at the sour taste, and wondered if wine could go bad enough to poison a person. This chardonnay should've been thrown out a while ago, but she wasn't the kind of woman who felt okay about throwing out wine. She'd never really drank until she was in her midtwenties. She'd grown up in a conservative, religious household, and neither of her parents drank. Not even a beer. Once, just after college, she'd gone with them to a party for a work friend of her father's who wasn't affiliated with their church, and they'd had champagne sitting out in pretty glass flutes. Sammie had picked up one and sipped at it while she talked with people, letting the flavor sit sweet and bursting on her tongue, actually enjoying herself as the buzz crept up her throat and made her head feel soft and easy. When she'd finished the glass, her father laid his hand heavy on her shoulder and whispered in her ear: *Why would you let everyone see you do that? What possessed you? This is not how we raised you.* Her mother in a corner, staring sternly into space but radiating disappointment. Her father took his hand from her shoulder, then smiled and called out a hearty *Bob, how you been?* and shook hands with Bob, who was clutching a sweaty bottle of beer.

It wasn't the first time she'd noticed the inconsistencies between how she was expected to behave and how her parents allowed other people to move around them in the world. It took many years for her to understand that the ways she was still allowing herself to be boxed in by them meant that she was still under their control. She didn't speak with them anymore, not really, except for brief spurts of communication. Samson was the only one they really kept in contact with, which Sammie allowed because she never wanted to be the kind of mother who decided her son's life choices for him. He could go to church if he wanted, could spend time with his grandparents if he wanted—that was all up to him. It didn't mean she had to.

She'd learned early on that it was important to build her own family. In high school, she'd had an English teacher who'd seemed different from all the others. She'd championed Sammie's writing, encouraged her to read more, gave her books and CDs and asked how she liked them. There was a reference librarian at their small public library who'd sat with her and helped her pick out colleges, researching financial aid options when she wasn't sure her parents would help with anything. It wasn't until later that she realized that these women were queer, too—that the reason she'd felt so understood and embraced by them was that they'd gone through the same problems she was experiencing. To be queer was to build your own community. To embrace the people who loved you for yourself and didn't expect you to change to suit their hang-ups.

There were things she missed about her parents. The soft glow of a candlelight service as everyone in the congregation stood together in the dark and sang Christmas carols. The family meals they'd shared on Sundays, heavy with fat and butter. But that was pretty much it. She didn't miss her relationship with her mother, which had always been stilted and fraught and full of passive-aggressive jabs about Sammie's weight or her clothes or her lack of femininity. She certainly didn't miss interactions with her father, who was gruff and abrasive at the best of times, and downright hostile with Sammie on occasion. It was a relief to leave them. *It felt freeing* is what she told herself when she spent holidays without them, or when she had to tell people they were estranged. People always assumed that their distance was a direct result of her queerness, that being gay had been the deciding factor, but the truth was that it was a lifetime of dismissals and disappointments that drove her, at last, to say goodbye to it all.

A second glass of wine and she was still sober. Not even tipsy, which seemed unfair. She decided to pour a third and sit outside. It was a nice enough night, aside from the mosquitoes, and she just wanted to stare up into something bigger than herself for a moment, to make herself feel smaller and less important, to make her universe widen and remind herself that, in the grand scheme of things, the feelings she was having would not last forever, that they were nothing more than the smallest passage of time.

She sat down on the back step off the patio and slopped wine directly onto her knee.

Okay, maybe I'm a little drunk after all, Sammie thought. *I'm getting dumb and philosophical.*

Their house had three backyard neighbors: one directly behind them, separated from their yard with a waist-high chain-link fence, and two others bookending the yard with tall, expensive wooden fences that blocked any view of their windows. Sammie didn't know much about the woman who lived in the place directly behind them, only that she owned two large rottweilers and occasionally hosted a man for the weekend, probably a boyfriend; every now and then she spotted him mowing the grass or fixing a sagging gutter.

But that night, like most nights, there was nothing new to see. Just the lemon glow of the porch light, flickering erratically as a huge moth battered against it. How strange that she always wanted to be home, Sammie thought—because when she finally got there, it felt like she was being smothered under a pillow.

Sammie got up and wandered across the unkempt lawn, feeling the dead grass crunch beneath her bare feet. It hurt a little, but not enough to make her want to go back in the house. Alongside the fence ran a long, soft mound of upturned earth, the path of a rampant mole. She let herself rest there as she leaned against the chain-link fence and looked into the house beyond. The windows mirrored the setup of her own house: Two on the right-hand side, probably bedrooms, with a single pane above. To the left, wide curtained windows, likely the dining room. In the middle, a kitchen window. Sammie had noticed that a bright light was always on in this particular room, no matter the time of day. Sometimes, if she leaned over her own sink, she could look through her kitchen window and see the other woman at hers. Both of them doing what women did in their homes: Washing dishes. Preparing meals. Filling a glass with wine.

She set her own wineglass on the ground, burying the base in one of the molehills, and in one abrupt movement jumped the fence. It clanged loudly enough that she paused on the other side, waiting for someone to shine a spotlight on her, or for the woman's two giant dogs to come bounding out of the back door to tear her to shreds. But there was nothing. Even the cicadas kept up their nightly ritual, shrieking in the treetops at the brim of the oaks.

Sammie stepped carefully through the yard. The grass was just as crunchy and dead on her neighbor's side, but it wasn't her yard, and the last thing she needed was to stub her toe on a rock or stumble over a garden hose. Through the dark, in the middle of the yard, she spotted an abandoned pot sitting half-buried in the dirt, with the remains of some kind of plant—a succulent, Sammie thought, maybe aloe—expired in the surrounding soil, or maybe just hibernating. She stretched her hands out in front of her, as if she might run into an unseen barrier, and after a moment she did: a gossamer spiderweb stretched between an oak tree and one of the azalea bushes lining the side of the yard. She swung her hands down to clear the way, wondering if the spider had landed on her clothes, and kept walking.

The moon was high, smudged behind a lake of gray clouds. The air was thick, a Florida spring that felt more like summer. It was so damp outdoors that every step felt like wading into a warm lake, pushing against a wake that wanted to drag her back to shore.

Finally she reached the house, close enough to see right into the kitchen window. She saw the fridge, bare except for a single pizza flier held by a magnet shaped like a bright blue pelican. The floors were hardwood, and she could see the edge of a blue-and-green braided rag rug on the floor in front of the sink. The sink, Sammie thought, was truly beautiful—one of those gigantic farmhouse sinks so deep you could wash a baby in it. That's what they always said, *a sink big enough to bathe a baby*, but when it really came down to it, you could probably bathe a baby in any sink you pleased. That was the thing about babies, they were small. Sammie had always washed Samson in a tub, though. A little plastic thing she had to wash afterward. It seemed like a tremendous waste of time: washing a baby and then having to scrub that tiny bathtub, too. But then there were a lot of things about having a baby that never made sense to Sammie. There were so many tasks she'd always wondered about, things other mothers seemed to pick up so easily while she struggled, miserable.

Sammie stood on her tiptoes and peered farther into the house. Beyond the kitchen sat the entrance to the dining room, and beyond that the edge of a living room, with a beige leather couch. The same as her own house, but nicer; it was like looking at the life she'd always envisioned herself having. This wasn't the kind of house that had kids, she decided. No clutter. No art on the fridge door. No leftover spoons or crusted mugs or plates clumped up next to the drying rack. No baby bottles or stuffed animals. No sippy cups. Everything neat and clean and tidy, put exactly where it was supposed to go.

The woman came around the corner with a mug in her hand, spooning something from it into her mouth. Sammie whipped back as if she'd been struck and pressed her body against the wall directly beside the window, praying that the woman hadn't seen her. The sink came on, and a spoon clanked against the bottom of the sink, and then Sammie heard the sound of the woman's voice, singing some sweet song Sammie didn't quite recognize. She relaxed a little, relieved that she hadn't been spotted, and let herself slide down the wall, still listening to the woman sing loudly to herself, calling out to the dogs.

This is ASMR, Sammie thought, *I could fall asleep right here*, and then she jolted, because for a minute she'd actually done it: fallen asleep outside her neighbor's house, sitting in the damp mucky dirt below the kitchen window. She got up on shaky legs and looked again into the kitchen, now empty, and looked back across the yard. In a panic she sidestepped the overturned patio chair and headed for her house, feeling like she was Alice trying to climb back through the looking glass.

When she got to the fence, she waited a minute and looked over into her own yard: the stunted orange tree growing crooked in the corner, the cracked birdbath, the wealth of disintegrating chimes Monika had put up when they first moved in, before she changed her mind and declared their patio *too humid for actual human life*. There was her own bedroom window, the window that looked into the small side room they used as a combined office. Her own kitchen window, dark, no light bleeding through to welcome her back.

Sammie jumped the fence again, picked up her empty wineglass, and headed back to her own quiet house.

7

It wasn't intentional. All the spying, the voyeurism. That's what she told herself, during and after—but especially after—her little nighttime trips over the fence. She even thought about telling Monika about them, because it was true. She did feel that way. But the part she kept inside and didn't reveal to anyone, at least not until later, was that she *loved* the fact that she couldn't get herself to stop. The chance to examine that woman's life from the outside, like how someone might observe an animal or a bird through binoculars: it was hers alone, something she could think about all day when she was alone. Touch. Turn over. That's what made it so irresistible. The secrecy of it. The inherent wrongness.

This flirtation with control was a heady, unusual thing.

Once she'd gone back inside the house that first night, it felt like slipping back into her clothes after walking around naked. Everyone was asleep. She hadn't been missed. Her wife, huddled beneath the covers on her side of the bed. Samson, when she opened his door, was sleeping in his usual way: flat on his back, the golden image of himself propped on the shelf nearest his own small head. As she leaned over him and smoothed the hair away from his eyes, a sweaty tangle caught in her fingertips. He rolled away from her hand, and she pulled back, wondering why she could never seem to touch her son in a way that elicited any feeling but pain.

Maybe that's what love is, she tried to reassure herself, slipping outside and closing the door behind her. *Maybe love is always a thing that's resting right on the edge of violence.*

Sammie spent the next day wondering when she could do it again. The prospect colored the rest of her life with unreality; a drunken, fuzzy haze that allowed her to believe the whole thing was a movie that only she got to watch.

The following night, after Samson refused to finish his math homework, Sammie found herself drifting to the kitchen window. She stood there for nearly an hour, basking in the golden glow from the other woman's house, unsure what she was even waiting for, but when the woman's shadow crossed in front of the sink, Sammie felt her heart skip in response. It made her wish she were under that window again, looking inside. Experiencing something outside herself.

Was it bad to look in on someone unannounced? To hide and watch?

Yeah, it probably is, Sammie thought, but the badness wasn't a huge deterrent. What would it be like to be looked at that way? Actually *seen* for once? Yes, she'd like to be seen in some kind of way. Be the snow globe someone held in their palms and gently shook.

Motherhood had seemed like it would give her that feeling, but in fact it had provided the opposite. It felt like her wife no longer saw her as an equal or a partner, no matter how much Monika tried to deny it. Her son viewed her as an obstacle to overcome. Looking in on that neighbor didn't make Sammie feel seen, exactly, but it gave her a strange measure of control. The viewing, and the way she chose to interpret everything she saw, was hers alone.

It started off sporadically. Sammie might be fighting with Samson over his homework, or arguing with Monika when she texted her way straight through dinner. Sometimes, Sammie was just experiencing that bad feeling she had more and more these days: a feeling that she'd settled into middle age, that she'd never go back to doing anything exciting or new again. And then she'd think of the neighbor's house and all of a sudden there she was, creeping across the lawn again. *Checking up on a friend*, she started calling it in her head, those nights when she felt like if she didn't do something right away, she'd just start screaming and not be able to stop. When she felt trapped in her own life, in her own brain. Heading over to the neighbor's house and peeking into a mirror image of her own home, assessing the woman's life and figuring out how her day had been, was like releasing a pressure valve behind her brain. Afterward she was nicer to her family; she was easier to be around. She smiled more. She slept better, was sweeter with Samson and more patient with Monika. Her dinners were made with care. She was more loving. She was just . . . *better.*

Besides, who was she really hurting? The woman had no idea what Sammie was doing. There was no sexual component; she wasn't some weird man who was peeping in her window for a lewd thrill, or masturbating, or something gross like that. If anything, Sammie felt she was checking in on her neighbor, making sure her life was going well. Yes, that was it; she was just making sure that this other woman—her mirror, her Alice in the looking glass—was succeeding. Just seeing a woman like her doing well gave Sammie a sense of satisfaction. Of hope.

One evening she'd done it before the sun had completely set. It was that gloaming that came over Central Florida, where the sky felt velvet, like it was touching the earth sweetly, and the colors were all sherbet-soft. She was putting a load of laundry in the washer and switching over some sheets to the dryer. Except, *fuck*, she'd taken too long to take the sheets out of the washer, had left them in the washer for two days, and now they were mildewed. The smell when she opened the lid was like a slap in the face. She'd have to wash them again—but what did it matter? she thought. Soon enough, she'd have to strip them off the bed *again* and wash them *again* and she'd forget them again, wouldn't she? Because she always forgot. She always forgot to change the fucking wash.

Bet that woman out back never forgets to switch her laundry, is what she thought in that moment, and she was suddenly arrested by the idea that she could walk over and see for herself.

So she threw those stinky sheets down on the floor of the laundry room, walked out the back door and straight across the lawn, and hopped the fence again. *I'm in a trance*, she thought, though that wasn't totally accurate. If anything, her mind felt loose and free; finally, she was thinking only about herself and what she wanted. In a life that had turned into a cycle of cook, clean, drive, fuck (and it was a *maybe* on fuck, the fucks were coming fewer and further between), and then sleep, this was like a moment of meditation.

Sammie's feet were bare. She brushed the fire ants from the top of her ankle and let the stinging sit in her brain while she peered inside that kitchen window again. Apple peels littered the woman's countertop. Had she made a pie? Cut up the apple on a plate and served the slices with peanut butter? Fruit flies darted over the garbage can. An open bottle of diet soda sat sweating rings. Sammie rested her hand on the sill and pressed her forehead to the window. The air-conditioning unit kicked on, and the house rumbled. She felt her chest loosen. She breathed easier. The woman walked past the doorway in an open silk bathrobe, bare breasts high and tight.

Those breasts have never fed children, Sammie thought.

The woman stopped next to the kitchen table and mindlessly picked her nose. Scratched at an itch on her arm. Oh, it felt like it was her own body doing the touching. Like she was watching herself. Sammie closed her eyes and carefully kissed the glass that separated them.

• • •

Monika had stopped coming to Samson's therapy after the first few visits. She claimed it was hard for her to miss work during the day, which Sammie knew was true, but it didn't make things any easier. So Sammie carted Samson across town every other Monday after school, and for a while she was grateful for another break in the routine, like swimming. She asked questions of the therapist, tried to stay informed. She gave Monika updates after every session. But it was frustrating how little she understood about what went on in her son's head. And if she was being honest, sometimes she felt like it could have been anyone driving her son to therapy. It didn't involve her at all, really, beyond the need for her physical body to drive the car. She was a mother, sure, but she might as well have just been an Uber driver.

I am the wheels, my heart is the engine, Sammie thought as she sat for hours while her son talked with the therapist. She was worried about Samson—she was always worried about him—but it wasn't like he came home from these visits any better behaved than he was going in. It wasn't like she understood him any better. He just stared at her with his buggy eyes, screwing up his mouth into a shape that looked like he'd tasted something sour. He acted like he'd rather live on the moon.

They both still bore the scars they'd gifted each other on their wrists, but Sammie was no longer worried that he'd tattle on her. If anything, she almost wished she still felt scared about it, just to bring some excitement back in her life, and that felt like one of the most fucked-up things she'd thought in a while.

One night, over dinner, Monika asked her about her hobbies. Wondered why she didn't take up some kind of exercise. Like running or something? Even swimming, like Samson? Sammie had calmly asked if that was a dig at her weight, and Monika sighed like Sammie was killing her, and she hadn't brought it up again.

They had sex that night, twisted up together in their sweaty sheets. Afterward, Monika put a hand on Sammie's belly and told her she loved her.

You know I think you're beautiful, right? she asked, and Sammie had said yes, but in her heart she didn't believe any such thing. Sometimes it was just that Monika knew what to say.

In the therapist's waiting room, Sammie stared blindly at the magazine she'd brought, waiting for Samson to emerge. Some celebrity she didn't recognize was on the TV overhead. The woman couldn't have been more than twenty-three, with hair up in a giant blond fountain of a ponytail and sneakers that were actually high heels.

"I'm super interested in making art," the woman said.

Sammie kept flipping pages—not really looking at the magazine, just staring at the pages blankly as her head filled with thoughts of the woman out back. The way she folded laundry on her kitchen table into small, neat piles. The way she left half-empty glasses sitting around with chunks of lemon spoiling inside them. The save-the-date for a wedding that had already passed, sitting on the counter with an unopened cable bill and some crumbs from a piece of toast or an English muffin. The woman had long dark hair; her belly was a little rounded mound, pouching out over the top of her underwear. She wore cotton bikini briefs and had two large moles directly over her belly button, which kind of made her torso look like an elevator button panel.

"All done for today." Dr. Kim and her son were standing side by side in the doorway to the office. Samson had on a blue polo, some khaki shorts, and white sneakers. His curly hair glowed golden in the sunlight from the office window. His face was shrouded in shadow.

He could be anybody, Sammie thought. *Who is this person?*

She slipped her magazine into her tote bag and held out her son's backpack for him to take, but he ignored her. Instead he walked over to the fish tank in the corner of the waiting room. He rapped a finger against the glass, two times, very hard.

"Not too rough," Sammie said, but her son kept on tapping, hard enough that she could see the ripple effect on the water inside. The tiny fish seemed stunned.

"Could I speak with you for a moment?" Dr. Kim asked.

"Huh?" Sammie was surprised. Not since that initial meeting had the therapist stopped to say more than just a quick greeting or to give a brief update on Samson's progress on their way in and out of the building.

"It won't take long. Just an update."

Sammie followed the doctor inside the office and told her son to stop bothering the fish. Samson kept tapping. *At least he doesn't have the doll with him today,* she thought. *If all these visits persuade him to give up the golden monstrosity, they'll be worth it.*

The therapist closed the door and sat down behind her desk, silent, as if she were waiting for Sammie to break.

This is what therapists do. They try to wait you out, see if you'll spill something. That way they don't even have to ask what's going on, you just admit it yourself out of guilt. Sammie crossed her arms over her chest. Then she crossed her legs, too. She stared at the woman, and the woman stared back.

I bet I can wait her out, Sammie thought, and then she coughed and asked for a glass of water.

Dr. Kim got up and poured her one from the dispenser. It was a paper cone of water, and the jug made a glugging sound as the water trickled down into it. When the doctor passed it to her, their hands touched. Sammie was surprised at how soft her skin was. Soft like a little kid.

"I wanted to talk to you about Gertie," she said.

Sammie frowned. "Who's Gertie?"

The woman sat back down and laced her fingers together. Sammie drank her water, icy cold and painful against her teeth, and stared at those soft fingers, their short rounded nails. *Gay hands*, Sammie thought, surprised. Why hadn't she ever thought that the doctor might be queer? Her dark outfits. Her blunt black bob. Her asexual wire-frame glasses.

"Samson has brought up his sister these last few sessions," Dr. Kim said, and Sammie squeezed the cup so hard water spilled from the top and ran all down the front of her linen dress.

The therapist handed her a wad of tissues from the box on her desk, and Sammie swiped them uselessly around the water saturating her lap.

"Samson doesn't have a sister," she said, blotting away at her dress. She wound up with a mess of soaked Kleenex bits all pilled and gunked, adhering to the navy fabric.

The woman's hands clasped together again on the desktop.

"He's mentioned something about a baby, the other baby. The girl baby."

Sammie swallowed over the mucus in her throat. "He calls her . . . Gertie?"

The baby had never been Gertie. She'd been a half-formed thought, a light in the swell of Sammie's stomach. She'd wanted to name that girl baby Hope, a bright, shiny thing, a soft, buttery dream of a child. She'd wanted a lot of things.

"He talks about her every session now. He says she lives inside him."

How . . . could he possibly know? About the other baby? Sammie's brain fought to process what the therapist had said. Her mind was in revolt. She'd certainly never discussed it with him. Tried not to think about it, ever.

That little light is inside Samson now, she thought. Except it wasn't as cute as that made it sound. That tiny flame of a heart had been snuffed out before it had had a chance to grow. Samson had extinguished the spark.

"It's not like that, whatever he's making it sound like." Sammie unclenched her hand; the crushed paper cup fell into her damp lap. "I was pregnant with both of them at the same time. She didn't make it."

The therapist just sat there, fingers twisted together. Those tiny hands. They were baby hands, weren't they? Too small and soft for a grown woman.

"You've talked about this with Samson, at home? You and your wife?"

Sammie shook her head. "Never. We've never talked to him about this. We don't even talk about it with each other."

But someone must have told him. Someone must have sat him down and talked with him about his sister. She would have been his same size now. She would have been in the fourth grade, had the same bright curly hair, would have loved kittens, maybe, or ducks. A daughter she might have understood.

You don't know that the baby would have been a girl, Monika told her when they discovered the light was gone, after that horrible after-noon in the doctor's office when the doubled heartbeats had ceased, leaving only one on the screen. But Sammie knew her own body, and she'd known that little girl, had felt the tenderness of that lost love.

"So you've never mentioned the baby? To Samson?" Dr. Kim picked up a pencil, tapping it staccato against the blotter.

"I think I'd remember doing something like that, wouldn't I?" It came out sharper than she'd intended, but the therapist didn't respond, just sat there tapping her pencil until Sammie wanted to reach over and break it in half.

"I need to discuss this with my wife," Sammie said, and got to her feet. Because that's who'd told him, obviously. Monika. Her wife must have said something. Sammie felt her blood coursing through her chest, down her arms, up her neck, and into her face. Her whole body felt hot, lava bright, like she was catching fire.

"Maybe the three of you would like to come in to discuss it further," the doctor said.

"That won't be necessary," Sammie replied tersely. She scrubbed all the lint and trash from her lap directly onto the floor and shouldered her tote. When she opened the door, there stood her son, arms all the way inside the fish tank, swishing the water around until it splashed onto the floor, soaking the carpet with gravel and tiny plastic plants. Fish flopped haplessly at his feet, gulping for air.

All the blood surged into Sammie's brain, so quickly she thought she'd pass out. Her legs felt disconnected from her body. She didn't realize she was hyperventilating until Samson's therapist reached over to touch her. When the woman shook her shoulder, as if to snap her out of it, Sammie's teeth clamped down on her tongue. The coppery taste of blood flooding her mouth pulled her back to the present.

Samson still stood there with his arms in the tank, staring impassively as the therapist crouched on the floor, trying to save the fish. Then he removed his arms from the tank. Water dripped everywhere, onto his clothes, the sofa cushions, the chairs. His sneaker came down on one of the remaining fish. The therapist made a deep, choked noise in her throat.

No, Sammie thought. *My girl's not in there.*

The cleaning people had shampooed the rug in the waiting room twice, but to Sandra Kim it still reeked of dead fish. She sat in her office with the door closed and sprayed some vanilla-scented air freshener over her head, wondering how long it would take for the smell to dissipate. The tank was gone. She'd thrown the whole thing directly in the dumpster. After the incident with Samson the week before, she wasn't sure if she could stomach seeing something like that happen ever again. It wasn't just that he'd stepped on the fish—that was a genuine accident, she'd seen it in his eyes. It was part of why she was seeing the boy: his propensity to act rashly and regret his decisions after the fact. She knew all of this and she forgave him for it. It was his mother's reaction that had bothered her. No, *bothered* wasn't exactly the word. His mother had scared her. The way she'd screamed, and how she'd looked at the boy immediately after, with a mixture of love and revulsion. And how, immediately thereafter, she snapped into a space where it seemed like nothing had happened. She even opened her pocketbook, prepared to pay for the session like they weren't all standing around in the watery remnants of a disaster area. No, Sandra wouldn't be buying any more fish for the office. At least not anytime soon.

8

Monika was supposed to be home by six for dinner, but she'd called to say she'd gotten "held up" at work. Sammie heard the quotation marks in her head. *Held up* could mean many things when it came to her wife, but there were more late nights now, less sex, less time spent together, more fighting, more space between their bodies on the bed. Always there sat Samson, a brooding lump between them. A physical divider.

It hadn't always been that way. When he was younger, still small and doughy-fresh, he'd sat between them like a bridge. They couldn't stay mad at each other, not with a baby to coo over, to share firsts with: first tooth, first solid food, first steps. They'd loved holding him on their laps, taking turns stroking his pudgy limbs, marveled over his tiny toes and rounded belly. Monika had hung one of those plastic baby swings in the tree out back, and Samson screamed with laughter every time they pushed him in it. One of his first words was *again*, because he always wanted more. They'd recorded him saying it one sunny afternoon, laughing and happy. He'd been perfect, a baby who slept soundly through the night, and when they tucked him in and snuggled together in bed, they'd known they were lucky.

All of this was what made his shift into a ball of angry energy so bewildering.

Sammie hadn't wanted to bring up the fish tank incident over the phone. And she really didn't want to talk about what the therapist had said about their daughter. It wouldn't do any good. For her wife, that baby was long gone. She'd never existed, not really. Monika had never felt her inside her body: the goodness, the small fluttery strength of her. She only thought of Samson and how lucky they were that he'd survived.

Don't you know he ate her? That's what she'd always wanted to say, but even when she was wine drunk she knew enough not to say such a thing aloud. Anyway, the doctor hadn't said that Samson cannibalized his sister; he'd called it "resorbing." What's the difference? Sammie wanted to know. He'd still consumed her, just like he did everything else. Consumed time. Consumed space. Hungry even when he was eating. Just needing so much from her.

For dinner she made chicken and yellow rice, which Samson barely touched. He took only a single sip of his milk, then left it there in front of him, warming to room temperature, before wiping his hands on the tablecloth and leaving the table. Sammie cleared the table carefully, wiping off all the fingerprints and putting together a plate for her wife, which sat lonely, covered by a limp paper towel inside the microwave.

"Do you wanna watch a show together?" she asked her son, who shrugged and climbed onto the other end of the couch. They were both wearing their pajamas. Sammie's body wasn't sleepy, but her brain felt tired. Being a mother made her so goddamn tired. It was as if she could never get enough sleep, never enough rest to feel truly herself.

Impulsively she reached across the couch and dragged him to her. He sat wooden for a moment, then progressively loosened as they leaned into each other. The show was a special on Animal Planet, something about dog breeds. It was a nice enough program, just cute videos of animals running around or sleeping, nothing too violent or stressful. Samson watched with his usual rapt attention. Sammie leaned forward, resting her face against the crown of his head. He smelled like the baby shampoo they still bought him, the stuff that was reminiscent of candied cherries or grapes or some other kind of fake fruitiness, which promised *no more tears* and left his hair in a tangled mess.

Her son leaned back into her, and she held him there, feeling the still-soft flesh of his arms under her palms. He still felt a little like a baby, even beneath all that boyish muscle he was developing as he grew.

I do love you, she realized, inhaling his sugary scent. *Oh, thank God, I do love my son.*

They sat like that for a while, till it was later than she normally let him stay up. She forgot about the woman she'd been spying on, forgot about the incident with the therapist, forgot about the problems with her wife. She just let herself sit still, let herself be gentle, enjoying the simple fact that she was a mother. They fell asleep that way, lulled by the dogs scampering on-screen and the deep cadences of the narrator and his endlessly patient account of every canine particular: how much the dogs should weigh, what kind of food worked best with each breed, which played best with cats, with other dogs, with small children.

Sammie woke several hours later, pins and needles threading through her legs. Samson had sprawled on top of her, his weight a heavy mass that trapped her against the sofa cushions. She extricated herself slowly, trying not to wake up her son, until he finally rolled off her and turned into the back of the couch, throwing an arm up over the cushions. His skin was covered with upholstery patterns; the circular imprint of a button pressed into his warm pink cheek, damply embroidered there.

Sammie stumbled into the kitchen and turned on the light. The clock on the microwave announced it was just past one in the morning. Monika wasn't home. Her dinner was still sitting in the microwave, congealed and cold beneath its napkin wrapper. Sammie picked up the plate and put it in the fridge, not sure what she was trying to save. Monika would never eat it.

Her phone was plugged into the charger in the kitchen wall. There were no missed calls or voice mails. No messages. She sent Monika a quick text—*WHERE ARE YOU*, in all caps—then had a glass of water and stared out the window over the sink. It was the same kitchen window she used to peer into the other woman's house. What would that woman think if she looked inside Sammie's house right now? Would she think Sammie's life was pathetic? What would she see, exactly? A young woman who'd once had ambitions and dreams beyond her home, but now was—what? What was she, exactly? *A mother*, Monika would have told her, but even that rang hollow to Sammie. Wasn't Monika a mother, too? And she had a whole other life. Other friends. Other people.

There it was again, that need to slip out of her skin. She wanted to wander over to the neighbor's place and peek inside. Probably the other woman would be asleep, but that way Sammie could spend some time escaping her own head. Looking at all the things that littered that woman's kitchen, thinking about how she was living, whom she was loving and how. Her private life, laid out for Sammie's inspection.

She slipped on a pair of her wife's loafers, lying forgotten by the sliding door, and wandered out into the muggy Florida night. The bugs were shrill in the trees overhead. At some point while she slept it must have rained, because the ground was saturated and damp, the wet grass soaking her shoes and slapping against her bare calves where the weeds had grown too high again. She was wearing only a nightshirt, but she didn't care. The moon overhead was a bare sliver, a tiny scraping of light that curved like a fingernail.

She climbed the fence, easier than ever, and settled herself outside the woman's window. It was dark inside. It was time for sleep, time to rest, yet here she sat, an audience for someone else's life instead of participating in her own. It felt so much worse to be inside her own head, inside her own body, she thought—and that's when the kitchen light flipped on. There was the other woman, the neighbor, staring at her through the window.

They both screamed. Sammie stumbled back, tripping over a tangled loop of coiled garden hose, and fell, sprawling out on the muddy ground. Suddenly she heard barking, loud, and Sammie realized she'd forgotten about the dogs, that the neighbor might set them loose in the yard, where they'd find her cowering in the muck and devour her. Her mind flooded with images from the dog show she'd fallen asleep watching with Samson: the sound of rottweilers, their fierce nature as guard dogs, how they could chomp down hard enough to break a human arm.

Sammie crawled to her feet and sprinted across the yard. When she went to climb the fence, she found her arms wouldn't work properly. Her fright made her clumsy, and she fell down, scraping her thigh on the chain-link fence and catching the hem of her sleep shirt. She ripped it free and ran up to the back of the house . . . where she slammed right into Monika, standing on the patio, still in her work clothes. Her wife caught her by the arms and held her there for a moment—to keep her upright or to keep her from running away, Sammie couldn't tell. She looked confused, Sammie thought. Maybe angry.

"What the hell are you doing out here?" Monika hissed, and then the lights came on over at the neighbor's. The back door opened, and the dogs scrambled out. They made it to the fence in seconds, barking and growling, leaping so high that one of them almost made it over. Sammie screeched and grabbed onto her wife's arm; after a moment, Monika broke away to meet the woman, who was running up to the fence and yelling.

Sammie watched from afar as the woman shouted at Monika, gesturing wildly. She couldn't make out what they were saying, but she didn't dare go inside, worried that if the dogs spotted her they might actually clear the top of the fence. Her wife kept talking to the woman, and after a while she appeared to calm down. Eventually the woman turned and went inside with her dogs, slamming the door behind her. The lights shut off abruptly.

Monika came back to the patio, breathing heavily. "What the fuck was that?"

"I don't know," Sammie replied, which was true enough.

"You don't know?"

Sammie shook her head, though Monika probably couldn't see her in the dark. "What did you say to her?"

Monika sighed and scrubbed her hands over her face. "I told her you were sleepwalking. That it's a chronic condition and you do it all the time. That you've never made it all the way out of the house before."

Sleepwalking. That was kind of what it felt like, anyway. A dreamy, otherworldly, out-of-body experience.

"Okay," Sammie said dumbly, and Monika asked if that was it. If there was anything else she wanted to tell her.

"No," Sammie replied, truthfully, and then they both walked inside.

Monika grabbed a seltzer from the fridge. It fizzed open, and she caught the spill with her tongue. Sammie's feet were filthy from the mud and the wet grass, and Monika was staring at them.

If she says anything about the fact that I've ruined her loafers, I am gonna throw something, Sammie thought, and that's when she noticed the creases on her wife's cheek. Deep, furrowed indentations, the kind that happen when you fall asleep on fabric. On a wrinkled pillow. On someone's chest.

"Where were you all night?" Sammie asked.

"I don't know," Monika replied, and Sammie laughed.

"Sure you don't."

Neither of them really knew each other, did they? Sammie looked at her wife's creased face, her mussed hair. Her sleepy eyes squinty and tired behind her thick-framed glasses. Who was this woman? Who was *she*? What the hell were they doing?

They walked into the dining room together, and there sat Samson at the table, eating from a full carton of vanilla ice cream. The golden doll sat beside him, Styrofoam face covered with its own soupy mess of ice cream.

"That's so cute," Monika said. "Look at the two of them. Twins."

Sammie reached over and grabbed the doll's head. Then she set it down on the floor and smashed it flat with one loafered foot.

9

Then came the unraveling. Somehow, it was easier than all the knotting that led up to it. All the stress, the angst, the wondering: such a relief for it to finally slip loose. It was as if stomping on that Styrofoam head had unleashed everything.

Monika pulled a few of her things into the guest room for the night, then a few more in the nights after that. They had plenty of space, and Monika was hardly ever home, anyway, and this way they could take some time to think about things, to make decisions about the future in a way that felt less claustrophobic. At least that's how Monika put it, as she pulled her work clothes from their shared closet, and for once Sammie was happy to let her have her way.

Now, in the early mornings, Sammie sat alone on the couch and sipped at her tea, watching the sun streak caramel and melon on the floorboards they'd chosen together. A unit. *Wives*, that's the word Sammie was looking for, wives who'd built a house and a family together. Now to crimson and gold, then a sharp yellowing, like butter spread on toast. God, it was beautiful, the light that early in the morning; she'd never been a morning person before, but now she thought she might be. She sipped her tea, slow and careful, so it wouldn't burn her tongue. Monika was gone, or she was out of sight; it didn't matter, not just then. There was all the time in the world. No need to rush. All that mattered was the tea, the light, her brain unknotted and still.

Down trotted Samson. He stopped at the foot of the stairs and yawned, scratching at his belly with his free hand. The other clutched the headless idol, no longer his likeness but still strangely sentient even without eyes. Wasn't the soul supposed to be lodged in the eyes? Sammie had always heard that, but she thought it might live in the mouth: that rough, wet opening where anything could spill out, lies or truth.

"Good morning," Sammie said. "Sleep well?"

Samson stared at his mother and stuck his wrist into his mouth, worrying the scar there with his own sharp little teeth.

Summer

10

Sammie scraped at the wet beer label with her fingernails.

When is the right time to tell a date you're still married? she wondered. *First date? Third date? That couldn't be right. Wasn't third date supposed to be the sex date?*

This was a first date, and there probably wouldn't be a second.

They were at a cramped high-top at the back of a trendy bar downtown, far from her house in the suburbs with its lazy evenings of boxed wine and casseroles. Neon lights sprayed pink and baby blue across the wall behind them, splashing their faces purple. The woman across from her, Myra, had a red wine smudge of a smile every time she opened her mouth. The lights made her teeth look rotted. It should have been unattractive, but Sammie kept staring into that cavern and wondering what it would feel like for the teeth to rest on her jugular.

Oh, someone bite me, she thought, and peeled some more of the label.

"What do you like to do for fun?" Myra asked, shouting over the music. "What kind of stuff do you like?"

Sammie repeated what she'd already told the woman through the dating app: she liked movies (not really, mostly she rewatched shows she'd already seen a million times), she liked cooking (okay, reheating food and adding cheese or butter and some herbs to spice it up), and she liked hiking (a blatant lie, unless she counted walking outside to the patio for a drink after dinner). The hiking bit was a weird lie, but it had a purpose: for some reason dykes loved hiking, or so she gathered from the dating app.

"I guess I don't have time for many real *hobbies*, you know?" she said, and that was mostly true. She watched TV, she did the crossword every morning even though she usually cheated and always gave up halfway through, and she liked to go online and look at ads for free kittens in her area, even though she hadn't gotten up the nerve to adopt one yet. They seemed like a lot of work, and she wasn't sure Samson would be all that thrilled to help out with one.

Myra was very much Sammie's type, which was another way of saying that Myra looked very much like Monika. They had the same dark, curly hair. They both wore the same chunky glasses. They both carried themselves like they didn't care who was looking at them, because they knew people would look at them no matter what. Sammie went for this type over and over again—and on the first date she always grew frustrated, because they all had the same problems as Monika, too.

The server brought over a plate of buffalo wings, and Sammie picked at one while her date dug in gleefully. Myra had spicy wing sauce all over her mouth and chin, dug up all under her short fingernails. *Guess we aren't fucking tonight*, thought Sammie, imagining all that orange gunk burning her pussy raw. But then the woman stuck one of those fingers into her mouth and sucked off the sauce enthusiastically, while making intense eye contact, and Sammie wondered if they might after all.

Myra worked for one of the theme parks, something to do with client relations; she mentioned free tickets, but Sammie wasn't a big theme park person, even though—or maybe because—she'd grown up in Orlando. She told Myra she was in marketing, which was not untrue, although at this point her work had dwindled down to copyediting emails for various political campaigns and ghostwriting the occasional technical manual. The work was dull, and the end product was usually pretty bogus, but as Monika pointed out (more often than Sammie would have preferred), no one was going to want to fuck her if she spent all her time complaining about her shitty job.

"You want another beer?" Myra asked, waving for the server before she could answer. That was how Sammie knew they would fuck, that sudden intensity of command. When they made eye contact again, she smiled broadly and put her hand on Myra's arm.

They each drank two more beers, and Myra finished off the chicken wings while they made small talk. It was the same stuff she discussed with all her dates, and she found it hard to remember if she was telling any given woman something new or repeating things she'd already said. They covered all the greatest hits: where are you from, do you have a favorite book, what's your go-to drink, what kind of music do you listen to—and then, there it was, the one about kids and ex-lovers.

"I have a son," Sammie said, and when Myra didn't bolt, she sketched in the picture: He was sixteen. He was an okay student. He was a championship swimmer, could be competitive, might even make the Olympic circuit if he put real effort into it, but he was just a sophomore in high school, so he was keeping his options open. "I guess I should say a junior now—it's summer break. I keep forgetting that."

"Kids are nice," Myra said, and then they didn't talk about that anymore.

Sammie didn't mind. She didn't know what she was looking for out of any of these dates, but it wasn't another mother for her son. *He already has too many mothers*, she thought, and then she felt bad, because that wasn't true, and it seemed like she was being a bad lesbian even to think it. But it was so hard, navigating the intricacies of parenting with another human being. When it came to raising Samson, she and Monika had wildly different opinions on almost every decision. Monika thought she was too hard on Samson; Sammie thought Monika was way too lenient. Monika gave Samson spending money; Sammie thought he should work for it. When Samson acted out at school, Sammie thought he should face some consequences for his actions, but Monika usually just shrugged it off and wouldn't entertain the idea of punishment. Sometimes Sammie wanted to climb in her car and drive away, to start all over again.

"What kind of music do you like?" Sammie asked, forgetting if that was ground they'd already covered. "Country music," Myra said; she had a monthly lesbian meetup that she attended in cowboy boots and a hat, a response that made Sammie wince. She immediately finished her beer and asked for the check.

They split it evenly between them, which seemed right even though Monika never would have let Sammie pay, and then they stepped out into the swamp of the Florida evening.

"Fuck, it's hot out," Myra said.

Sammie nodded and pulled her tank top away from her stomach, already feeling the sweat bead along her hairline and neck.

Myra, who was from Miami, kept talking about how wild the weather was in Central Florida, how the thunderstorms were especially bad that year, and Sammie just kept agreeing, though she'd seen way worse Orlando summers. They walked down the street together, weaving their way past pedestrians. There was a sign for pizza slices up ahead, and Sammie found herself wishing she could have one. *Maybe later I'll order a pizza for me and Monika—then Samson can have leftovers for lunch*, she thought, but then she shut that line of thinking down. She still had a hard time knowing when she was supposed to be taking care of the family and when she was supposed to be looking after herself.

Myra had parked a block away, but Sammie had shelled out for a spot at the adjacent garage to make sure she wasn't late.

"Well, I guess this is me," Sammie said when they reached the building, and then Myra pushed her up against the brick and kissed her.

It wasn't great, but it wasn't terrible. Sammie leaned into it. She tasted beer on the other woman's breath and then the aftertaste of the buffalo wings, a weird, spicy tang that made her suddenly hungry. Myra pressed into her, hard, harder, and then Sammie's head was jammed against the wall.

"You like that," Myra whispered, and Sammie nodded because she guessed she did, wasn't that the kind of thing she usually liked, though her hair was getting pulled and her neck hurt and she barely knew this woman.

They made out like that for a while, the midweek downtown crowd filtering in slowly around them as the night progressed, and no one stopped them or bothered them, or made lewd noises, or tried to interrupt them.

The thing about meeting women from the dating app was that it was always like this, too much or never enough, Sammie thought as Myra ground her hips into Sammie's, making a growling noise like a stomach that wanted pizza.

Sammie's phone buzzed, and she used that as an excuse to separate. Myra breathed heavily into her face, eyes sleepy with desire. Her lips hung open, wet and red and slick with spit. Between her teeth, Sammie spotted a sliver of chicken. One more kiss and she'd be eating from the woman's mouth like a baby bird.

She pushed against Myra's chest. "Lemme check, it could be my kid."

Myra leaned away just enough so Sammie could dig into her back pocket for the phone. There was her wife's face, staring out at them both. It was a picture that she'd taken several years ago, when they were on a beach trip with Samson, using one of his swim events as an excuse for a family vacation. In the photo the sun was setting behind Monika, her curls fiery in the dying light, and she was laughing. Sammie wished she could remember what was so funny.

"Who's that?" Myra asked, turning the phone toward her.

"My ex," Sammie replied. "Not a big deal."

"She looks good."

Of course you'd say that, Sammie thought, *you look just like her.* She was still thinking about that trip: how they'd screamed at each other for most of the car ride; how Samson had disappeared for part of the first day and they'd panicked until they'd found him on the shore poking away at a dead jellyfish; how she and Monika had gotten blisteringly drunk in their relief and exhaustion. That picture, the one on her phone? She couldn't even remember taking it. That's how drunk they had to be just to enjoy each other's company.

Or was it? Sometimes her old memories of Monika felt tinged with the current doleful colors of their semidetached life. Memories that used to make her smile now brought her frustration.

The call went to voice mail. Then Monika called back.

"Do you need to take that?" Myra asked. "It's okay if you do. I understand."

"No. I'll call later." Sammie put the phone back in her pocket and slid her arms around Myra's neck. They locked there comfortably, just like they always did around Monika's, just like they always did with these women who were clones of her wife.

Her pocket buzzed and buzzed. It almost felt erotic, that insistent vibration while she kissed a woman she didn't know on a busy street in front of a bunch of strangers. It started to feel better to her then, good enough she got wet, and for a moment she thought about having Myra take her to the back seat of her car.

But they separated when a truck sped past, nearly clipping another car, the two of them honking like a couple of angry geese. If Sammie hadn't been so aggravated about losing her chance at an orgasm, she might have laughed.

"Can I call you?" Myra asked, and Sammie said yes, though the magic of the moment had faded. Now, instead of aroused, all she felt was empty. The smell on the street wasn't one of romance; in fact, it smelled like someone had pissed against the side of the garage right where they were making out. *My clothes are going to reek like a public toilet*, she thought.

Sammie walked inside the garage with her keys clutched in her fist, the way her mother had taught her as they navigated the parking lot by the public library when she was young. When she saw a man get into the elevator before her, she knew it wasn't smart to be alone with him—regardless of his well-pressed suit—so she took the stairs.

You can never tell about people, Sammie thought. *They could be monsters in disguise.*

The air was close in the garage, heavy with fumes from the cars of office workers who had recently left for the day. Sammie's body felt like it was shutting down, too. She'd stop at a McDonald's, she decided, and wouldn't worry about getting a pizza for everyone else. Samson was at his summer job at the bowling alley—something Sammie had insisted on and that he'd been lucky to get, through an acquaintance of Monika's—so he wouldn't be expecting dinner. And her wife—

Ex, she corrected herself, unlocking the car and climbing into the driver's seat. Her ex-wife, though they weren't formally divorced. They were exes now, and she needed to remember that, to stop using the past tense and think in the present. To move forward. God knew Monika had been, for years already.

She threw her phone down onto the seat beside her and noted the missed calls. Four of them. Monika knew she was on a date tonight.

They'd had the stilted conversation over the kitchen counter as they un-packed the groceries Sammie had brought home, even though it was Monika's turn to buy. *Sounds like you've got a type*, Monika joked. Monika, who always had dates, who sometimes let them pick her up at the house, even though they'd agreed not to bring anyone over until it was someone serious, someone they wanted to introduce to Samson. Yet there was her wife, climbing into some dark sedan while Samson did his homework upstairs.

Let her wait for a while, Sammie thought. *See how she likes it.*

She drove home slowly, taking the long way around the lake that cut through their neighborhood. It was pretty out despite the heat. The stars were blinking up in the cloudless sky and the moon was shining through the oaks. An owl swooped low, alighting on one of the Spanish moss–laden branches, giant yellow eyes illuminated by her headlights. She'd been drinking—just a couple beers, but why chance it? And any-way, this gave her time to roll down the windows and smell the dank, mineral sharpness of the lake and think about what she'd say once she got home. *Home*, a strange word for a place that felt so cold, where the three of them orbited one another like they didn't even speak the same language.

Sammie stopped at the drive-through a couple of miles away from her house and ordered the meal she liked: two cheeseburgers, fries, and a Coke. It was date night, after all; why shouldn't she take herself on a date? Eat her favorite garbage food, pour herself a glass of wine, and then tuck herself into bed. Maybe fuck herself with one of the vibrators in her nightstand drawer. Actually have an orgasm. Go to sleep peace-ful, calm. Rested. Wouldn't that be something? Best date she'd had in years.

Pulling up to the house, Sammie noticed that none of the lights were on. Not even the ones for the front porch, which was always notoriously dark and generally full of tree frogs that tried to leap at her when she opened the screen door. Every summer she had to worry that some sticky projectile would jump directly into the nest of her hair or down her top as she left, some clammy amphibian clambering over her breasts as she tried to yank down her shirt to free it. She spotted one as she pushed her key into the lock—a huge one, pale and sickly green, its throat pulsing grotesquely.

"Don't even think about it," Sammie whispered, and the frog chose that moment to jump, just barely clearing her head. Sammie screeched and nearly dropped her keys.

She got the door open and walked through the pitch-black entry-way. She didn't bother calling out for anybody; Monika always left the hallway light on when she went to bed, and Samson refused to re-spond when called. He only showed up when he felt like it, which was hardly ever. Her mother used to tell her—back when they were still speaking—that daughters did things out of obligation, but sons never did anything without incentive. At the time, Sammie told her she was full of it, that that was just gendered nonsense, but now that she had a son who did whatever he wanted, whenever he wanted, she'd begun to wonder.

Sammie turned on the kitchen light, blinking at the brightness of the fluorescents. She unpacked her meal and wolfed it down right there at the kitchen counter, stuffing the cheeseburgers and hot, salty fries into her mouth, slurping down the Coke. The kitchen smelled like lemon cleanser, which surprised her; Monika never did any chores, and when she did deign to take out the trash or bag up the recycling, she expected a huge thank-you. Maybe it was just some new cologne she was smelling.

Monika went on dates all the time. So frequently that it verged on pathological, Sammie thought. She wished Monika would see a thera-pist, like Sammie was doing every other week.

After hoovering all that fast food, she felt disgusting and bloated. She worried she might not fit into her dress for her next date that weekend—this one with a different woman, who'd seen her only through the carefully curated pictures she'd posted on the dating app. It wasn't that the pictures weren't of Sammie. It's just that they were from a while ago, back when she'd looked a little younger and fresher. There was the one of her in a bikini top at the beach, cropped just above her stomach. Then there was the one taken from behind as she lifted up her old friend Bonnie's Persian kitten, showing off her ass in a pair of tight jeans that didn't really want to button anymore.

She washed her hands, then picked up her phone. Seven missed calls, but no voice mail. That left a knot in her stomach that had nothing to do with the cheeseburgers. She hit redial, and Monika picked up after half a ring.

"Why the fuck haven't you answered your phone?"

"I was on a date, remember?" Sammie said. "I told you last night."

"You can't ignore calls just because you're fucking someone."

Sammie laughed. "You think I was fucking someone on a first date at a shitty downtown bar? What, like in the bathroom? Am I you?"

"No—you're a mother, whether you like it or not," Monika said. "You can't just turn off your ringer whenever you want."

"I don't do that. You know I don't." Sammie heard noise on the other end of the line—some kind of loud music and people shouting to be heard over it.

"Wait, are *you* in a bar?" Sammie asked.

"I'm not at a bar, *Samandra*, I am at the bowling alley dealing with your son."

There was that horrible knot again. "Wait—what happened? What did he do?" Sammie forced herself to pause, take a breath. "Is he okay?"

"Just get the hell here." Then she hung up.

"Oh, you fucking *bitch*." She slammed the phone down, harder than she should have, and then had to scramble to catch it before it fell onto the tile floor. Whatever Samson had done, she hoped it wouldn't get him fired.

The bowling alley was only a twelve-minute drive away, but Sammie hit every red light on the way there. It was a Wednesday, but when she pulled into the lot the place was packed. League night, she remembered as she looped around the side of the building to look for parking. Finally she pulled in between a rusted Buick with a Jesus fish on the bumper and a monstrous blue pickup truck taking up a space and a half. She squeezed out of the car and made her way inside.

The bowling alley smelled bar-familiar, like cheap beer and cigarettes, even though smoking had been banned for years. It made the place feel weirdly cozy, like hanging out in a friend's shitty garage in high school. It reminded her of making out with Karen Pullman at a sleepover junior year. Everyone already asleep after sharing a couple Millers and a single cigarette. Sometimes, when she was really desperate to get off, Sammie would think about that sticky, beer-flavored kiss.

She walked up to the counter, littered with shoes waiting to be put back in their cubbies. Brandon, the manager, was running the main register. Sammie and Monika had hung out with him a few times. He and his partner, Marco, came over for game nights at the house. They were lucky that Brandon had offered Samson the job. Hopefully whatever her son had done now wouldn't spoil their relationship.

She gave Brandon a wave, and he nodded back as he talked with a couple at the bar. At least he'd acknowledged her. That was something. She followed the hideous carpet runner to the concession stand. That's where Samson worked, loading up hot dogs with chili and passing out foil-wrapped cheeseburgers, french fries, and Tater Tots. Most nights he came home smelling like a convenience store. She liked that smell, better than his usual antiseptic chlorine odor.

A girl Sammie didn't know was working the front counter. She passed two fizzing Mountain Dews to a preteen boy, who was so jittery he spilled one of them down the front of his T-shirt as he walked away.

And that is why I never let my kid drink soda, Sammie thought.

"I'm looking for Samson?" Sammie asked. The girl—BRITTA, her name tag read, with a glittery teal heart over the *i*—jerked a thumb over her shoulder. There was her son, kicked back in an orange plastic chair, flicking his finger aimlessly against a laminated health code sign about hand washing. Monika was sitting with him, arms crossed over her chest. Her hair was shorter, Sammie noticed, buzzed up the sides, curls falling down over one eye. It was the same haircut Monika had insisted she hated a few years back—"the hipster lesbo," she called it.

"What's going on?" Sammie asked, leaning over the counter. Britta huffed as she wiped down the counter with a questionable-looking rag that reeked of Pine-Sol. Sammie craned around her so that Monika could hear her. "Should I come back there?"

Monika got up. "Stay there," she told Samson, who just kept flicking at the sign. She came around to Sammie's side of the counter to talk, as Britta scrubbed a little too vigorously at a coffee stain on the counter a few feet away.

"Hello, can you please tell me what's going on?" Sammie asked. Monika told her to lower her voice, glancing at the girl.

"Brandon's gonna come over to talk to us in a minute, and we all need to be on the same page," Monika said.

"And what page is that?" Sammie never knew what the hell was going on when Monika was in charge. Sammie knew she meant well, but she was always making decisions without consulting Sammie, without explaining herself, and then steamrolling through on the assumption that hers was the best possible idea.

"It's not that big a deal." Monika grabbed her arm and turned her away from the counter when Britta came closer, blatantly leaning in to listen. "Samson got into a disagreement."

"What kind of disagreement? Just tell me what happened."

Monika was doing that thing she always did when she got stressed, pulling chapped skin off her lips until they were nearly bleeding.

"He got into an argument with a girl who bought snacks. Someone from school."

Sammie felt her shoulders tighten. "Of course."

Monika stopped picking her lips and frowned at her. At least Sammie had gotten her to stop. "Listen, you know he has trouble there. Kids don't understand him. It's not his fault."

"I know he *causes* a lot of this trouble himself. That's one thing I know."

"This girl . . . she doesn't like him. She's claiming he spit in her drink before he gave it to her."

"Well, did he?"

"How can you even ask that?" Monika stopped talking and turned around to stare down Britta, who was nearly sprawled across the counter by now.

"Do you mind?" Monika hissed.

"I'm just saying," Sammie said. "Seems like something he'd do."

"You have absolutely no faith in your son. Do you think maybe that's part of the problem?"

Brandon was finally working his way over, weaving between some kids who were running between the lanes, batting a balloon back and forth like a volleyball. He waved at them, then held up a finger as he stopped to direct the kids out of the way of the league bowlers, who were glaring at them like they might commit a murder.

Monika leaned in close to her again. She had coffee on her breath—something Sammie used to find attractive, back when it was the scent of her wife finally coming home from work, but now she just associated it with all the times she'd been out cheating on her. She wondered what little tics of hers bothered Monika now that way.

"Just let me do the talking here, okay?"

"I wouldn't even know what to say," Sammie replied, which was true.

Brandon came over and hugged them both, apologizing for the wait. "Wednesdays here are a nightmare," he said, wiping his brow with an embroidered handkerchief. "Had to settle a dispute over some joker's receipt."

"Perks of running your own business, am I right?" Monika was using that used-car salesman voice she affected with clients; Sammie found it transparent, but she had to admit it worked. Most people wanted to be treated like VIPs. It was why Monika was so good at her job.

Brandon smiled. "It's hard work. You get that."

Sammie noticed a smudge at the corner of his mustache, a yellowy mustard blob. She turned to look at her son, who'd managed to pry free the poster and now was peeling the laminate off its backing in strips. He didn't look up when she called his name, not even when she shouted.

"He never listens," Britta said, leaning over the counter again. "Like, I'll ask him to get me something for a customer three times and he'll just stare at the wall."

"Could I get a Diet Coke?" Sammie asked.

"Yeah, sure." Britta filled a cup with crushed ice and fountain Coke and slid it over to her.

Sammie passed her a few dollars and gulped down several sips, feeling the carbonation burn her throat. Samson's hair was getting long again, she noticed. Most of it was stuffed under the baseball cap that was part of his uniform, but some of it hung down over his collar, bleached white from the sun and pool chlorine but crunchy and unwashed.

"Listen," Britta said, pouring her own drink. "For real, that girl? She's the worst. She was bothering me. He didn't do nothing wrong."

"Samson," Sammie called, and her son ignored her, again, wrapping the tattered poster around his hand.

"Well, what should we do here?" Monika asked. "Samson is saying he didn't do it."

Brandon sighed, scratched at his mustache. Some of the mustard came off under his fingernails and flaked onto his polo shirt. "It's a weird one. Sometimes it's hard with the high school kids 'cause they get into it all the time."

"Kids are always fighting, then the next day it's forgotten," Monika replied. "You know how it is. They're just messing around. Or they like each other and don't know how to show it. Hormones, right?"

Sammie didn't think it had anything to do with hormones; most likely it had to do with the fact that their son didn't know how to manage his anger. But she knew better than to argue about it.

"Samson loves the bowling alley." Monika looked at Sammie and raised her eyebrows, nudging her along.

"It's true. He really likes it here, and it's so great for his work ethic. I know he really enjoys working with you. And you were so nice to give him a job in the first place. We're so appreciative of that."

Sammie wasn't sure if he really liked it all that much, but it was good for him, and it definitely kept him busy. *Busy is better*, Sammie thought. Busy kept him out of trouble. She thought of her mother then, how that thing about idle hands being the devil's playground was her favorite cliché, but the gist of it was true. Busy kids had less time for mischief. Busy kids probably didn't spit in a Coke.

"It won't happen again," Monika said, which Sammie thought was a bold promise. Samson did whatever he liked.

Brandon sighed. "I mean, I guess. He shows up, and I don't wanna take time out of the schedule right now to look for somebody new. Especially with all this league crap going on."

"Thank you so much." Monika shook his hand. It was a vigorous shake. Monika was always trying to get men to take her seriously. Sammie echoed her thanks, and then Brandon was all smiles and affability again, like nothing had happened. *Were there ever any repercussions?* Sammie wondered, but she was tired, and all she wanted was to go home and think about how Myra's mouth felt on hers.

"You can go ahead and take him home," Brandon said. "Have him come in for his next scheduled shift. We'll start fresh. Brand-new day!"

"Absolutely," Monika replied, shaking his hand again. "We'll have him back to you this weekend. Thanks, buddy."

Sammie thanked him again as well, which felt excessive, and then looked back at her son, who was tossing bits of shredded poster in the air like confetti—what they always called Florida snow. She remembered playing with him when he was a kid, taking hunks of Monika's papers out of the shredder and throwing them onto the floor, daring him to make a snow angel. But when she lay down and smiled at him, swinging her arms back and forth on the carpet, he looked at her like she was an idiot, then turned and left the room.

"Clean that up," she told Samson, who rolled his eyes and came out from behind the back to stand beside Monika.

"Sorry about the mess," Sammie said to Britta, who'd already gone to collect the broom.

"I'm telling you," Britta called over her shoulder. "He does dumb shit like that all the time. But it's no big deal. It's just a boy thing."

Is it? Sammie thought, looking over at her son. He looked angry and uncomfortable. He scratched at his arm and his nails left behind red welts. *Maybe it's just a Samson thing.*

Monika's car was full of boxes, documents she needed for work, so Sammie walked Samson back to her own car. The giant truck was still there, crowding its way into her parking space.

"Careful when you get in—you don't have much room there," Sammie said.

Samson slammed open the back door—he *never* wanted to ride up front with her—and Sammie heard a metallic *crunch*. She looked over and saw a huge dented scratch in the truck's glossy paint job. She couldn't bring herself to yell at him, not when she'd wanted to smack that truck, too, for taking up so much space. So she just started the car and pulled out before anyone could stop them.

"If I had my own car you wouldn't have to drive me like this," Samson said.

Sammie was startled by the sound of his voice, which was gravelly and lower than she remembered; she had a hard time reconciling the shrill notes she remembered from his childhood with his steadily deepening adult baritone.

"Your mom and I still would have had to come out here tonight."

No response to that. Sammie looked at him in the rearview mirror, watching the shadows play across his face. She didn't understand most things about her son, but one thing she did know was that he was handsome. Traditionally handsome, people might say, if he ever smiled. But he didn't. Not even for school pictures. He hadn't needed braces, his teeth were so straight and perfect. He had ruddy cheeks that never developed any serious acne, and big blue eyes that matched the shape of her own dark brown ones but somehow looked better on his masculine face than on hers.

"Did you spit in that girl's drink?" Sammie asked.

The mirror-son shrugged at her in the rearview.

"I really pray to God you didn't, Samson."

"You pray to God?" Samson parroted, mimicking her trembly falsetto.

"You can't just . . . do things like that. Especially not to girls. Even if you don't like them."

Samson just picked at a thread coming loose on the back of the passenger seat.

"If we find out it's true . . . your mom would be furious, you know that, right? She told your manager you'd never do something like that."

"Mom's a bitch."

"Stop it," Sammie said, grip tightening on the steering wheel. She could feel the anger building inside her body, blood rushing to her face. "Don't talk like that about your mom."

"Why not? You talk about her that way."

"I do not," Sammie said, trying to keep her voice calm. "I do not do that."

"You're such a liar."

Sammie took deep breaths, in through the nose and out through the mouth, the way her therapist had taught her after she'd mentioned having panic attacks. She hadn't wanted to tell the woman that they were less about anxiety and more about rage—this lavalike anger that made her whole body feel like it might combust. Some days she worried that she'd burn up from it from the inside out, implode like a collapsing star.

"I don't know why you guys think I'm deaf or something. We all live in the same house. You've said that to each other a million times, and you know what, you're right. She's a fucking bitch."

How often had Samson heard them fight? She tried to be careful around him, but sometimes she got so mad that she forgot he was there. Not even forgot he was in the house—sometimes forgot he existed. She and Monika said things they didn't mean during those horrific fights: called each other terrible names, accused each other of awful things, swore and spat like feral cats. She stopped being a mother during those moments. Stopped being Sammie. All she could feel was her anger.

Desperate to change the topic, Sammie decided to ask about the girl.

"Who was she? Someone I know?"

Samson snorted and punched the seat. Sammie shifted around uncomfortably.

"Don't do that," she said, though she knew that would just make him do it again.

"It's no one you know. You don't know anyone."

"I might."

"How could you? You don't listen when I talk. You don't know any of my friends. Any of their names."

Was there any good way to talk with a child? Except he wasn't a child, was he? He was something else. Part of her, obviously. She could see it in the structure of his face and even in some of his mannerisms: the way he set his jaw when he didn't want to do something, ran his hands through his hair repeatedly when he was frustrated, chewed the inside of his cheek when he was working through a problem in his head. These were all hers, still hers, but the rest seemed like his own thing. As if he'd created himself.

"Do you know what it's like—what it's *exactly* like—to spit in someone's drink? It's forcing someone else to take your bodily fluids. It's assault, Samson."

"You are so *stupid* sometimes. Spit isn't jizz."

She'd hit a nerve. Usually she couldn't get him to show any kind of inflection in his voice, but this time she'd heard it go up, heard the mad buried under all that apathy.

"It comes out of your body," she said. "It's a fluid someone didn't ask for. Didn't want."

"Spit can't make babies."

"No, but it requires consent."

"You don't know anything about it," Samson replied, turning to face the window. "You're gay. You don't know anything about men's bodies. And you don't listen to anything I have to say, so why should I listen to you? You didn't even ask me what was wrong. Whatever you have to say is pointless."

And that was it. For the rest of the drive, he sat staring out the window in silence. She tried talking to him, tried changing the subject, but she might as well have been talking to a wall. That's what talking to anyone in her house felt like, Sammie thought—like trying to reason with a piece of furniture. If you talked and no one listened, were you even talking at all?

They pulled up to the house, and Samson climbed out of the car before she'd even turned off the ignition. From that point on, she knew, everything would be a rerun. She'd go inside and ask Monika what they should do about Samson, and Monika would say he'd already been punished enough for something he didn't even do, and Sammie would insist it wasn't right, that he didn't respect them because they never gave him firm boundaries, and Monika would say that Sammie didn't have a backbone anyway, and how did she actually plan on enforcing anything when she couldn't even get her own life together, and then they would all drift away to their separate corners of the house.

The lights were on when she walked inside. Monika was sitting cross-legged on the couch, already engrossed in some cable news show.

"Good night," Sammie said to the air, to no one, to the moon.

Brandon had seen Samson spit in the girl's drink, but he hadn't wanted to get involved. That's what he told Marco that night over dinner. (Fish sticks, again. Brandon was sick to death of reheated frozen foods.) He'd called it a little lovers' quarrel, and Marco had rolled his eyes—heterosexuals, right?—and they'd both had a laugh over it. That was good, because they'd been having fewer laughs recently. The kid was a fine worker, showed up on time. And he was respectful, always giving him a "yes sir" and a "no sir" when questioned, which Brandon thought showed good character. The two moms were smothering the boy, that was clear as day. They'd shown up in high dudgeon; he'd worried they were going to cause a whole huge scene right in the middle of the alley. That was the last thing he needed when the league tournaments were starting. The really bad one was that Monika, who was a lawyer, and could be a right bitch about things. So, yes, Samson had spit into the girl's drink. Brandon had seen it; he wasn't blind. But that girl and her friends were always making trouble at the bowling alley. She was constantly trying to needle the league bowlers, too—wearing short skirts, bending over to pick up a ball, flashing a slip of panty and a large amount of ass. The girl was kind of a bitch; maybe it wasn't such a bad thing that she got some back once in a while. Marco asked him if he wanted any more fish sticks, and Brandon said yes, even though he was sick of them, because that's what you did when you loved someone, he thought. You said yes and pretended to like it.

11

Sammie hated summers, all that time between spring and fall stretching like years instead of months. It was hard enough to get things done when Samson was in school, but when he was out it almost felt like Sammie was in jail.

"Why do you think you feel that way?"

She was in her therapist's office, again. Talking about Samson and Monika, again. Talking, but never solving anything. Therapy was like being in limbo, yet she dragged herself back every other week. *I'm a masochist*, Sammie thought. *That's the only explanation.*

"Because then I have to think about his problems and there's no room for mine. Because the two of them invade my space all the time, they wind up taking up all the room in my brain, too."

"Have you considered moving out?"

"Maybe."

All the time was more like it. It was foolish, the two of them still sharing that house, when they'd been split up for years. Sammie knew that well enough. But the alternative was so complicated: How to divide up all their things? How to co-parent their son? How to make a decent living on her own when so much of her time was spent tending to Samson? Their life was a series of intricate knots, and she couldn't face the challenge of pulling them apart.

If she was being honest, she also didn't want to give up the still-sweet moments that happened. The way she and Monika helped each other with little things like picking up dry cleaning or ordering takeout. Seeing her wife's face first thing in the morning over coffee, still soft before the day ahead turned it hard. She wasn't sure what it would mean to give all that up completely.

"Think about it some more," the doctor said.

"I will. I am gonna."

That was Sammie's usual answer, and then as soon as she was out of the office she pushed it from her mind. The thought of changing her life exhausted her. Easier to just forget about it until the next time her therapist brought it up.

Sammie had been seeing the same therapist since she and Monika had seen her as a couples counselor, back when they were still trying to make their marriage work. This was when Samson was still in middle school—when it seemed important to salvage their marriage, if only for his sake. Aja Brewer was gay, like them, and it seemed better to go with someone who would understand the dynamics they faced as a queer couple raising a child. It had been easy enough to stay with her after Monika had decided things were over between them. Monika hadn't wanted to go on with therapy on her own—she supported Samson's ongoing sessions, but Sammie could tell she thought adult therapy was for weak-minded people who couldn't solve their own problems—so she didn't care that Sammie kept the same slot with Aja after they split.

Aja was fine, as far as therapy went. Sammie was attracted to her, that was one problem, but weren't most people attracted to their therapists? Who wouldn't be flattered by someone who sat and listened—like, *really* listened, not just waited for their turn to speak? Like Samson's therapist, Aja wasn't very pushy; she allowed a lot of room for self-discovery. But where Dr. Kim was petite and dark and quiet, Aja had wild, curly hair and bright clothes and liked to poke fun at herself. She sometimes made jokes in session, which was nice. She talked about herself, too, and offered up glimpses of her own life.

Sammie's only disappointment was that she'd expected Aja to understand the dynamics of living with an ex—that even if she might not endorse it as a therapist, she would understand it as a queer person. Heterosexual couples hardly ever did this kind of thing, but lesbians did all the time. They stayed friends. They dated all the same people. They kept living together after breaking up. There was a reason for the stereotypes, wasn't there? This was all just stuff they . . . did, all the time.

But Aja wouldn't let it sit there. So Sammie had to keep addressing it, when all she really wanted to talk about was why she wasn't able to enjoy having someone fuck her anymore.

"Let's talk about this at our next session," Aja said, slipping a hunk of frizzy red hair behind her ear.

"Okay," Sammie replied, but she thought, *Absolutely not*, and then thought of how she wished her therapist would bend her over and spank her with one of those thick file folders she always had stacked high on the corner of her desk.

On the way out, Sammie stopped to pay the receptionist and then checked her phone. A text from Monika, asking her to pick up Samson from practice.

Why? Sammie texted back, daring Monika to say something honest—*I'm going on a date and I can't be bothered to pick up our son*—but all she wrote was *I'm busy*, which could have meant anything. Sammie didn't need the words to know what was actually going on.

She drove across town to the same building she'd been taking

Samson to since his first beginner's class. They'd expanded it over the past few years, consuming all the suburban houses around it to make room for a gigantic pool. It was sad, seeing all that old Orlando architecture—those retro ranch houses with screened porches—bulldozed to make way for faceless commercial buildings and mini McMansions that could have been plopped down anywhere in the United States. Sammie missed all the wild Florida foliage that used to clamber over every front yard, too—the bougainvillea with its bright pink spray of blossoms, huge leafy stands of palm scrub housing thousands of lizards. These new places, with their clean green replacement lawns, had none of the charm of those old places, with their crumbling birdbaths and plastic hummingbird feeders, their squirrels running through weedy acorn-riddled grass.

The chlorine hit her as soon as she opened the outer door to the gym. It was an overpowering scent, one that singed her nostrils and puckered her face. The house she grew up in hadn't had a pool, but her family frequented the neighborhood community pool and the local water parks everyone went to, so that smell should have felt like a happy Florida thing to Sammie. But ever since Samson had started swimming, back in elementary school, she'd come to associate the smell with feelings of duty and obligation. Instead of carefree summer days, the smell of chlorine reminded her that she was getting older, that her life belonged to her kid.

There was Samson, lean and muscular at the far side of the pool. He was standing alone, as always, but at least in his sleek aqua swim cap and his navy swimsuit he looked like he belonged. That was the thing that puzzled her, how he never seemed to fit in with the rest of the group. He was good-looking—better-looking than the other boys, she thought—and she knew she wasn't fooling herself about it, since she found her child ugly so often in his disobedience. He was toned from years of swimming, and when he swam he was charismatic, even graceful. But out of the water there was something stiff in his body language. As a child he'd had a dancer's casual poise, but after puberty that seemed to change overnight. Now he stood too straight; his arms were braided with muscles, but when they weren't powering him through the water, they appeared jerky. His neck was tense, turning his head uncomfortably far when he looked around, owl-like and blinking. His gait was almost unnatural, as if he were walking in a stop-motion movie. Sometimes she wished she could just move his limbs for him.

He spotted her then, up in the bleachers, and she put up her hand. He acknowledged her with a brief nod, something he almost never did, and she squelched a smile. She watched him ease into the water, buoyant and loose. Oh, but there—this was where her son could shine. The pool did something to his body; he looked like himself there, sliding down beneath the blue of the water. When he turned, flipped, kicked, it was as if his body had been constructed for just such a purpose. A merman. A shark. A barracuda fixed on an achievable goal.

His teammates crowded around at the other end of the pool. They dunked one another, sputtering as they emerged, shaking free of one another's hands. Laughing and yelling. Not Samson. He didn't goof off with the other boys, although he got along fine with them. He went out with them to parties, got rides home in their crowded cars. Sammie felt like he should be socializing more, but one part of her was relieved that he didn't spend too much time with his teammates. She was so ill-equipped to talk to him about his gender and all the issues that went along with it. She'd put off having the sex talk with him until it was too late. Monika hadn't done it, either. There was no one for him to talk to about his body, about puberty. All he'd had was a talk at school, which Sammie knew was a poor substitute for actual sex education.

That was the thing she'd worried about when it came to having a boy. Already the odds were stacked against them as a lesbian couple. People were already judging them, sure that a boy with two mothers wouldn't turn out right. Monika's attitude had always been to just prove them wrong. Raise their son, have him turn out beautifully—that would be the best *I told you so* of all. But Sammie wasn't so sure.

One thing she knew was that she had no idea how boys talked to each other. She was scared to find out. She knew they could be crude, especially in groups. Boys moved in packs; they talked smack, egged each other on. They could be disgusting when it came to girls and sex. She had a vivid memory of one Sunday morning at church, when she was twelve, and a boy in the middle of a group behind her kept trying to wedge a church bulletin through the crack of her chair and down her pants. She listened to them all whispering, snickering, laughing. It was her first encounter with the terrifying laughter of aggressive young men. She spent the whole service teetering on the edge of her chair. Her fear was a buzz in her ears, a live insect looking for a way to escape. The rest of the week, her lower back had felt like an open wound.

Samson popped up at the opposite end of the pool and flipped neatly, speeding down to the bottom and spreading his arms wide, powering himself along. No, she didn't want her son spending too much time with those boys. She imagined, as she did sometimes, what it would have been like to have the daughter she'd lost, one who'd share a Diet Coke with her in the bleachers. Then she remembered those boys in church, how they cackled as they preyed on girls like her, and she crossed her legs involuntarily.

At the end of practice, Samson walked over to her barefoot, swaddled in towels. One was slung across his chest like a sopping prom-king sash.

"You're still dripping," Sammie said, grimacing. "You can't get in the car like that."

"Where's Mom?" He slopped one of the soaking towels onto the bench beside her, spattering her shirt and her face.

"Something came up."

Samson grunted. "Something always comes up." He dropped the rest of the towels on the floor and yanked a T-shirt out of his green duffel bag. The bag was the same one Sammie had bought for him when he first started swimming. It was tattered and ripped, holes opening along the top where the zipper was beginning to separate from the cheap nylon.

"You should let me replace that," Sammie said. "Get you something bigger. Sturdier."

"I like this one." He pulled the shirt over his wet hair, and when his arms came down, Sammie saw the silvery flash of his scar against the deeper tan of his wrist.

"Are you hungry?" she asked, rubbing at her own wrist, and he grunted again. She rolled her eyes. He was so predictable.

"Pizza? Grunt once for yes, twice for no."

He leaned down directly into her face and burped, twice. "Had pizza for lunch."

Boys and their bodies. Too open. Too smelly. Too *much*.

"That's disgusting."

Samson dug around in his duffel bag and pulled out a Red Bull. He cracked the can and took several large gulps, belching again when he was done. She knew she should say something about it—so many chemicals, and it would keep him up half the night—but what good would it do? He'd drink what he wanted.

Sammie looked out across the water and imagined herself in there, facedown. Floating peacefully. Ears underwater, too, hearing nothing. Seeing nothing. Drifting.

"How about the Tex-Mex place?" she asked. "We haven't been there in a minute."

Samson stopped drinking and looked down at her. His lips were wet from the Red Bull, almost spitty. It reminded her of when he was a baby and she had to chase him around all day with a rag, wiping him down. "When we get there, can I have a sip of your beer?"

Sammie laughed, surprised. "Fine. One sip."

He did a double take. She'd surprised him, too. Good.

"Can I drive the car?" he asked.

"Absolutely not."

They walked out of the gym together and into the muggy Florida evening. Twilight was coming on, and the sky was lit up along the seam like a crack under a closed door, glowing golden light. The cicadas were screaming and everything smelled like heat and dirt. Sammie rolled down the windows, despite the muggy air, and let her hand slip along in the breeze. It was a quiet drive to the restaurant. Neither of them talked, but it felt nice to be still. To just exist in the moment. That was something she and her son had in common, something Monika could never understand: when they were alone, they were really alone, and they liked it that way.

The place wasn't far from home, shoved inside a strip mall with a T.J.Maxx, a supersized Publix, and a Baptist bookstore. They parked and walked inside, weaving through the after-work crowds of people leaving the supermarket with their loaded carts.

"We need to get toilet paper before we go home," Sammie said.

Samson opened the door to the restaurant and barged inside, almost knocking over an elderly woman with a very small child at her side.

"I'm so sorry," Sammie said, scrambling to help her. "Are you okay?"

Samson just walked on, marching over to the host station to grab a menu.

The woman nodded and put an arm around the little girl, who looked to be about four. She had a bright blond ponytail and big brown eyes. She didn't make a sound as the woman took her hand and led her outside. Sammie held the door for them, then followed Samson up to the front.

"You need to be more careful. You're bigger than a lot of people. You're not a kid anymore—you're nearly a grown man."

"Am I a man? When you get mad you say I'm acting like a child. Pick one."

"Man-child," Sammie retorted, and the hostess came by to seat them.

Wedged into a red leather booth in the back corner, Sammie ordered a beer and Samson got a Coke. Over their menus, Sammie assessed her son.

"You need a haircut," she said.

Samson frowned. "Not this again."

"Why do you refuse to take care of yourself?"

The drinks showed up. He pulled half the wrapper off his straw and blew the other half at her. "Why do you think taking care of myself means doing exactly what you would do?"

Sammie had to laugh at that. "What I would do? You see how I dress." She gestured at her own clothes: pants she'd owned for ten years, a shirt with a coffee stain that had never properly bleached out. "It's not about me. What I care about is you learning to be an adult."

"You never care. You talk over me. You think you're listening, but you only hear what you want to hear."

Samson focused on dripping minuscule drops of soda onto a napkin. Slowly they formed a pattern, a spiral winding tightly inward. Sammie picked her phone up and scrolled through the dating app. This was the most her son had spoken to her in weeks. And she wasn't screaming at him. She knew she should stop nagging him about his appearance, but it was hard to stop, like picking at a scab. In a way, she thought he liked it, too. They both got something from it, a weird satisfaction from goading each other on. Monika couldn't stand it when they argued in front of her. She'd wind up leaving the house, going for a long walk or even a drive. It was one of the things they fought over most: *What about your callous treatment of Samson?* Monika chided her. *How exactly is it callous that I want him to have an ounce of self-respect?* she shot back.

In therapy, she talked a lot about the fact that she didn't know what she wanted out of her relationships with Monika or her son. She missed

the way they'd been together early on; it was an ache like a slowly healing bruise. Aja wondered if things had ever been that rosy. No, that
wasn't the way she put it; what she asked was, "Is that what really happened?" Which forced Sammie to consider the idea that many of her
memories had been turned into nostalgic stories in her head, cleansed of
the same animosity that tinged their current life.

Sammie beckoned to their server, an attractive blonde in her early
twenties. When she came over to take their order, Samson wouldn't say
a word, just tapped at his menu.

"He'll have the chicken quesadilla," Sammie said, forcing a smile.
"And I'll have the nachos. Sour cream on the side." That was another
thing she wasn't supposed to do: talk for Samson. Back when they were
going to couples counseling, Monika brought it up plenty, and Aja supported her: Samson needed to speak for himself. They were supposed to
prompt him to do his own talking. Remind him, every time. But Sammie
got so exhausted with all the nudging that she just gave up and did it for
him. *Wasn't it easier that way?* she'd argue, and Monika would say,
Easier for who?, and they'd be in the same fight all over again.

"You said I could have some of your beer." Samson pointed at her
pint glass, nearly empty.

"Next one."

Sammie ordered another from the server and felt the warm fuzz of it
creep up her neck. She was still on the dating app, swiping past faces she'd
already seen a million times. It was so boring, but she couldn't help herself. Whenever she sat down for more than five seconds, there she was,
back at it again. The app never gave her a good feeling—most of the time
it made her feel terrible—but every time she deleted it from her phone she
thought about Monika going out on dates, so she added it back and kept
on scrolling, looking for someone who'd finally catch her attention.

She set her phone down on the table, with the app still open, and
picked up her new beer.

"Ugly."

"What?"

"Ugly." Samson tapped hard on the table in front of her phone.

"That's rude."

He shrugged. "Ugly."

The woman wasn't someone Sammie would normally swipe yes on, but now she felt like she had to, on principle. "Who are you to say who's ugly and who's pretty? How would you feel if someone pointed at a picture of you and said 'ugly'?"

He didn't answer. It seemed he'd used up all his words in the few sentences he'd managed to get out before the food arrived. Sammie finished her beer and asked for another. Three was a lot, even if they were light beers, but she figured if she finished all her nachos it wouldn't matter. She'd be fine to drive.

Her phone lit up on the table. A message. Probably from the woman she'd swiped on, a woman with long dark hair like hers. A woman whose face looked pinched, who looked too much like herself.

"What about you? Are you dating anybody?" Sammie asked.

"Gross, Mom."

Even she knew the question was annoying. She sounded just like her own mother, asking her about boys. Sammie had hated that, the way her mother's nostrils had flared every time she'd said the word *date* to her daughter. It was mortifying to talk to her mom about boyfriends (and she hadn't even had any). About her body. About *anything*. Every probing question from her mother made Sammie furious.

I don't want to be like her, she thought. But that didn't solve her problem with Samson.

"It's not gross to be interested in people," she said finally.

No response. Samson was tearing apart his quesadilla, stacking the pieces in giant piles. She'd be lucky if he ate three bites. Buying him food always felt like such a waste of money. He never appreciated good food, even the Mexican food everyone else loved. One night she'd tried buying them all expensive lobster tails as a treat.

Why can't we just have burgers? he'd groused. *Why do you have to make everything fancy?*

"What about that girl Britta? From work?"

Samson pretended to gag, and Sammie rolled her eyes at his dramatics. But then he leaned over and actually started choking. Sammie reached across the table, not sure what to do, nearly upending their drinks. He was hacking and wheezing, hands at his throat, and then he spat an entire wad of chewed quesadilla right back onto his plate. Her son sat back and grinned at her, then took a quiet sip of his Coke.

"Fuck you," Sammie said. She'd never spoken to her son that way before, but wow, did it feel good to say that aloud.

His eyes widened, those eyes that reminded her of her own, but he said nothing. Sammie ordered another round. She wasn't hungry, but oh God, she needed another beer. She had the server take away Samson's plate before the wad of half-chewed food made her sick.

Samson spun her phone around on the table in front of them until she grabbed his wrist to get him to stop. He stilled, a statue in his seat, and Sammie rubbed her thumb against the smooth slickness of his scar. Her teeth. This was her wrist, her body. What was his was actually hers, wasn't it? She'd made that body with her own—grown it, birthed it. She pressed down suddenly against the mark, hard, and when he shuddered she wondered if it felt like pressing into a deep bruise.

She let go. "One sip," she said, pushing the new beer across the table. "I mean it, just one."

Neither of them looked around. They stared at each other as he took a large gulp from the glass. It was still icy cold, and she wondered if it would give him a brain freeze, like she used to get when she drank Slurpees too fast from the 7-Eleven down the street when she was young.

"Let's play a game," she said. "Truth." She hadn't planned on starting up a truth-or-dare game with her son—Monika would be horrified—but Sammie found the idea of sharing another secret with her son kind of heady. Another thing Monika couldn't have access to. She was fully drunk now—a stupid thing to do when she had to drive them both home, but maybe they could just sit a little longer in the restaurant. She could order more food, even though she'd barely touched her nachos.

"Okay, I'll start," she said when he didn't answer. "Truth. Have you had beer before?"

In her tipsy state, his face seemed made up of disparate parts. The large nose. His excessively thin eyebrows, so blond they were nearly invisible. The ears poking out from under his mop of scraggly hair. She wondered what his mirror would have looked like, had she ever made it to sixteen. Hope: that little glimmer, the baby who would always live with her because she lived on within Samson.

"Yeah, I've had beer." He picked up her glass, without waiting for a response, and took another sip.

"I figured." She took the beer back, holding it between her palms to keep it away from him. "No more for you."

Would her girl have acted this way? Whenever she brought up the baby with Monika—after Samson had done something terrible at school or on the playground or at swim practice—her wife insisted that gender wasn't the issue, that no matter its sex (Monika always called her *it*, because she refused to name a baby who "didn't exist"), Hope might still have grown up to be a problem child. That she'd likely have made things even harder, with two kids and only two of them to raise them.

Kids aren't dogs, she countered, frustrated with Monika but also with herself for getting caught up in the same old argument. *It's not like they're a pack of wild animals. They're not going to outnumber us.*

"Truth," Sammie pressed on. "Have you ever had a girlfriend?" She stopped herself then, shook her head. "Or boyfriend. Whichever."

He shrugged.

"Shrug, shrug. That doesn't count. You have to say yes or no."

"One sip per answer," he said. "Then I'll do it."

"Fine." She could do this. She could sip her way through a dozen questions without finishing a beer, and then she'd finally get some answers out of him.

She signaled the server that she'd like another beer and, once the woman was out of sight, pushed her own across the table.

"Okay. Let's do it."

It went that way for the next half hour. He answered her questions, at least partially. No, he hadn't dated anyone, though the face he made when she called it *dating* told her she should have called it something else. No, he didn't know what he wanted to do with his life, didn't know if he wanted to go to college, didn't know what kind of job he wanted. Yes, he did like swimming. That was something she'd always wondered: Did he enjoy it at all, or was it just something he was good at?

"Your grandparents made me do gymnastics. For years. It was horrible."

"That's stupid."

"Yeah, I hated it. But I was good at it, so they made me keep doing it. The only reason they finally let me stop was that I got boobs and your grandpa said the uniforms were too revealing."

"Weird."

"Yeah, I know."

She was good and drunk now, matching her son sip for sip, and now they had to drive home. By her last count she'd ordered six beers, and when the server had dropped off the last one, she'd brought the check as well—setting it right down in a pool of suds Sammie had sloshed out onto the table.

"Truth," she asked. "What's your favorite color?"

Samson stared at her, then laughed. "You're kidding, right? You don't know my favorite color?"

She sat for a minute and tried to think. He wore a lot of blue. "Is it blue?"

He laughed again and rubbed his face with both hands, like she was exhausting him. "Mom. I've told you this a million times."

Sammie shrugged. Maybe he was right; maybe she was a terrible listener. "Refresh my memory."

"I like green," he said, taking another sip of her beer. "Green like frogs."

"Like Kermit the Frog."

Her son made a low croak, and she realized he was emulating frog noises. She listened a little closer, until the croaks came together into a bastardized, silly version of "The Rainbow Connection." She burst out laughing. *When was the last time I laughed with this kid?* she wondered. And then she was about to cry.

"Let me drive," Samson said. His shape swam in front of her—one Samson, two Samsons. It reminded her again of her daughter, Samson's mirror, and she swallowed past a lump in her throat. Oh, he looked prettier that way, through her tears. The lights around them blinked and spun out, giving her son a fuzzy Christmas halo. It might have taken some beer to get there, but it felt like she and Samson had finally connected, if only for a moment.

Sammie paid the check, then pulled herself out of the booth and attempted to walk soberly out of the restaurant and into the sticky Florida night. Then, as she stepped off the curb, a Honda hatchback braked suddenly to let a woman with a grocery cart pass, and Sammie stumbled into the car. In frustration she kicked at the car's tire, missed, and sprawled flat on her back.

It was nearly dark, but the sticky black tar of the asphalt was still hot enough to sting her hands. She sat there on the ground, her purse spilled around her. One tube of lipstick rolled away under a parked car. She held up her hands to her face, unsure if she was burned or scraped or what. Samson stood at the edge of the sidewalk, looking down at her.

A man loomed over her, blocking out what was left of the dying light. "Oh my God, are you okay? Do you need help?"

She held out one of her hands, the one she thought might be bleeding, and he took it and helped her to her feet. When she leaned back to get a closer look at him, she swayed so badly he had to grab her arm to steady her.

"Is there someone who can drive you?" he asked.

He has a nice face, Sammie thought. Bearded over and fuzzy with pink cheeks, like a dark-haired Santa Claus. She realized she was laughing out loud when the man frowned at her.

"Yes," she said, shaking off his hand, trying to pull herself together. "My son here is driving us home."

He stepped back and helped her collect the things from her purse: some loose tampons, a roll of ancient mints, her wallet, which had burst open and spilled out receipts and her driver's license, a picture so old it looked like it was from three lifetimes ago.

"Samson. C'mon."

Her son took his time walking over to her, and even when he reached her he avoided eye contact. The man handed her purse to her son—or, rather, thrust it at him, jabbing the leather satchel into her son's gut when he didn't immediately take it.

"Pay attention, son." He leaned in close to Samson's face. "Show some respect."

"We're leaving," Sammie said, grabbing the sleeve of her son's T-shirt and dragging him away from the man, who suddenly seemed much larger and more aggressive.

"Asshole," Samson said. He wasn't even quiet about it, and suddenly the man was charging back over to them.

"What did you just say to me, you little prick?"

"Thank you for your help," Sammie said, smiling a smile that felt like almost all teeth. "Thank you. So much. I've got it from here."

The man muttered something under his breath—*bitch*, maybe? Sammie couldn't be sure. The interaction had sobered her up, faster even than falling to the pavement. She took her purse and dragged Samson across the parking lot, dodging a couple of kids running between cars—who let their kids run loose in a busy parking lot?—when she realized that Samson had stopped.

"What?" she said, spitting out the word like a bullet.

"Mom. The car." He pointed back the way they'd come. "The car. It's over there."

There it was, they'd already passed it. She was still drunk. It felt like all the wind had been knocked out of her. She collected herself and followed her son back to the car, fishing around in her purse for the keys until he took the bag and found them himself.

She climbed into the passenger seat as he got behind the wheel, shoving the seat back until it clicked so hard she thought it would break.

"Do you even know how to drive?" She probably should have asked him before she'd had all those beers, but it was too late now.

"Mom showed me," he said. Then he started the car and backed them out of the spot, maneuvering them easily through the parking lot.

"Fuck. I was supposed to get toilet paper."

"Mom's gonna be pissed."

"Yeah, I know." Sammie sighed and messed with the radio. News, news, bad eighties song, country, news, news. "Wait, when did she even show you how to drive?"

"Lots of times. Since I was like twelve."

That sneaky bitch, Sammie thought—another first they should have enjoyed as a family—but all she said to Samson was, "Lucky for us, huh?"

Thanks to the beers, she wasn't white-knuckling the seat the way she might have if she were sober. It was weird to be in the passenger seat beside him, to watch his profile as the oncoming headlights glanced off his features and turned them to granite. Her boy, still as a statue.

"Turn here," she said.

"I know, Mom," he said. "We've lived in the same house my whole life."

"Right," Sammie said. "Sorry. I'm on autopilot."

They drove past the lake, a dark thumbprint out in the distance. No moon out, no stars. The trees flashed past in a cloudy blur.

"That was really embarrassing." Samson drummed his thumb twice against the steering wheel. "You embarrassed me."

Sammie's face felt hot. A tidal wave of shame rose up in her chest, threatening to drown her. "I'm an adult. It's okay if I have a drink sometimes and let loose."

"You fell down in a parking lot."

"Do you know how many times you've embarrassed me? Are we keeping score? Because your list is a lot longer than mine, Samson."

He swerved to avoid a dead armadillo, insides splattered in the middle of the lane.

"Do you wanna play the game?" Samson asked.

Sammie was transported back in time for a moment, back to when Samson was very young and she'd tried to teach him to play hide-and-seek. She'd explained the rules to him, her five-year-old who never listened. Told him to go find a place to hide and she'd count to ten. She turned to face the living room wall. Counted loudly, dramatically. It was sunny and hot and the light was streaming in through the curtains, hitting her square in the face. Outside was a bright blaze of green, all the azalea bushes in front of the house in shocking pink bloom. She remembered thinking how perfect it all was: her son was healthy, her house was her own, she loved her wife. Then she turned around and there was

Samson standing in the middle of the rug, right where she'd left him. Couldn't even play hide-and-seek with her own damn kid.

"The game?" Sammie asked stupidly, then remembered. "Oh. Okay. Yes."

"Truth," Samson said. "Why don't you and Mom get divorced?"

Sammie sat and let the words wash around in her head. They separated from each other, slipped out of sequence, slid between each other again like tiny goldfish in the bowl of her brain.

"That's not easy to answer," she replied, and then she thought, *Fuck it*, because what did it matter anymore? "I mean, I'm not sure. We're still attached to each other in so many ways. Somehow this seems easier than doing all that work. Maybe it's love." She shrugged. "Who knows."

They were driving past all the familiar places they used to go as a family. The streetlights flicked by overhead in a spastic blur. It was hot out, too hot to roll down the windows, but for a moment she wished she could, just to feel the air like breath against her neck. Florida felt like that to her sometimes: like something alive, a panting dog, a being that took time from her but also lavished her with affection. Made her feel secure in its love, even when it was pissing all over the floor.

"Truth," Samson said, eyes on the road, hands at ten and two. "Did I kill the baby?"

Sammie felt like the car's airbag had gone off directly into her chest. "Oh my God."

"Did I eat her?" Samson drummed his hands against the steering wheel. Sammie watched those eight fingers sprawl out, tapping and crawling. "Cannibalize her?"

"Stop it."

"Did I eat her? Mom? Did I?"

Those spider fingers, creeping, tapping, scurrying. She reached out to smack them, just to make them stop, to get him to quit before she lost it completely—and then her own hands were wrapped around the steering wheel and she was turning the car to the side of the road.

Neither of them made a sound as they grappled for control of the car. For a moment, Sammie's drunken strength won out. The car moved jaggedly to the right, bumping over the edge of the curb. Cars honked behind them and in the next lane. They skirted the edge of the guardrail and bright sparks flew, metal shrieking on metal. Then Samson wrestled the wheel back, shoving her into the passenger seat with his right arm, and it was over.

They were only a minute away from home. Sammie stared out the window as Samson drove carefully down their street. He put the blinker on and turned the car gently into their own familiar driveway.

It was pitch dark, but Sammie somehow managed to catch the keys when Samson tossed them to her. Inside their house every light was on, as usual. Monika was curled up on the couch with one of the mystery novels she loved.

"Did you guys get dinner?" Monika asked without looking up. "I'm starved."

"I ran into a car in the grocery store parking lot," Sammie said. "Scraped up the bumper."

"What?" Now she had Monika's attention. "How bad is it?"

"We're fine, by the way."

"How bad is the car? The insurance is gonna go through the roof." Monika set down her book on the couch, dog-earing one of the pages. "Honestly, you're so irresponsible. You know this affects me, too."

"I'm going to bed," Sammie said, and left her wife where she sat, yelling after her.

The drunk woman was sprawled out on the pavement like a goddamn puppet with its strings cut. Mike was a nice guy, he'd seen her fall and gone over to help. He would have done the same thing for his own mother. Or his grandma, he supposed, that's who'd mostly raised him. This lady's kid was a punk, though—that much Mike knew for sure. Standing there looking embarrassed while his mom was lying down in the street like a kicked dog. Mike had never been embarrassed of his mom acting that way, would have liked the chance to help when she needed it, to support her, but she'd died in a car wreck not too long after she left him with his grandma. Never even got to know her. This kid didn't know how good he had it. He was an asshole, too, talking to Mike that way. Probably he didn't have a good father figure. He shouldn't have gotten in the boy's face—he'd looked scared, and then that scared his mama, who was just trying to look out for him. Mike just got so mad sometimes. He was sure the woman loved her boy. And the kid loved her, too, he could see it from the soft look on his face when he eventually helped her to the car. Mike went home and drank a few beers, and then called his grandma, who asked if he'd come over and fix her stove. It was rattling again.

12

There was no smoking in the bar, but the whole place reeked of cigarettes. That's mostly what Sammie was fixated on. The smell wouldn't
leave her nostrils, though the drinks helped with that. Astringent bite of
gin, then the smoke. Gin, smoke. It almost felt nostalgic, or at least it
would have if she still had the youthful stamina she had back when she
was partying in her twenties.

She was hiding out in the back corner of the lesbian bar. Even though
it was Saturday night, it was still early, and the place was nearly de-
serted. She'd forgotten how everyone always showed up to bars late.
Back before she and Monika started dating, she'd pregame with friends
at her shitty apartment for hours before they left the house, drinking
vodka and Crystal Light from plastic Slurpee cups she'd collected from
the gas station. Sometimes people would puke before they'd even gotten
out the door. Wouldn't even see the inside of a bar before 11:00 P.M.
She'd stumble home at 3:00 A.M. and sleep off her hangover, then wake
up in the morning and walk down the street in her pajamas for three

cheeseburgers from McDonald's. Then she'd do it all again the following weekend.

Now it wasn't even ten and she was swirling a plastic drink straw in her gin and tonic. She'd asked for extra lime and more tonic after the bartender had given her a particularly heavy pour, and the woman looked at her like she'd asked for dog shit in her drink.

She sat in the red vinyl booth, grimacing at the medicinal flavor of the gin, wishing she'd ordered something sweet instead. She looked back over at the bartender, who had a spiky short haircut, shaved up one side, and a nose piercing. She was wearing tight black jeans and a ripped tank top with a black bra underneath. Her eyeliner was thick and dark, with cat-eyed corners.

Sammie fidgeted in her seat. She tugged down the hem of her skirt, berating herself for the hundredth time for not wearing jeans. She was overdressed, she knew it. The thing was, she'd looked at herself in the mirror while she was getting ready, stared at all that long, unkempt hair, assessed her face with its steadily encroaching wrinkles, and wished she looked . . . different. No, not different. Pretty. She could admit it here, just to herself, after too much gin in the back of a mostly empty night-club. She'd been desperate for the feeling she used to get when she was young and women looked at her the way she was looking at the women around her now. A hungry look. One that made her feel wanted, like she was as necessary as oxygen.

Downing her drink in a hurry didn't make it taste any better, but at least she could get another. Sammie climbed down out of the booth, wincing as her sweaty thighs peeled free of the vinyl. Her blouse had rucked up out of her skirt and she hurriedly stuffed it back in, nearly overturning her cup of ice onto the floor. That was another mistake: the skirt, the ruffly sleeveless top, even the stupid kitten-heel sandals. She felt like an imposter. The women who were slowly making their way inside were all dressed like the one behind the bar—ripped jeans, oversize shirts, little tank tops. Sneakers. So many pairs of boots, even though it was Florida and their feet must be sweltering.

And, God, they were young. So young she felt herself aging as the minutes passed, as if every second of the clock sprouted another gray hair on her head, produced another wrinkle, yellowed her teeth to butterscotch. It wasn't as though she had some painting of herself in an attic, aging while she stayed youthful, no; it was like these young women were sucking the life out of her and she was the hideous figure in the painting, gnarled and monstrous.

"Another gin and tonic," Sammie told the bartender, smiling with her mouth closed in case her teeth were as yellow as she feared. "Make it a double."

The bartender gave it to her without comment, putting it on the tab Sammie had already opened, then went back to talking to a dark-haired woman in a tight shirt who looked an awful lot like Salma Hayek.

She took another swig, and her lipstick left a dark scar along the side. When she went to wipe it with her thumb, it smeared across the entire lip. It looked like the drink had some kind of horrible STD. That was another thing—she'd worn too much makeup, or maybe she couldn't remember how to put it on. When she sat down at her vanity mirror and looked at her bare face, all she could think was how she needed to cover it up. The makeup she owned was old, too. Tubes of stuff from weddings, or things she'd bought for parties long ago. When she'd opened her mascara, the makeup inside was so ancient it had clumped into a solid mass.

Monika never would have had this problem. If Monika even went out to clubs like this, which Sammie very much doubted.

You have to stop trying so hard, Monika always told her, but what the hell did she know? She'd never had to try a day in her life, not for anything. Her parents had paid for college, then grad school, then law school. She'd gotten a job at a firm where the partners knew her father.

Growing up, she'd traveled all over the world—so many places that Sammie could never think of a new place for them to go that Monika hadn't already seen.

Still, it had also been nice that Monika knew so much, that she was always able to pick out something fun for both of them. She knew how to choose things Sammie would like: a special restaurant where they could share a plate of spicy crab legs; a ski trip where they hardly left the room, just drank hot chocolate and watched the snow fall softly outside the bedroom window. Sammie had seen snow so rarely in her life that it seemed almost like an illusion—as if Monika had a special world built just for her.

She sucked at her drink—slow sip, slow sip, make it last. More people were coming in now, which was good, although most of them were in couples or groups. Sammie felt like the only person who'd come alone.

She wondered, not for the first time, how different her life would have been if she hadn't had a kid. Before they'd had Samson, she and Monika had been friends with a huge group of gay people. They'd had dinner-party friends, people they'd gone out with to bars and restaurants, out to the theme parks for Gay Days, picnics and weddings and brunch. But when they started telling people they were thinking about getting pregnant, their friends—even the ones who were coupled up themselves—had expressed polite interest, then gradually stopped calling them to hang out. By the time Sammie was pregnant, the friends she'd considered to be her closest had begged off until she was just hanging out with her wife most weekends.

Having a baby meant no longer being able to socialize at Sunday brunches, because your kid would scream so loud you'd have to leave the restaurant. It meant not getting invited to Pride parties, because nobody wanted to get naked and act wild when you were sitting there with your baby. No more Saturday nights at the gay bar, because you had to stay home and breastfeed. It was as though your friends all thought you'd aged out of queerness just by creating a family.

There were mommy groups, sure, but they were populated by straight women who didn't understand her. She felt excluded. Those women had husbands. They drove minivans with those little stick-figure family window clings on the back: husband, wife, children. They talked about the men they found attractive in movies and TV shows. Discussed birth control methods. In one embarrassing group meeting, there'd been a discussion about blow jobs.

Sammie missed her life before the baby. She missed her queer friends.

Everybody today seemed so young, so goddamn *young*—everyone coming into the bar was an infant. She choked on her drink when she realized she was thinking of them sexually and they were her son's age, or close to it.

The woman checking IDs at the door was wearing mauve lipstick that made her look like she was dressing up in her mother's makeup. The older butch who'd done the full-body check before she entered the bar had touched so perilously close to her pubic area that Sammie had gotten a little turned on, which made her wonder when the last time was that she'd had decent sex. She forced herself to think about something else—it was too maudlin sitting there at a nightclub wishing someone would fuck her when everyone in the place looked like they'd just graduated high school.

"Is anyone sitting here?"

"No," Sammie said, scooting all the way into the booth to make room. "Just me."

"Okay, cool." The woman was young and blond, with short hair, and she was with three other friends who all threw their bags onto the table. They didn't sit down with Sammie, just stood at the edge, setting their drinks on the tabletop and looking out into the steadily crowding room.

Sammie wasn't sure what to do. Her drink was almost empty, and now she felt trapped in the booth behind these women, all standing there with their backs turned on her. She pulled out her phone, just for something to do, and up came the dating app—mortifying when everyone she might possibly match with in Orlando was probably right here in the area's only lesbian bar.

The woman she'd been out with a few weeks ago had messaged her again. Myra. Her text was just a bunch of question marks, since Sammie hadn't responded to her last three messages. For a moment Sammie got nervous, wondering if Myra was at the bar that night, seeing her in her embarrassing getup, and then decided probably not. That was the thing—nobody her own age was there.

When the young blonde leaned down to retie her friend's boot, Sammie tossed her phone into her purse and scooted out of the booth. The girls swooped in and took it over as if they'd been waiting for her to leave.

The throb of the music felt like a second pulse in Sammie's body. She dropped her empty drink at the bar and collected another, just to give her hands something to do, and then moved along the perimeter of the room. She wiped her lipstick off on the back of her hand—too red, too orange, too loud for her own face—and then scrubbed that smear off her hand with her cold fingertips. The music was unrecognizable, but felt good, felt *gay*, that was the word for it, and all those bodies moving together were like a single organism, as though they had all been ingested by the place, had become part of it. She finally felt herself settle into her skin.

Outside the bathroom, two women were making out. Sammie stood there for a minute watching them. They were the same height and both wore jeans. One had her hands in the other woman's back pockets. The other had her arms looped around the other woman's neck, running her hands through her hair. That was something she missed—not just the fucking, but how easy it was to touch another person when you were in love, or at least on the cusp of falling into it. She thought of how Monika had always set her hand on the very base of her back, in the perfect place, touching her exactly the way she wanted. Those wide palms, her long, strong fingers, the same ones she used to twist the lids off jars for Sammie in the kitchen.

She was close enough to this couple that she could smell them, their hot skin and spit. She could stand there all night and they wouldn't even notice, they were so focused on each other. When she realized she was actually leaning into them, nearly touching one of their shoulders, she made herself walk outside to the patio.

Different music, but it was still pretty much the same. Deep bass, pulsing beat, nothing words. Half-finished drinks passed between sweaty hands. Plastic cups perched on tables or concrete lips of planters, half-dead palms and scrub in dirt stuffed full of cigarette butts. The air was thick with humidity, the damp of it frizzing up her hair and making her face oily and slick, makeup like a second skin skimming over the top of her flesh.

A song came on that she actually knew. *Fuck it*, she decided, she was gonna dance even if no one wanted to touch her. Then it was a whole crowd of women dancing all together.

Her drink sloshed onto her skirt. Suddenly someone was behind her, grabbing at her waist, and she pushed back into them, the cradle of their hip holding on to her snugly. She felt locked in like a puzzle piece. She had missed it so badly, this feeling of want, and when the song was over and the arm abandoned her, she felt bereft, loose in a sea of other bodies that only a moment before had felt so welcoming.

Again, she wandered. Sammie wondered if there was anyone at the club she might recognize, and sometimes she felt like she did, but the haircuts and clothes seemed wrong. She couldn't tell if she was remembering a person or a memory or just the idea of a lesbian, something she might have seen in a movie or a TV show. Maybe even something from online.

A drag performance was underway in one of the front rooms. It was getting crowded, so she stood at the back, too nervous to push her way in. All she could hear was the music—another song she recognized— but there were people pushing past her, struggling to see, so she left to get another drink while the bar was empty.

The bartender who'd served her came over and poured her another, smiling when Sammie pulled a folded ten out of her purse and slid it across the bar. *Oh, she's cute*, Sammie thought, and leaned over until she spilled half her drink along the bar top.

Embarrassed, she took her drink and left the woman to clean it up, slipping back along the wall at the edge of the dance floor. It was darker there, and almost beautiful, with the lights playing colorfully along the ceiling and across the dancing bodies. There was a woman near her leaning against the wall, too. She had her hands shoved deep in the front pockets of her leather jacket. She was a little older, like Sammie, but she had a different energy. Like she was alone and she wanted to be, or like she was waiting for someone to come to her. Sammie thought of Monika, with her no-try energy. Sammie wished she was like that. She always found herself gravitating toward women who were in control, who could tell her exactly what to do and make her like it.

She'd met Monika at a party thrown by a mutual friend they'd since lost touch with—Bianca? Breanna? Sammie couldn't remember. They were in the kitchen of a tiny apartment, the air-conditioning struggling to keep up with the Florida swelter, the roomful of bodies trying to navigate around one another and the cheap IKEA furniture. Her future wife had been holding a beer and another woman's arm. Sammie remembered that most of all: Monika's hand wrapped around that woman's elbow, a faceless person who meant nothing to Sammie beyond the way Monika moved her around the room. Gently, but with authority. As if she knew what the woman would want without her having to say anything at all.

Sammie glanced again at the woman leaning next to her. She had black hair shorn close to her scalp. She had on dirty jeans and big butch boots, and the T-shirt under her leather jacket was for a band she didn't recognize. In contrast to her clothes, her face was sweet and soft, dotted with dark moles. But it was her eyes, large and liquid, that Sammie wanted on her. The woman never looked her way, didn't acknowledge her at all. But Sammie knew she could feel her there. This was one of those women who could tell people wanted her and didn't have to do anything to make it happen. They came to her.

The music dipped to a deeper throb. More people spilled onto the dance floor, bodies slick with sweat, air filled with the scent of perfume mingling with worked-up deodorant. Sammie missed being pressed close against someone, encountering the damp aroma of a person's skin, that hot, cooked scent that let you know exactly what they would smell like when you were finally tangled up in bed together.

When the woman pushed off the wall and headed for the bathroom, Sammie trailed after her. That body was a beacon. She would have followed it anywhere. Even thinking about that body meant thinking less about her own. Maybe it made her feel more present in her mind and less like an animal—or, no, that was wrong. Maybe more animal and less mind. Focused purely on need. For once not letting her brain fuck it up with any unnecessary thinking.

The line for the bathroom had freed up. Once the music started feeling like sex, everyone had decided to just deal with their full bladders. Sammie remembered when weekends had felt like this, before Monika, and even after, with Monika, because hadn't sex with the two of them been great? Like someone else was grabbing the controls inside her and operating them expertly.

Sammie stood next to the woman in line, then edged even closer, near enough to count the freckles on the woman's neck. The woman was wearing small studs in her ears. How would that feel, to put her mouth around that soft lobe and trace the sharp edges of the jewelry with her tongue?

At the party where she'd met Monika, she'd followed her movements around the room out of the corner of her eye. When the other woman inexplicably left for the night, Sammie knew it was fate. She followed Monika out through the sliding glass doors and onto a rickety balcony. There were no chairs, just a shitty plastic table and an ashtray full of scummy rainwater. It overlooked a parking lot where a tow truck driver was methodically working his way along the rows of the complex. Monika leaned over the side of the balcony and said, *Oh fuck, that's my car,* and that's when Sammie had slipped her hand right into the back pocket of Monika's jeans. And Monika had made a noise that sounded like a question mark, but had taken over from there. Sammie wasn't sure how she got home that night, but it hadn't mattered, because she'd found the one. That feeling she'd been missing.

The DJ put on a song that everyone loved. Another woman got out of the line, still aching to pee, but refusing to miss out on the dancing.

The leather-jacket woman had a chafed spot on her neck, a blushed line where her collar kept rubbing at the crease of skin below her skull. Sammie threw her empty cup into the overflowing garbage can and slipped her fingertips along that soft, injured spot. The woman jerked when she felt it—didn't just move away, but actually spasmed, as if Sammie's fingers had electrocuted her.

"Don't," she said, but she didn't turn around.

There was just the single word; Sammie couldn't even be sure she'd heard it properly. It could have been someone else, a noise from the stall, someone yelling something out on the dance floor.

Yes, it had to be someone else, Sammie thought, hands still chilled from holding her drink, and she ran her palm along the woman's neck and cupped it there along the irritated spot.

The cold will help, she thought, and flashed back to Samson burning himself on the stovetop when he was eight years old. She'd stuck those burned fingers into her mouth to soothe them, just as now she was sticking her cold hand onto the woman's poor neck, even as all she could think was *But couldn't this woman soothe me, couldn't she do the thing I need right in this moment, give me what I want and make it good?*

The woman shuddered. Sammie took her hand off her neck and put her mouth there, pressed her lips against the chafe as she circled her arms around the woman's waist. She was so solid, it felt like Sammie was anchored to something, and it felt so good that she didn't even really hear the woman's voice—*don't, don't, stop, don't*—until another set of hands was on her shoulder, someone else behind her, forcibly removing her from the woman's body.

She was escorted away from the bathroom by a body that was larger than her own. The woman hustled her past the bar until they were standing near the door, back by the bouncer who'd touched her so intimately, by the people who'd taken her money to come inside.

"When someone says stop, you stop."

"What?" Sammie looked up at the woman: tall, rail-thin, with shoulder-length gray hair and wire-framed glasses. Lean, hawkish nose. Age spots on her neck. The strobe lights bouncing off her lenses made her eyes look like they were made of glitter, as if she had no real irises and all she contained was the energy of the room.

"Are you drunk? Do you need me to call you a car?"

"No," Sammie said, shaking off the woman's hand. Her fingers were long and thin, stronger than her own. "I don't need a car."

The woman leaned down close to Sammie's face, and now Sammie wanted to be the one to lean away. Because the woman looked like every time her mother told her she'd done something wrong, looked like the people at church when she'd done something inappropriate. For a moment she was paralyzed, like she couldn't stand to live in her own skin another second.

"You have to listen when someone says stop," the woman said. "You fucking know that. Don't be like a man in here, grabbing at people like they're your property."

Like a man, Sammie thought, steadying herself. Is that how she'd been acting? How could she be acting like one of those entitled assholes when all she'd wanted was comfort?

"Come back when you remember how to act."

Sammie laughed at that, and the woman stood up straighter. God, she was tall.

"I know how to act. Have a good night."

The woman frowned, then hitched up her pants and walked back toward the bathroom. Sammie thought she might own the same pair of slacks: gray cords, low on the hips. Maybe they were the same age. No, the woman was definitely older. Sammie looked around and saw plenty of people her own age in the bar. Plenty of older dykes, too. Sammie paid her tab, gave the hot young bartender a huge tip, and wondered if all these older women had been there all along. Maybe she just hadn't been looking for them.

Back outside, the air pressed against her, warm and sticky. She broke through the line waiting to get in, dykes huddled together in cutoff shorts and sneakers, hair short and long and curly and cropped and shaved.

Her car was in the lot across the street. Once she was behind the wheel she felt horribly sober. She watched the line crawl antlike into the building, which was festooned with pink and turquoise neon lights, some shaped like flamingoes, some like palm trees. It was gay Central

Florida, and she wasn't part of it. She didn't know where the hell she belonged, but it wasn't there.

She fished out her phone, found Myra's number, and pressed call. She picked up after the first ring. Myra asked what she wanted, and Sammie said she wanted to come over, and Myra said, "What, like right now?" and Sammie said yes.

Myra texted her the address, an apartment near International Drive, that haven for people who frequented places like Ripley's Believe It or Not!—the tourists who only came to Florida to pretend, who never ventured into the actual city.

It would take at least forty minutes to get there. She plugged the address into her phone, but before she pulled out of the parking lot, she begrudgingly sent a text to Monika and Samson.

Be home late.

Chloe hated her job at the bar, but the tips were good, and her girlfriend said they needed the money. Sabrina didn't know what it was like. Having to make small talk and mix shitty drinks for hours while her hands froze in the ice and how she had to smile real nice just so someone might throw an extra few bucks her way. What did that mean in the grand scheme of rent? But Sabrina was in grad school and she had student loans, and Chloe was the one who brought in steady money, so she worked those late nights when all she really wanted to do was be home eating pizza with her girlfriend in front of the TV. There were times it was worse than others. Like that night, the drunk lady who kept making passes at her. She was sweet, but way too old for Chloe. Her eye makeup was running and she just seemed so . . . sad. She'd left a massive tip, but even watching that lady wander the room—like she had no idea how to hold her own body and she just wanted someone, anyone, to prop her up—made her think that that'd probably be her someday. If things with her and Sabrina didn't work out. She didn't wanna be some old dyke bothering young girls at nightclubs. She didn't even want to be at nightclubs, period. So she texted Sabrina, asked if they could make popcorn. Pocketed her tips—even that extra ten from the drunk lady, she really was nice, even if she was a little embarrassing— and drove straight home. Home, Chloe thought, was a very nice word.

13

A gated community. What a pain in the ass.

She sat outside the apartment complex next to an empty security-guard gate and the minuscule pad where she'd need to punch in the call box. She'd already tried texting Myra and there was no response. Forty minutes of driving and she was aggravated and tired, all the night's alcohol only serving to make her surly and out of spirits, plus a little hungry.

A pizza delivery driver with a lighted Domino's sign atop his beat-up Camaro pulled in behind her. She put her car into gear and looped around, pulling back up behind him as he jabbed a number into the call box.

When the gate opened, Sammie rushed through behind him, barely squeaking past as the gate clanged shut. Monika would have a fit if she hurt the car again, and she had a point; she paid the car insurance, and she'd gotten them a good rate. Sammie was lucky if she remembered to pay her bills before they were on their way to collections.

Myra lived in one of the generic apartment complexes that peppered the landscape closest to the theme parks. They were nice enough, with palms and scrub and flowering greenery, but the buildings were so tall and crammed together you could barely see the skyline, and it was almost impossible to tell them apart. They came in an assortment of pastel hues, salmon and minty-ice-cream green, the occasional pool stuffed between buildings.

For a while, when she was little, her aunt had lived in town. Sammie's mother would drop her off at her apartment while she went to Bible study or did the grocery shopping. Her aunt had already been married twice by the age of thirty. She was pretty—hot, even—in a way that seemed exciting to Sammie, whose own mother wore potato-sack dresses that draped to her ankles. Aunt Stella had a head full of hair spray and tight-fitting clothes, neon-colored and low-cut. Her nails were painted a bright candy-apple red. She let Sammie splash around in the water while she lay out in a deck chair, suntanning her slick, bronzed flesh.

Every weekend, there were kids who stood outside the locked gate to the pool area, like a litter of lost puppies. Sammie wanted to open it for them, but her aunt wouldn't let her.

No, honey, she said, flipping over to tan her other side. *We can't let them in. If they drown, then I'm responsible.* Her thighs and back were covered with red stripes from where the deck chair had cut into her skin. She untied her bikini top and let the straps drape. Sammie avoided looking at her bare breasts, but still caught their shape from the corner of her eye.

After that aunt moved away, Sammie never saw her again. She moved in with a man and chose not to marry him. Her mother stopped speaking to her entirely. Never mentioned her again. *That's how easy it is for someone to delete you from their life*, Sammie thought, following the curve of asphalt around Myra's complex, squinting to read the apartment numbers as they slipped by in a blur. *Just pretend they never existed.*

As she rounded the final curve behind the complex, she pulled into the first parking space she saw, only to see it was a resident-only space. That was the last thing she needed, to get towed all the way across town from her house, so she slammed the car into reverse and pulled out, almost knocking over the pizza guy as he grabbed the stack of boxes from his trunk.

"Jesus," he yelled, kicking her bumper. "Fucking watch it, you dumb bitch."

Sammie pulled back into the spot, scraping the front of her car against the curb. She ducked down so that the pizza guy wouldn't see her as he headed into Myra's building, and waited till he drove away before getting out of her car. *Fuck it*, she thought when she wondered if someone would tow her. *Fuck it and fuck that guy.* As she climbed the stairs, she thought about her son's anger. Samson didn't often get explosively mad, but when he did, it was like a firecracker. Men got angry so fast—but no, she thought now, maybe that's not right at all. Maybe they're just quicker to show their anger. Women learn from a young age to choke theirs down and swallow it.

Would her daughter have stifled hers, too, like Sammie? Would she have been patient when her brother chose to be angry? Would he have been the kind of brother who struck his sister, or one who protected her from harm?

Well, he ate her, didn't he? she thought. *There's your answer.*

She walked the long third-floor walkway to Myra's apartment and then stood, waiting outside the door to catch her breath. She found a tube of lipstick in her purse and hurriedly put it on, smoothed down the flyaways in her hair that inevitably stuck up in the humidity. She wished she wasn't wearing her bar clothes. She wondered if she smelled like smoke or spilled gin. But it was too late to worry about any of it now.

She knocked and waited. She could hear more than one voice behind the closed door, which gave her pause. What did she actually know about this woman, other than her name? She was Myra Santos, though Sammie had entered her name in her phone "Myra Tinder." Sammie hadn't thought to ask if she lived alone or with a roommate. God forbid an ex-wife.

The door opened and her question was answered. A girl, maybe thirteen, stared dumbly at Sammie as she stuffed a slice of pepperoni pizza into her mouth. Her dark hair was slopped back into a messy bun, and she wore a paint-stained UCF shirt.

"Ma," she yelled, dripping sauce on the floor. "Lady for you."

The girl turned around and disappeared into the apartment. Was she supposed to follow her inside? Should she leave? And then there was Myra in a plain gray T-shirt and baggy gym shorts, barefoot, inviting her in. It was too late to do anything but stay. Again, she was floored by how much the woman resembled Monika. Same curly dark hair, cut short and buzzed up around the back and sides. Same dimpled baby face and button nose. The biggest difference was that Myra was a little taller. It felt strange looking up at her; she kept glancing at her chin, expecting to see a pair of eyes.

"Sorry it's such a mess. Wasn't expecting anyone."

"That's okay. I'm sorry to intrude."

"You're not intruding." Myra took her hand and led her past the living room, where the girl had curled up on the couch with her laptop and another slice of pizza. She was watching something loud. Something with a laugh track.

The apartment wasn't huge, but it seemed comfortable. It had a small dining room with a sliding glass door that opened onto a balcony overlooking a massive pool. The brilliant green-blue of the water shone like liquid turquoise. For such a hot weekend night, Sammie expected to see a crowd of people down there paddling around. When Sammie asked why no one was out there enjoying the water, Myra muttered, "Pool closes at ten," and then led her into the kitchen. It was small, too, but fairly new, with granite countertops and a stainless fridge covered with kids' artwork—a finger painting resembling a radioactive sunset, some graded essays, pictures that had been turned into magnets. Sammie couldn't remember the last time she'd put something of Samson's on the fridge. Had she ever? Or was that just Monika? Her wife was often sentimental in ways that Sammie never managed on her own.

Myra got them both beers, and they stood drinking them on opposite sides of the kitchen: Myra near the hallway leading to the bedrooms, Sammie leaning awkwardly by the counter near the sink.

"It's nice," Sammie said when she couldn't bear the silence any longer.

"What was nice?" Myra asked.

"The apartment," Sammie told her.

"It's okay," Myra said, and then they both were quiet again.

"How long have you lived here?" Sammie finally asked. She'd been pulling nervously at her beer label. "You like it?"

"It's fine," Myra said.

There were no dishes in the sink. No crumbs on the counter or sticky rings from juice glasses or half-empty cans of soda collecting ants. A loaf of Publix whole wheat bread sat neatly twisted inside its plastic wrapper next to the microwave. Three boxes of cereal, all sugary junk she'd never buy for the house, were lined up on top of the fridge. She wondered what was in the fridge: Cold cuts? Leftover pizza? Was there whole milk or skim or did they drink almond because of allergies? It was weird to be in this strange apartment with a woman she didn't really know. She thought she'd long since relegated Myra to a casual fling. Now here she was, making idle chitchat with her as her kid sat in the other room.

"Why haven't you been texting me back?" Myra stared down the hall, avoiding eye contact.

"Let's not do that."

"Not do what?" Myra asked, and then Sammie set down her beer and crossed the short distance to kiss her.

It went on like that for a few minutes. It wasn't like before; this time it felt much better, somehow, than their first kiss, downtown on the sidewalk after that one boring date. But then Myra pulled away and held her off when Sammie tried to press back against her.

"My daughter is home," she said. "We can't."

"Why not?"

Sammie stared at Myra's face. It wasn't Monika's, but it was still attractive, especially now that she was seeing her in the comfort of her own home. Sammie pinched the fabric of Myra's T-shirt, feeling the woman's waist; she touched the soft give of skin at her stomach and felt Myra start to fold.

"Ma, I need a drink."

Myra shoved her off abruptly. Sammie pulled back, and there was the daughter, peeking around the corner of the kitchen entrance. She was pretty, in a young, disheveled kind of way. Big dark eyes. That skin teenage girls boasted, smooth as unformed clay. Myra opened the fridge and grabbed a bottle of orange juice, poured her a glass that she'd scrounged out of the dishwasher.

"No more videos," Myra said, handing it over. "It's late. Bed."

The girl made a face like she wanted to argue, but Myra put up her hand—a gesture she'd tried a thousand times on Samson, though it never worked. The girl stopped herself, collected her computer and her juice, and kissed Myra's cheek good night before wandering down the hallway toward her bedroom.

"God, how did you get her to listen?" Sammie asked. "I can't believe that worked."

"You have a girl? I can't remember." Myra got out a box of crackers from the cupboard, a block of cheese from the fridge. Started cutting up precise slices that Sammie could imagine nestling neatly inside a lunch box. Her brain always did this—separating herself from the sexual behind the trappings of being a mother. She could feel her attraction to Myra in danger of slipping away, crowded out by questions about car pools or colleges or school districts.

"I have a son," Sammie said, picking up a square of cheese. She was already having second thoughts about coming, wondering if she should leave, but she was hungry, and she'd driven all the way out there. She wondered if Myra might offer her a slice of pizza.

Myra made a sandwich stack of the crackers and cheese. Bit down carefully with her palm cupped beneath her chin to catch any crumbs from falling on the tile. Monika would have let anything fall on the floor and waited for Sammie to pick it up. Then she'd say something like, *Samandra, you don't have to clean it, I'll get it later*, but if Sammie didn't clean it up right then they'd be walking barefoot on crumbs for days. Her son was the same way; he'd been neater as a young child, but now he'd leave a mess in the sink until it started to form its own bacterial colony.

She looked up and realized Myra had been asking her a question.

"What was that?"

Myra sighed. A cracker crumb fell from her lip onto the tile. She wasn't so perfect after all, was she? "I said, do you have a picture?"

"Oh." Sammie patted at her side and realized she was still wearing her purse. "Yeah."

Myra pulled a snapshot off the fridge as Sammie dug around for her wallet.

"This is Dani at softball." It was a picture of her daughter, wearing a batting helmet and a massive grin—one of those sporty pictures they took of kids when they were on teams. Samson had some, somewhere. Sammie wasn't sure the last time she'd seen one.

"She's cute," Sammie said. "Looks like you."

"She looks like my ex-wife." Myra stared down at the picture like she wanted to hug it, though her daughter was right down the hall. "Dani's twelve. I only get her on the weekends. Every other big holiday."

"Oh, wow. That's rough." Sammie couldn't imagine. She'd never had to deal with that kind of separation—one of the upsides of living with her ex. Their holidays were weird, sure, but hadn't they always been weird?

She was doing it again. Thinking in *always* and *never*. Forgetting things like the waffles they made Christmas morning after opening gifts. The time Monika put whipped cream on the end of her nose and chased Samson around the house like she was gonna kiss him and smear it all over his face. How listening to her son laugh reminded Sammie how big her heart could feel: massive, a ballroom of feeling.

She opened her wallet to look for a picture of Samson. All she could find was one old shot; he couldn't have been older than thirteen, around the same age as Myra's daughter. It was his official school shot, standing in front of a gray backdrop in an oversize blue polo shirt, his hair a wild mess of curls down to his collar. He wasn't smiling, but he hardly ever smiled in pictures. His face was pale, his natural rosiness washed out by all that gray. Sammie had never like the shot—it looked nothing like her son the way she imagined him—but Monika insisted they order at least one enlargement for the dining room and a selection of wallets. And that's how this one had landed in her purse.

"Is that him?" Myra asked.

For a moment Sammie held the picture to her chest, embarrassed by it. "It's from a while ago. I never wind up putting the new ones in my purse," she fibbed. Finally she handed it over.

"He's very handsome."

"He needed a haircut. Still needs a haircut."

There they were, doing what moms always did: talking about their kids, because what else was there? Myra got them a couple more beers, though Sammie knew she shouldn't drink any more if she was going to drive home.

"You're lucky you have a boy," Myra said. Sammie laughed, sure she was joking. She wasn't.

"Boys are not easier," Sammie replied. "They're like wild creatures that live in your home. They eat all your food and destroy anything they can throw."

"Girls kill you here." Myra tapped at the space over her heart. "They know all the things to say that get you right in the soft spots."

Sammie wondered what kind of venom a twelve-year-old girl was capable of inflicting on a mother. What it would have been like if her own girl had lived. Would she have withheld affection when she didn't get what she wanted? When Sammie was young, she'd done that to her own mother. In middle school, every day for a solid month, she'd told her mother she hated her. She was tired of behaving the way her mother wanted—clean, silent, pretty, smart, feminine—and she'd lost the ability to squelch her anger.

One day, after her mother wouldn't let her attend a sleepover, she'd yelled it again: *I hate you!* And then her mother had yelled the same thing, right back in Sammie's stunned face. She had a look in her eye that Sammie hadn't seen before. And when Sammie burst into tears, her mother said in that same awful, grating tone: *See? How do you like it?*

"That's very gendered thinking" is how Sammie responded now, though she wasn't sure what she really knew about it. All she knew was Samson, and he was hard, but Samson was his own animal.

"I don't know. I mean, I'm not a perfect mom. People always expect so much of you when you're a gay parent."

"I'm definitely not perfect," Sammie replied. "Like, not at all. I just think boys are hard. Maybe because I didn't grow up around them. At least, not in my family."

That was something Monika had always emphasized: that they had to be model parents, especially as lesbians raising a boy. For some reason people weren't that skeptical about seeing a girl being raised by a family of women, but for lots of folks it seemed like a foregone conclusion that two lesbians raising a boy would inevitably fuck it up.

It was quiet in the apartment except for the loud noise of the fridge clicking on, a buzzing that rattled the cereal boxes, and then she and Myra were making out again. Seemed like it didn't matter that Myra's daughter was home after all.

Sammie turned around, pressing her back to Myra's front, and Myra fucked her against the side of the kitchen counter. She breathed hard in her ear, and Sammie was about to come when Myra asked her, in a voice that was close to Monika's but wasn't exactly, if it was good. Wondering if it was actually good made her think about her pussy and about the fingers in it and made her realize that her ribs hurt from being shoved against the granite, so she faked an orgasm and then they were done.

Sammie drove home with the cruise control set, paranoid about getting pulled over and having to take a Breathalyzer test. There weren't many other cars out on the road, just her and the other people wandering home from their nights out. She didn't even turn on the radio, just sat inside her own head as the lights of downtown flashed by, lit up pretty in a mess of construction that never seemed to be finished.

Back home, she turned off all the lights Monika had left on—kitchen, back patio, hallway, stairwell—and then opened Samson's door, just to see if he was home. There he was, buried beneath a mound of sheets and a dirty comforter. (Samson refused to do his own laundry, and Sammie refused to wash his sheets for him, so they were at a filthy standstill.) On the shelf by his bed sat the remnants of his old golden doll—its caved-in head long since detached from the body, though the two pieces still sat together like some deconstructed trophy. His face and a fluff of hair poked out from the front of his covers. Sammie was suddenly seized by the memory of how terrified she'd been whenever she left him sleeping as a baby, worried he would suffocate the minute she left the room. She'd often woken him by sticking her finger under his nose to see if he was breathing, making sure that he hadn't died in his crib—a habit that infuriated Monika, as it was so hard to get him to sleep in the first place.

She didn't reach out to touch him now, but she did stand there for a few minutes, watching his chest rise and fall beneath the blankets, thinking that all that really separated life from death was a very fine gray line.

Myra wasn't sure Sammie liked her all that much, but she liked the way she felt when they fucked. It was a big change from her ex-wife, who'd had a lot of things to say when it came to sex with Myra and none of it good. This was the first time she'd been with a woman since Tiana, and she'd missed that feeling. Although it hadn't felt like Sammie had been all there for it, the way she'd turned around and presented her back to Myra, like she didn't want to see her face while they touched. She worried that she wasn't doing it right, that maybe she'd forgotten how to fuck someone or that her fingers weren't doing what she wanted. But then she asked Sammie if it was any good, if it was nice for her, and Sammie had made such a sweet, soft sound, such a good-sounding yes, and then orgasmed right in her palm. It was a powerful feeling, the one she always had when she made Tiana come, and for a moment she felt whole again. She didn't really understand Sammie—how closed-off she seemed, how guarded—but she thought she could get to know her. At least, she wasn't against trying. And that made her happy, she guessed. That she felt ready to try again. That felt like something. Hopeful.

14

The boys were all yelling and swearing at one another. They called each other pussy, constantly. Pussy this, pussy that. Sammie was a dyke and she didn't say *pussy* as often as these teenage boys. She wished she'd brought earplugs, even though it was illegal to use them for driving.

She'd gotten roped into chaperoning after two other moms had called in sick. Monika had been next on the list, but she suddenly had "something big" come up at work, spinning out some spiel about an important client and the timeliness of getting it all before a judge. Sammie knew so little about Monika's job that any or none of it could have been true. So Monika volunteered her for it—*It should be easy for you,* she said, *since you work from home.*

With three hours left on the trip, she was finally getting used to driving the big rental van, one she'd paid for when she realized she didn't want all those monsters eating fast food in her SUV and wiping their hands off on her car seats. Already she'd stopped and bought them all Chick-fil-A—reluctantly, because of their donations to anti-LGBTQ charities, but everyone in the van was clamoring for it, and she didn't want to get into a whole thing over it. So she supplied them all with fried sandwiches and chicken strips and boxes of waffle fries, but didn't get anything for herself, so she could tell herself she'd taken a stand.

But now she was starving, her hunger aggravated by all that delicious-smelling salt and fat, and starting to regret that she'd volunteered in the first place.

"Don't do that," Sammie hissed when Samson wedged his way between the front seats and started messing with the stereo. "I'm driving."

Samson ignored her, plugging his phone into one of the outlets, fiddling with the knobs, and suddenly music was blasting loud enough that Sammie felt like she'd been slapped. She yelped, clinging even harder to the steering wheel.

Her son squeezed back through the seats, trailing a tangled and knotted aux cord that kept brushing her arm and bothering her. She could no longer hear the boys and their conversation, which was good, but now she had to deal with the sonic reckoning of the music, so bass-heavy that it shook the sides of the van. She turned it down a little, and when the groans started up from the back seat, she turned it up just a hair to placate them.

A few more hours and then they'd be at the hotel. She could drop them off with their swim coach, who had the paperwork and could check them all in. Four boys to a room—she couldn't imagine what the place would look like after two days of that. She pitied the poor maids. Sammie would avoid it entirely, free to huddle up in her room, to decompress or nap or, most likely, just stare at her phone. She was still on the dating app. She was also still talking to Myra, though they hadn't hooked up since the night Sammie went to her apartment two weeks earlier. It felt easier to text; she could pretend to be a different person that way, sexier, more competent. It also allowed her to control the conversation.

Super fun and super sexy, Sammie thought, brushing her greasy bangs out of her face.

They were headed for a summer competition up in the Panhandle, in a small town near Pensacola that Sammie'd never heard of. There were plenty of places in the state she didn't know anything about, even though her family had lived in Florida for generations. They'd traveled around for youth group trips when she was younger, stopping at the beaches on either coast, but the peninsula was so big and overwhelmingly disparate that you could drive forty minutes in a single direction and become completely disoriented. She remembered a trip to Jacksonville, where she'd marveled at the houses, brick and squat, and the plants, which seemed strangely foreign—still green and wild, but shaped wrong. For a moment she worried that they'd wandered out of the state.

Sammie wasn't sure whether she'd acclimated to the noise of the stereo, or if she was just going deaf, but suddenly she felt able to handle the loudness better. The boys had settled down a little. They were still messing with each other, but eating the food seemed to have worn most of them out. One by one, they were settling into sleep like a group of hibernating bears.

There were six of them in the van, or maybe nine or thirty-seven; she wasn't sure from the yelling and bodily functions. There was Samson; the twins, Rodney and Alex, with their shaved heads and acne-riddled faces; Marcus, who'd already taken his shoes off even though his feet smelled awful and the boys all shouted at him to put them back on before they suffocated; and two others with Play-Doh faces and dark blond hair, whose names Sammie couldn't remember. Tim? Peter? Honestly, they could have all been named Brad or Chad and Sammie would have believed it. Teenage boys always looked the same to her, all big, loud mouths ringed with metal braces, arms and legs gangly as Gumby. They all told terrible jokes that ended with some ingenious punch line like "Go fuck your mother!" Does it count as a joke if one boy just farts on another boy? Sammie wasn't sure, but the kids all thought it was hilarious.

Her phone chimed in her lap, and she felt a frisson of satisfaction, wondering if it was Myra again. They had been texting a lot, but mostly it was sexting. Things were easier that way, Sammie decided. It made her feel better about the whole situation. She didn't want to talk about their kids or their personal lives, their jobs or hopes and fears about the future. That was too much like what she'd already done with Monika— what she was *still* doing with Monika, despite their separation. Does it count as a separation if two women just live in the same house together?

Sammie reached down to grab her phone. She knew it was dangerous to text and drive, and she usually only texted at stoplights, but there was no one else on the highway, the weather was nice, and the roads were straight and smooth. *What could it hurt?* she thought, bringing the phone up to her face as she tapped at the screen with her thumb.

It was from Myra, and it wasn't just a text. It was a picture. A close-up of the woman's cunt, to be exact. Sammie stared at it, mouth agape. She wasn't sure why she was shocked, exactly. She'd asked for it. The night before, after a few glasses of wine, she'd been uninhibited enough to text Myra all the things she wanted to do to her. In one of those messages, she said she wished she had a picture of Myra's pussy to look at when she touched herself. Myra hadn't sent one right then, but she'd responded that the request made her wet. Sexting wasn't something Sammie had done much before—she'd definitely never done it with Monika—but sexting with Myra was fun.

Sammie stared at the image so long that it started to look less like a pussy and more like a piece of modern art. A sculpture, maybe. All those pinks and reds, the cloud of dark hair, the glistening wetness, the heart of it purple and dark. The way it wanted to open, or looked like it might. She'd never taken a picture of herself like that. Definitely had never been sent a picture like that. She wasn't sure she'd ever even seen her own in quite that way. She remembered, as a teenager, bending over in front of the full-length mirror in her bedroom in an attempt to see between her own legs. Her blood had rushed to her head, and she tried to hurry, hurry, hurry, because her bedroom door had no lock and she could only imagine what would happen if one of her parents barged in and saw what she was doing.

Sammie wasn't a prude. She watched porn. Usually when she was sure nobody would be home for a few hours. But a majority of the stuff she watched didn't look like this. Nothing so close-up. There was always some action involved—never just a cunt without fingers, or a tongue, a face lapping between the legs. Always a larger body blocking the opening itself.

Sammie turned the phone to the left, then switched the angle again, just to see if it made a difference. She was surprised to find herself aroused by it. She hadn't expected that. Hadn't thought just looking at the part where they fucked would make her feel so turned-on. For a minute she forgot where she was and what she was doing. There was nothing but the picture on her phone, her breath labored in her throat, and the rumble of the car on the road beneath her.

"Ms. Lucas, can we stop to use the bathroom?"

"Jesus!"

One of the boys had leaned between the seats. Sammie dropped her phone and grabbed the wheel with both hands, overcorrecting and drifting onto the shoulder for a second. She didn't dare look down to see how the phone had landed.

"Trey. Yes. Next rest area." That was his name. Not Tim, but Trey. The shock had shaken his name free in her brain. "Buckle up, please."

He went back to his seat, leaving behind a strong waft of his deodorant or body spray or whatever it was those boys all used, the stuff that smelled like musk and cheap cologne and gym locker.

Her heart beat in her ears. Finally she glanced down at her phone—mercifully, it had fallen facedown. So at least Trey hadn't seen it on her lap. But what had he seen when he came up behind her to ask the question? Would he tell the other boys in the car? Would they tell their parents? Sammie didn't think she'd care if she were ostracized from school functions—she truly hated spending time with all the other parents—but an awful nausea spread through her belly when she imagined what people would say about her. Because it was different, wasn't it? A gay woman looking at a dirty picture in the front of a car full of teenage boys?

Sammie spotted a sign for a rest area a few miles ahead and turned down the music to tell the boys they'd be stopping. When she pulled in, there were only two other cars in the lot: a newer-looking black sedan and a big pickup truck with a Confederate flag sticker splashed across the rear window. The man who presumably owned the truck was in the middle of a grassy outcropping next to some picnic tables, smoking a cigarette while a yellow Lab ran gleefully unleashed around the periphery of the lot.

"That dog is gonna get run over," Sammie muttered, but what she thought in her head was, *That'll serve him right*. It was a shitty thing to think, especially about a dog that had no control over its owner's bad decisions, but Sammie couldn't help wanting something bad to happen to the man.

She waited until all the boys had climbed out, then locked the van and followed them up a winding path to a forlorn warehouse-looking building that housed the bathrooms.

At least it looks too new to be a hangout for serial killers, Sammie decided.

"Go use the restroom," Sammie told the boys. "And you can pick up whatever snacks and drinks you think you'll need for the rest of the trip. If you're not back in the van in the next ten minutes, I'm gonna leave and you'll have to call your parents to come get you. I mean it, I'm serious."

They ignored her, as they'd been doing all day. The boys took a right when they got inside, heading for the men's room. She took a left and walked all the way down to the last stall in the women's room. She could hear someone talking in the stall next to her and assumed it was the owner of the other car.

While she was sitting there on the toilet, scrolling through her texts, a chubby little arm appeared from under the divider and reached for her shoelace. She yelped, moving her foot out of the way, but the tiny hand kept waving and grabbing. That's all she could see, a disembodied baby arm, and for a moment she had the crazed thought that she was in a horror movie. She envisioned the arm, free of a body, flopping and crawling across the bacteria-laden floor, then climbing directly up her pant leg. A tiny sticky baby hand reaching up to pat her cheek. Sammie finished peeing and pulled her jeans back on, praying the baby stayed where it was. She did not want to have to deal with a child while her pants were still around her ankles.

Luckily the toddler's mother finished up and collected the child from the floor.

"Sorry about that," the woman called through the door. "She's so fast now. I forget that she can get away from me so quick." She made a bunch of smoochy noises against her baby's cheek. Then they left the bathroom without even washing their hands.

Sammie left the stall and washed her own. As she reapplied her lipstick, she noticed how haggard and washed-out she looked. She fluffed her flat, frizzy hair, then decided to message Myra before she got back into the van.

She wasn't sure what to say, especially since she was sober, so she quickly pulled up her shirt and bra and snapped a picture of herself. With her arms squeezed at just the right angle, it almost looked like her breasts were a full cup size bigger. Perkier, too. She yanked her shirt back down and fired off the picture before she lost her nerve.

Outside, the air smelled fresh and clean compared with the ammonia scent of the bathroom. Three of the boys were still at the vending machine, buying Cokes and an actual mountain of candy and chips, though she'd fed them lunch only an hour earlier. She didn't see Samson or the twins, but she figured they were already over by the van. The day was sunny and hot, but the sunshine felt nice on her skin. The sky was such a brilliant blue it almost hurt her eyes when she stared up at it, and maybe that's why she didn't notice right away that the woman from the bathroom was hurriedly stuffing her child into the car.

The baby was screaming. Wailing, really. It was the kind of shriek that kids made when they were startled or handled too roughly. Sammie watched the woman throw herself into the front seat, purse tangled around her neck, then start the car and speed out of the parking lot.

Sammie turned around and there was Samson, peeing all over the side of the building. Dick in hand, he was drawing swirl after swirl on the pale-colored brick while the twins pointed and laughed, one of them in such hysterics he nearly fell down in the grass.

"Samson!" she yelled. The twins stopped laughing and looked chastened, but not her son. He just kept on pissing, streaking up the wall, until he'd finally emptied his bladder. Then he waggled it in his hand to get the last drips off before stuffing himself back into his pants.

She was so furious her hands were shaking. No wonder that woman had stormed off in anger. Her son had to take out his dick in front of a young mother and her toddler, because . . . why? Because he could? She slid her phone into her back pocket, shoved her key fob at one of the twins, and told them in a curt voice to go wait in the van. Then she walked over to her son, who was still admiring his handiwork.

She wanted to push him. He was bigger now than she was, big enough that if he pushed her back he could knock her over. That had never been a worry before. There'd never been a time when she didn't think she could physically make him do what she wanted him to do. She realized she was rubbing at her wrist, the same one he'd bit all those years before, and she knew that if they bit each other now, he would win. No contest.

Instead of pushing him, she turned him to face her. His expression was blank, impassive. He never looked like he got any joy out of the things he did, which genuinely confused her. Why do such awful things if there wasn't even any satisfaction to be gained from doing them?

When she was young and wanted to rebel, she got a lot of pleasure from defying her parents. Especially her mother. Like the time she'd told them she was sleeping over at the house of a friend from church when she was actually out drinking with a couple of girls from school. It was her first time drinking, and she only went because she'd been obsessed with the girl who invited her. Amanda, that butch girl from the soccer team; Amanda with her long ponytail and thick legs; Amanda with the low, raspy voice that made Sammie feel like her heart was going to catch on fire. They drank beers in that carport together, the two of them, and Sammie was just working up the nerve to put her hand on Amanda's knee when suddenly Amanda's mother pulled up in the driveway.

What do you have to say for yourself? her mother asked, hands in the air. Amanda had shoved her beer behind her back and tried to hide it, but not Sammie. No, she held hers out proudly, and as her mother approached she even dared to take a big swig. Her mother slapped the can out of her hand, but Sammie just smiled. That night, she smiled the whole way home in the car. She smiled when her mother and father yelled at her in their living room, and she smiled as she went directly to bed. It had felt like a rebellion. It had felt like *something*.

But there stood her son, with no expression on his face, no sign that he cared at all about what he'd done. And maybe that was what felt so disappointing. There was no passion inside him. It was like he was hollow, like one of the chocolate Easter bunnies she got for his childhood basket.

He looked at her and said nothing. She looked at him and said nothing. And then she said, "Sometimes you disgust me." She hadn't planned on saying it, but out it came anyway, like vomit. She felt better after she'd said it, and she wasn't afraid to admit it to herself. It was like she'd unearthed something rotten from the core of her being.

Monika would never have said a thing. Monika was the nicer mother. The better one.

"You were looking at a pussy on your phone," he replied.

Her eyes widened.

"In front of my friends. Looking at it while you were supposed to be driving me to a swim meet."

Somehow, Sammie laughed. "I bet your phone is full of them."

"It's weird when you do it."

"Is it? I'm a person. I have a body. I like sex, too."

"Gross."

"It's not gross." Everything involving sex was always gross when it came to your children. She was so tired of feeling like a body split in half. Sometimes feeling like a mother, with the body of a mother doing all the things a mother was supposed to do, and the rest of the time trying to be a fully realized person: someone who had sex, someone who liked her body and wanted other people to see it, someone who took care of herself.

Sammie didn't take very good care of herself.

"Don't touch your dick in front of other people," she said. "Only do it if you have consent."

"Consent to piss?"

"Yes, Samson. Consent to touch your dick and piss in front of another human being."

"Fine." He pointed at the van. All the other boys were waiting, staring out at the two of them going at it in the parking lot. "Can we go now?"

"Yes. But no more music." Sammie had a splitting headache.

• • •

Their coach was an hour late. They'd stopped along the route for gas and food and souvenirs at one of those kitschy Florida rest stops where they let people pet baby alligators and buy "homemade" marmalade and packages of real Florida oranges. The coach, who was from Connecticut, thought all the touristy stuff was cute. Sammie was tired. All she wanted was a bath and her bed, but instead she was trapped in the lobby of a Holiday Inn Express with another frazzled mother and four more teenage boys to add to the six she'd brought along.

"I should have rented a van," the woman said, and Sammie was glad she'd made at least one good choice. The kids were all hungry again. They were like garbage disposals. After thirty minutes of complaints, the other mom—a woman named Matilda who wore a varsity swim T-shirt and had her graying hair wrenched in a topknot that listed dramatically to one side—decided to order them all pizza just to shut them up.

Finally they quieted down, strewn around in the lobby chairs and couches as they demolished several boxes' worth of cheese and pepperoni. Sammie picked at a slice, oozing orange grease onto a paper plate, and drank some coffee the women at the front desk were nice enough to offer. The coffee was good, but it wasn't enough caffeine to keep her awake. Soon, the length and stress of the day pulled her into a fuzzy headspace where everything felt like a weird dream.

Matilda was on the phone with her husband. She was giving him step-by-step instructions on how to heat a casserole Matilda had left for him and their daughter, a girl named Kaylee or possibly Haylee. "No, you have to preheat the oven," she kept saying. She sounded like she was trying to train a puppy, not a grown man who should know how to work an appliance in his own kitchen. Even Monika would never have called to ask how to use a stove. *What was wrong with men?* Sammie wondered. *Did having a wife automatically turn them into babies?*

In strolled the coach with the remaining boys, who swarmed the pizza boxes—scrounging through looking for stray slices, scraping bits of cheese off the cardboard, consuming the remnants like a pack of wild dogs. The coach was a middle-aged man with an oily, thinning head of hair and severe rosacea. He had patchy facial scruff that looked like a failed attempt to bring his beard in contact with his mustache. He barked loudly at the woman at the reservation desk until she got their rooms squared away. Sammie got up from her chair, wondering if she'd need to do anything else that evening or if she could head back to her room to read and possibly masturbate.

"Look at these boys, all worn-out," Matilda said. She was finally off the phone with her husband. "Aren't they sweet? Reminds me of when Josh was little and he'd run around all day until he'd finally pass out on the rug."

Matilda's son, Josh, was a short, bulldog-faced freshman. He usually sat in grim silence, trying not to be noticed by the other boys, who repeatedly dunked him in the YMCA pool.

The coach handed out their room keys and paired up the boys in groups. "Josh will just stay with me," Matilda announced, slinging her arm around her son's neck. Sammie winced in sympathy for the kid, who'd be dealing with the fallout of this maternal betrayal for weeks.

She and Samson made brief eye contact.

At least I'm not that kind of mother, she thought.

Sammie made sure Samson had his stuff—the same garbage duffel bag he always used, which reeked of chlorine and mildew—and then split off, sprinting down the hallway to make the elevator before any of them could follow. The building itself was only three floors, so there was no chance she'd be far enough away from their rooms that she wouldn't hear them yelling or breaking furniture, but Sammie didn't care. Leave all that to Matilda, or maybe even to the coach. Let him parent for a while.

The room itself was fine: two double beds, with dark green polyester floral spreads, and a balcony overlooking the parking lot. Off in the distance she could see the glowing beacon of a Cracker Barrel. The thing about Cracker Barrel, she noted sadly, was that they didn't serve alcohol. She threw her stuff on the bed that was closer to the door and peed in the dark bathroom, then went back downstairs and asked the clerk where she could find a convenience store.

"There's a 7-Eleven a block away, direction of the interstate," the woman replied. She had her hand behind her back and a guilty look on her face. One of their pizza boxes was sitting on the counter behind her, partially opened.

"Listen, have as much as you want, you deserve it," Sammie said, and then she decided to walk all the way down the road to buy cheap wine.

She came back with cabernet as well as a six-pack of local beer the cashier had recommended, along with a family-size bag of Funyuns, the spicy kind that made her fingers turn red. She brought it all back up to her room, juggling the packages while trying to dig her key out of her back pocket. Once inside, she locked the door and kicked off her shoes, digging her toes into the suite's ugly brown carpet. She turned on the TV but dialed the volume down until the couple on HGTV were whispering their way through an argument about granite countertops. She sat down on the edge of the bed and proceeded to drink directly from the bottle of wine. It had an image of a cartoon bear on the label, but for five dollars it wasn't bad.

Her phone was full of texts from Myra in response to the photo she'd sent from the rest area bathroom. She'd sent back a slew of images, stuff that was increasingly horny, to the point that Sammie didn't even know where to begin. She was starting to wonder if she liked all this sexting more than actual sex. When she texted dirty messages to Myra, she could be whatever kind of person she wanted: fearless, in control, sexually confident. She could text things she'd never in a million years say aloud, ask for things she'd never have felt comfortable with in real life. She could tell Myra exactly what she'd like to do to her, how she wanted to fuck her—bent over a table, using different kinds of toys. She named a variety of rubber cocks she'd seen only in porn. The only toy currently in her possession was a small, discreet vibrator, one that might pass for a computer mouse if her bag ever got examined by airport security. Several times she'd even suggested that she wanted to slap Myra or choke her, things she'd never done before and had never imagined doing to another person.

Myra had sent a close-up shot of her ass. It sported a vivid red handprint that she'd apparently administered herself. Sammie found the picture extremely erotic. For a moment, she considered what it might be like to slap another person like that. Was it something she even wanted to do?

She texted that she wanted to slap Myra's face and pull her hair while she fucked her from behind. Then she messaged her wife to say they'd finally gotten checked into the hotel and reminded her to PLEASE (all caps) water the plants out back so they wouldn't die like last time. She texted Myra another picture, this one of her mouth, and told her she wanted to bite her tits. Then she threw her phone down on the bed and went to sit on the balcony.

A family of four was pulling their luggage from the back of a silver minivan in the parking lot below her room. Two young kids ran screaming as their father chased after them, roaring like a monster. The mother was attempting to organize everything into a single stack, which kept toppling over. The smaller of the two kids ran into the suitcases and fell over, scraping his knee; then he started sobbing until his father picked him up to airplane-zoom him over his sister's head. The mother stood there looking like she wanted to tear out her own hair.

Sammie held up her beer in solidarity. "Cheers to you and your thankless job," she said, and then took a long pull of the IPA—sour and sharp, with a strange aftertaste of olives.

Cars raced past on the distant highway. The sun sank through the clouds, producing a smear of princess-colored frosting: baby pinks and violets and vibrant coral. She knew those pretty colors were due to pollution, but in that moment she loved it. Loved to see all those Florida cars sliding past, heading for places far away, different lives, other cities.

It's nice to be away from home, even for a little while, Sammie thought. *To view it through a haze of nostalgia.*

The family marched off, and the parking lot was quiet again. She listened to the sound of the highway until it was interrupted by other noises—vibrations, a crisp hi-hat, and suddenly she was listening to the same thumping, abrasive music her son had plugged into the car stereo earlier that afternoon. In the room below her, she heard the sliding glass balcony door screech open. The song swelled out like a yell, frightening a couple of birds off a nearby palm.

The boys were talking. She couldn't make out much of the conversation, which was fine with Sammie. Their discussions always involved something she felt required to address—their lewdness, their language, the disparaging way they spoke about women, the misogynist swagger of their music.

Was her son boorish when it came to women? She didn't think so, but how could she know what he was like when she wasn't around to police his behavior? It wasn't something she wanted to think about, not at the moment. Not when she had a drink in her hand, the sun setting beautifully down below, and nothing ahead of her for the entire evening. There was no one she had to be other than what she wanted to be, what she wanted to enjoy. That was enough.

A strong smell wafted up from below. The boys were smoking weed, right on the balcony. She'd never smoked up as a teenager, hadn't even known any friends who did, though God knows she would have if anyone had offered. She didn't care that the boys were doing it now; she used to get high all the time at parties, and she still smoked occasionally at home herself, breathing through an open window in her bathroom so Monika wouldn't smell it. Mostly she just hoped she wouldn't have to deal with any fallout from the boys doing it so publicly. They were probably drinking, too, and at least one of them would puke on the floor, which was whatever, they could deal with it later, but if they were out smoking on the balcony, anyone could see them. If the little minivan family called the police, where would she be? Spending her entire weekend making sure her son didn't get expelled.

She cleared her throat, affecting a raspy Andie MacDowell growl, and started talking in a loud stage whisper. "Excuse me, officer? I'd like to report someone smoking marijuana at the Holiday Inn Express. Next to the interstate, off one of the balconies. Yes, please send someone right away."

"Oh shit," someone yelled. The sliding door slammed closed, and the music shut off. Sammie belly-laughed, delighted with herself. She set her bare feet up on the balcony railing and wished she'd brought some nail polish so she could do her toes. Maybe she'd find a place in town to get them done while the boys were at their meet.

She finished her beer and went back inside to get another, abandoning the empty on the desk next to the card with the wi-fi access code. She texted Monika about what happened with the boys—her wife would laugh; she was usually the one pulling pranks, not Sammie—and then she undid her pants, shimmying out of them and her underwear. She spread her legs, tilted her phone, and took a picture of herself, a close-up of her pussy. She examined the image for a second, then thought *fuck it* and sent the picture to Myra, with that exact caption:

fuck it.

Sammie took a long, hot shower. She used all the terrible hotel soaps that smelled like lemons and musk. She shaved her legs and under her arms, and then she washed her hair a second time. It was nice to be in a bathroom that wasn't hers. Different lighting, different toiletries, different towels. She could be anyone, just a traveler on her way out of town. One of those people out on the interstate, heading for their own lives, very different from her own.

After, she stood wrapped in a towel, drinking the rest of the wine straight from the bottle. The breeze coming through the open sliding glass door was hot and sticky, but the air promised rain, so it felt marginally cooler than before. She loved Florida thunderstorms. Everything was so electric, like the sky could break open and smash everything to bits. She hoped it would. She wanted the kind of rain that slashed sideways and stung skin. Booming thunder. Lightning that cracked so hard in her ear it sounded like a slap. Almost hoped they'd lose power. She could sit out on that balcony, finish her drink, and feel the wind sweeping through as the sky broke open, smell that mineral aroma of the earth changing, shaping into something new.

When she picked up her phone again, she had two missed texts. A cry-face laughing emoji after her fake call to the police and a bunch of exclamation points; that one was from Myra. The other, in response to the close-up of her pussy, was from Monika:

We need to talk.

The boys were good kids, but after hours in the car with them, Craig was over it. He had no idea how parents did it. All day long. Nights. Weekends? No, thanks. Not for him. He'd gotten them safely to the hotel and there were the two moms. Jekyll and Hyde, he'd taken to calling them in his head. The one was so nice. Matilda. Made him cookies. Invited him over for dinner. Loved her husband, a great guy, but the son could barely turn a single lap without floundering like he might drown. The other mom was a real piece of work. Sour look on her face, like she'd just eaten a lemon. The sweet talk never worked on her. He liked her wife a little better. She was up front about things. He could have a conversation with her without all the passive-aggressive bullshit women liked to throw his way. Craig didn't approve of their lifestyle, but as long as he wasn't forced to talk with them about it, what did it matter? Politics were politics, just keep it out of his face. And Samson could swim, goddamn it. Best on the team, even if he was a little weird. Never made jokes, not like the other boys. Didn't really date. Probably from having two moms. Would screw a boy up, living with that much estrogen. Well, that wasn't Craig's problem. At least the woman working the desk at the hotel was cute. Little blond thing. When she gave him the room keys, he'd gone ahead and slid her his number. Would be nice to have a dinner companion for the evening. The boys wouldn't need him. Not with the moms there. They could handle it fine. Kids were their job.

15

When she thought back on the worst moments in her life, it seemed like they'd all started with that same short sentence: *We need to talk.* A phrase designed not to start a dialogue but to end it. Though it implied that the listener was being invited to contribute to a discussion, what it really meant was that the other person had already come to a decision.

It wasn't a conversation; it was an apocalypse.

Sammie spent the night thinking about the text Monika sent her. She didn't bother messaging her wife back. What was the point? There was no undoing what she'd seen. Instead she sat inside her own head, thinking about how to defuse the situation. She still had a whole day left before she got home and had to deal with things, one more night to spend restless and sick, staring out at the glow of the parking lot. Insomnia until the sun hit the horizon.

She spent the next morning, lightly hungover, watching teen boys scarf down continental breakfasts—making toaster waffles, picking up syrupy sausages with their hands, downing biscuits slathered in jelly from tiny plastic tubs. Sammie couldn't eat. She drank black coffee and felt sick—sickened by their mouths and bodies, sickened by her own.

Instead of bailing on the swim meet, she decided she should go. Just in case Monika asked her about it or heard about it from the other mom. Instead of getting a pedicure or grabbing a drink somewhere, she sat with Matilda (wearing another of her swim team shirts, this one with a picture of a shark holding a stopwatch and the slogan *Take a bite out of time*, which made Sammie want to die). Samson did well, but he always did well. Sammie sat up in the stands, as she'd done for years, and watched him place first in nearly every event. Matilda sat with her, grabbing her hand every time their boys got into starting position, like she might jump out of her own skin over the prospect of them even competing—which would have struck Sammie as sweet if she wasn't pre-occupied with what was waiting for her at home. The boys leaped into the water and pulled themselves back out again. The whistle shrieked. Everything smelled like chlorine. People in the stands yelled or cheered and screamed. It was hard to tell who was angry and who was happy.

Her son emerged from the water, hauling himself onto the pool deck. The mop of curly hair under his regulation navy swim cap made his head appear misshapen. He didn't need her cheering for him, did he? He never looked for her in the stands. Never showed any need for reassurance. When he swam, he was alone. Completely in his own head. Some-times she wondered: If he let her in, even a little bit, would she actually give a damn?

Her phone buzzed in her pocket. She didn't check it, sure it was Myra. Monika wouldn't text again unless it was an emergency. When they were first together, she used to message her, or call her, just to say she was thinking of her, to mention some small thing she loved about Sammie. These days, she never messaged unless they needed milk, or if she couldn't pick up their son from school or work or practice, or if

Sammie had forgotten to pay the water bill. Monika only texted when Sammie fucked up.

Back in the pool, Samson had already pulled ahead of his competition. Her son, the shark, the submarine.

"Look at that! Look at him go!" Matilda grabbed her arm again, cutting off her circulation. "He's so good. Your boy is so good."

Sammie let her do the cheering for both of them. Stared at her son, the water. Felt her phone buzz. Wondered how her life was about to change.

They placed high, of course. Everyone on the team, but especially Samson, who people congratulated over and over again. He took the praise so quietly it seemed almost gracious, but Sammie thought he just didn't care what other people thought. It was kind of a blessing, she guessed. Sammie cared way too much about everything. She wished she cared less.

On the way home, the boys all fell fast asleep in the back of the van. It wasn't even that late, before six in the evening, as the sun burned low through the greenery along the highway. Her son was back there with them, zoned out and immobile. Long eyelashes fluttering as he moved through whatever dreams were happening in his head.

Recently, she'd tried to get Samson talking about friends. *Do you have anybody you care about?* she'd asked. He stared at her like she'd grown a second head, then turned away, draining his juice box and then blowing spit bubbles from the plastic straw at the passenger window.

What I mean is, do you have a friend you like best? No answer. She knew there was no one. He'd never asked to have a friend over for a sleepover. She couldn't imagine him going to prom with his close friends, or asking to room at college with a buddy. It was funny, come to think of it—that's what Monika had always said about Sammie, that she never seemed to make friends. Sammie had been satisfied just spending time at home with her wife, but it was never enough for Monika. *I don't want to be those lesbians*, she'd say when Sammie complained about her going out with her friends. *I think we should have our own lives.*

She had no idea what Monika would say when she finally got home. It was mortifying that her wife had seen her exposing herself that way by sending that picture. Their sex had always been good, but definitely on the vanilla side. And Myra had texted about meeting up again, which Sammie felt uncertain about. It was so much easier to deal with their mutual attraction over text, at a safe distance. What would it look like when they met again in person? Sammie wasn't sure, but already her stomach was queasy over it. She had never quite accepted the prospect of dating someone new while her teenage son was still living under their roof, as if the two facts were tugging her in opposite directions.

Samson would have scholarships to multiple colleges—places in state, but also places clear across the country. Sammie encouraged him to keep his options open. She had a gut feeling that once her son was grown and out of the house, she wouldn't feel like a mother anymore. You're only a mother if you're mothering.

She glanced back at Samson, leaning against the window in his hoodie, the gray one with the pockets in the front, the one she called his kangaroo pouch. His hair glowed bright, but it was still too long, too unruly. In moments like this, when she caught herself wishing he was different, she was reminded of how her parents had controlled her body, how her mother wouldn't let her wear anything out of the house that looked too "butch" or even cut off her hair.

And she'd wanted to cut off her hair. Had almost done it, several times, but there was something inside her brain that told her she'd look hideous if she went through with it. She knew that was stupid. It made no sense, especially because she was so attracted to women with those haircuts: shorn so short it looked buzzed. Her whole life she'd kept her hair long, even though it wasn't her preference. If she made herself think about it, she'd find her father there, lodged in the back of her brain: *Pretty hair, pretty mind. Pretty hair, find a husband. Pretty hair, find someone who'll love you.*

And her hair had been one of the first things Monika loved about her. On that first night they went home together, Monika held her fist in Sammie's hair as they fucked for hours. In the morning, as they lay naked in bed drinking coffee, Monika ran a gentle hand through that mane and sighed with delight. *Beautiful*, she whispered, and then they'd set down the coffee and fallen into each other all over again.

The road ahead was bumpy, one of those stretches of highway that was forever under construction. She tried to avoid the potholes, but once, when she caught a bad one, Samson's head smacked against the window and he opened his eyes. They looked at each other in the mirror for a long moment, until Sammie mouthed, *Go to sleep*, and for once, miraculously, he listened.

Monika wasn't home when they got back from dropping the other boys off at the Y. The van was due back at the rental place, but Sammie didn't feel like going alone, since she'd have to deal with the hassle of getting a Lyft home. She called and added an additional day of fare, planning to return it in the morning.

It was stormy out. The pressure in the air was so high Sammie could feel it buzzing electric on her skin, sizzling against her flesh. But the sky stayed pregnant, swollen with thunderclouds, refusing to rain. Sammie collected her dirty laundry and went to grab the sheets from Samson's bed. It had been months since she'd done laundry for him. She was his mother, wasn't she? Why did he have to turn everything into a battle?

As Samson took a shower down the hall, she stripped his bed and remade it quickly with fresh sheets from the closet. They smelled a little musty, but not too bad, thanks to the dryer sheets Monika liked to stick between the folded blankets. It was always a happy surprise to open the linen closet, shake out a new set of sheets, and be enveloped in the scent of freshness.

When she flipped out the blanket and saw that dryer sheet sail free, wafting gently to the floor, she burst into tears. She sobbed and pressed it against her hot face, letting the blanket soak up the mess of tears while she inhaled, inhaled, trying to breathe in that good clean aroma because, God, it was going to leave her soon, wasn't it? She would never have it again.

She felt a gentle pressure on her shoulder and she startled, dropping the blanket. It was Samson, wearing his favorite old robe, too short because he refused to get a new one his own size. His face had the same impassive look, but his hand on her was soft. He kept it there as she wiped at her face and pulled herself together.

"I'm sad," she said, unsure if she was telling Samson or herself. "I'm really fucking sad."

"Let's make the bed," he replied. They both took corners of the sheet and fitted it over the mattress. Then the woven blanket he liked. Then the comforter. They each took a pillow and slid on their respective cases. There was the bed, all made, and they'd done it together.

"I'm gonna make Kraft mac and cheese," she said. It was the one food he always ate without complaint.

She went downstairs to the kitchen, poured herself a glass of water, and watched night fall on her backyard. The woman who'd lived behind them had since moved away, and the fence around their own yard was overgrown with invasive plants and weeds, but Sammie didn't mind that, because it gave them more privacy. It also meant that she spent more time outside on the patio. She put the water on the stove, then walked out the back door and into the yard, looking up at the bats that were fluttering in and out of her neighbor's chimney. One afternoon, when she'd gone out to water some new plants she'd placed around the perimeter of the patio, she thought she'd seen a rat scrambling along one of the small palms, but it was just one of those bats. Tiny, the size of a hamster or even a bigger mouse, but sweeter-looking than she'd expected, and she'd been tempted to reach out and touch it. The bat made no noises, just scrambled quickly up the palm until it was safely ensconced beneath one of the green shard-shaped leaves.

She'd had her phone with her, and she'd taken a video of it to show it to Monika or Samson when they got home, but then she and Monika had gotten into it over who would empty the dishwasher. Sammie thought Samson should do it. Monika thought it shouldn't matter, that it should just be Sammie's job. Sammie remembered her mother saying that every household divided up chores between the husband and the wife, but then she realized she never saw her father do anything other than wash the car and hire some kid to cut their lawn every other week, and she got so mad she slammed the dishwasher door so hard it broke. She forgot all about the video of the sweet baby-faced bat until she was lying in bed that night, still fuming. It made her realize that she had nobody in her life to share beauty with, and the thought made her want to die.

"There's water boiling over on the stove."

Sammie jumped, startled, nearly knocking over her glass. Monika was standing in the doorway, backlit by the kitchen light. Sammie couldn't see her expression.

"Did you take the pot off?" Sammie asked, following her inside.

"Of course," Monika replied. She put her briefcase on the counter and shrugged off her blazer, draping it on one of the high-top barstools that lined the counter.

"Good," Sammie replied. "Thanks."

"What I said yesterday, in the text." Monika stopped talking, reaching up to massage her own shoulder. Her shoulders were always tense from work. "I don't know how to say this."

"Just say it," Sammie replied. Her stomach was fiery, full of acid. "It's fine."

"I have a girlfriend."

Sammie didn't know what she'd expected, but it wasn't that. She'd been bracing herself for a tirade about the lewd picture she'd sent, some jab about how she was an unfit mother. Not . . . whatever this was. "What does that mean?"

"It means I'm seeing someone seriously," Monika said. "It means we've been seeing each other for a while."

"Okay."

"It also means that I want her to meet Samson."

"Fuck you," Sammie said. "Absolutely not."

"He's my kid, too. You don't get to make all the decisions."

Sammie laughed at that. "I'm the one who carried him around in her body, Monika. I was the one who spent hours and hours in labor with him. So I'm definitely going to decide whether he gets to meet some total stranger my wife is fucking."

"She's not a stranger, and I'm not your wife."

"We're still married, you know."

"Not for long," Monika shot back.

Sammie told her to move because she needed to go inside and finish fixing dinner. As she pushed past Monika, she took a quick look at her face in the light. Not happy, not sad, but tired. Monika looked like she was over it, and much older than Sammie remembered. Maybe she'd looked that way for years and Sammie just hadn't been paying attention.

The pot she'd been using to boil water was sitting out on the bare marble counter. "Goddamn it, you know you can't just set this down without a potholder. You'll ruin the countertop."

Monika usually had a snappy comeback when Sammie tried to scold her—*It hasn't happened yet, has it?*—but this time she only replied, "I really want him to meet her."

Sammie put the pot back on the stove, waited a few moments for the water to heat enough to boil again, then dumped in the noodles and got some milk and butter from the fridge while she attempted to conjure a response. This wasn't going the way she'd planned. Not surprising, since the whole thing was an ambush. That was Monika's MO—spring things on Sammie so she'd have no chance to think about them first.

"I need to talk about this with my therapist," Sammie countered. When Monika paused, Sammie added that she wanted to meet the woman first, before Samson.

"Why do you need to meet her?"

"I'm his mother. I want to meet this person first."

She didn't look at Monika. If she did, she worried that she'd start crying, or start yelling, or throw the pot of mac and cheese against the wall. Then Monika would say she was being irrational, because every time she showed an emotion that was more than a shrug, Monika claimed Sammie was giving her a guilt trip and stopped taking her seriously.

"Fine," Monika said. "Let me know when you've had your appointment with Aja."

Sammie knew she should feel good, that she'd stood her ground and gotten her way, but what this really meant was that Monika was deeply invested in this new person, and that meant Sammie's life was about to change.

"Can I have a hug?" she asked. Her stomach hurt. "Just hug me."

She missed the comfort of her wife, the way holding each other always made Sammie feel right in her own body.

Monika held out her arms in a way that spoke of giving up more than offering comfort, but Sammie ignored that and just let herself be held. She dug her nose into the crook of her wife's neck and inhaled, as if she could trap the scent in her lungs.

"Your pot is boiling over again," Monika said, and let go.

Charlie missed her dog. He'd been gone awhile now, but he'd always made her feel so safe. Even when the woman who lived behind her did that strange thing, sitting outside her window and looking inside (she'd thought it was Brian again, her stalker ex-boyfriend, there to do something for real this time, maybe kill her like he'd threatened before), and the dogs had felt her fright and reacted before she could even give them a command. Maybe she would move. She'd never really gotten to know anyone in the neighborhood. That was partly her fault, she knew, because she was so scared of people after Brian. You could never really know who anybody was, could you? The neighbors from the back had always seemed lovely. Even though the one had done that weird sleepwalking thing, her wife had been nice. Talked to Charlie whenever she saw her out in the yard and gave her any extra tomatoes they had from their plant. A friendly wave. A kind hello. Their boy had even mowed her grass a few times after she broke up with her last boyfriend, Jose, and she'd had such bad carpal tunnel that she couldn't do it herself. He was a nice kid. Handsome. When she tried to offer him money for it, he just waved it off. A quiet kid, but it seemed like they were raising him right. She'd wanted kids herself: a girl, a boy, either, it didn't matter, but that didn't seem in the cards. Maybe she would move. Take the other dog, Belva, someplace new without so many memories. A yard she didn't need a neighbor kid to mow.

16

Sammie had told Monika she wanted to talk it over with her therapist, but when it was time for her next session, she never brought it up. Instead she talked about the trouble she had making connections with women. She mentioned the embarrassing thing she'd done, sending the photo to her wife instead of Myra. And then she talked about her struggle to have real conversations with Samson. It was hard to talk to him about anything important, because trying to get him to listen, or stay still while she talked about her problems, made her too tired to engage.

"Tired. You say that a lot. Maybe living in your own place would give you the time to process some of these things without wearing yourself out." Aja had on her chunky glasses, the ones that made her look like certain women Sammie sometimes watched in porn.

"I think it's better to wait," Sammie replied. "I don't want to stress out Samson."

"Doesn't your stress add to his stress?" Aja was chewing on the end of her pen. She was wearing new lipstick, Sammie noticed. It was the color of crushed cherries. All the porn actresses wore that same bright, smeary kind, which wound up dotting the insides of thighs and necks. She imagined her therapist taking off the glasses, shaking down her hair, and bending her over the desk. She needed to find some new porn, *or maybe a new therapist*, Sammie thought. She mentioned that she was still talking to Myra, but she didn't know if the relationship would go any further, but when Aja asked why, Sammie realized she didn't want to talk about that, either. *Why do I come to therapy?* Sammie wondered, and then she just stalled and talked about her parents until their time was up.

She paid and left, but she wasn't ready to go home. She drove around aimlessly, wondering what she should do with the rest of her day. There was no one she wanted to talk to. Monika wasn't available to her any longer, and she almost never knew where Samson was. There was Myra, but they were still getting to know each other—although that was really on Sammie. Every time Myra brought up a topic other than sex—kids, work, even the goddamn weather—Sammie inevitably changed the subject. Not that she wasn't interested in Myra. They'd been getting comfortable with each other on the phone, with good long conversations that felt warm and genuine, and the last time they'd gone out, they'd held hands at dinner. Myra was nice, and she was a good listener. Still, it seemed weird to call up a new girlfriend and unload on her about her troubles—especially when they all revolved around her ex-wife.

She found herself driving out to her parents' neighborhood. It was forty-five minutes away, the house where she'd grown up, right next door to the church her parents still attended. At least she assumed they did; they hadn't spoken directly for years. They still sent Samson birthday and Christmas cards, but the envelopes sat unopened for weeks, until Sammie finally opened them so he could deposit the checks they enclosed. Then they stopped sending checks, replacing them with the annual picture they had taken for the church directory—the two of them growing older and grayer every year, the frown lines deepening along their jowls. Sammie stared at her mother's aging face in those photos, worrying about the droop she'd started to notice in her own neck.

She passed the convenience store where she used to buy candy after Sunday school, before service. There was the road for the church, the same welcoming sign with its black-and-white lettering. A large retention pond sat winking sunshine, big enough to cough up thousands of mosquitoes every summer, but never quite able to keep any fish alive. Sammie turned down the drive, navigating the twisty single lane that led to the back of the property. The church itself was set on a corner lot, and the building emerged like a shrunken dollhouse as they approached. That's the way she'd seen it growing up, when they'd attended as a family—the three of them always walking, in the pouring rain or the blistering sun.

The building was just as she remembered it: white cinder block walls, dark shingled roof coming proudly to a tall point at the front, large black cross nailed to its surface. The only change she could see was that more portable buildings had been installed around the perimeter. They sat there, peeling and tacky, in direct contrast to the clean brightness of the church itself. FIRST BAPTIST CHURCH, read the marquee, and as she drove slowly around the building, she saw the traditional weekly greeting:

GOD SEES EVERYTHING!

Ominous, Sammie thought as she pulled past the portables into the gravel lot where she'd thrown rocks with her friends after Wednesday-night services. One night, she remembered, a boy had been struck in the forehead. Blood gushed everywhere, staining his temples and his cheek. All the other kids ran screaming, but Sammie just stood there, thunderstruck. He looked like what she imagined Christ on the cross to look like—that image from Easter, the one they showed on the overhead projector when it was time to show the *before* of Jesus. The tomb, the reckoning, Jesus clean again, standing around in his white holy robes—all of that came later. But it was that messy, bloody *before* that Sammie was fascinated by. The ugliness.

That night, Sammie had gone up to that boy and wrapped her cardigan around his wounded head. *I'm helping Jesus*, she'd thought, but when she took him into the women's restroom to get cleaned up, some older ladies inside started screaming: first at the sight of a boy in the women's bathroom, and then, louder, when he passed out in front of them on the floor. Once he came to, and the nurse was seeing to him, Sammie's mother screamed at her in front of everyone for getting blood on her church clothes. Brady Hudson—that was the boy's name, she suddenly remembered, and he'd carried a scar on his face after that.

After looping her car around the building three times, Sammie impulsively pulled into the gravel lot next to the church entrance. *What could it hurt to go in and look around?* she wondered. It's not as if anyone would recognize her. It had been years since she'd been inside the church. Besides, after she'd married Monika, it was like she'd never existed back home.

The air outside was heavy with the stench of decay from the retention pond, but inside those double doors the air-conditioning made it feel like winter. The church itself smelled exactly how she remembered. It was a scent she'd forgotten until she walked through those doors, but suddenly there it was: a mix of drying paint, dusty potpourri, and hot ink from an overworked copy machine. She could hear the copier all the way in the main office, running off stacks of church bulletins that would end up in the trash at the end of every service.

Her mind flashed back to a dead lizard skeleton she'd seen as a child, sitting in a corner of the hallway, under the water fountains by the restrooms. It stayed there for years, curled up next to the baseboard, as the church vacuums steered around it. *That's how you know people aren't cleaning properly*, her mother always said, pointing it out every Sunday morning, but they'd never stopped to pick it up, not any of them.

"Can I help you?" A woman leaned through the office doorway. *Probably the church secretary*, Sammie decided, and she shook her head.

The woman smiled and asked if she was looking for the nursery.

"Yes," Sammie replied, even though she absolutely was not.

The woman beckoned her down the hall, and she followed, walking the same carpeted path she'd paced thousands of times in her life. For a weird moment she felt young again, moving back through time as they passed the Sunday school classrooms, the posters of biblical scenes: pregnant Mary riding a donkey into Bethlehem; Christ at that long table, supping with his disciples on that fateful night before his crucifixion. She would never forget those images of the supper, the loaves and fishes of the miracle. Every time she had to sit through a service, hungry and waiting for lunch, she'd stared at that loaf of bread and wondered how good it had tasted. If Jesus could feed the masses, why was Sammie forced to sit through service every week with her stomach growling so loudly that her father always whispered for her to knock it off?

That was something she'd never forced her son to do: go to church. She waited to see if he'd ask on his own, see if he wanted it for himself, but it had never happened, not a single question. It was a rare decision she and Monika had agreed on: that their son should be able to choose for himself. He was smart, they both recognized. Able to see through the bullshit.

The woman had on a long jean skirt and a colorful striped sweater vest over a light denim button-up shirt. A bright red headband pulled back her respectable church hair, chin-length with choppy bangs. She wore fuchsia ankle socks, folded down to the lip of her bright white Keds sneakers. *Keds! What decade have we landed in?* Sammie wondered.

Those church office jobs were largely nonpaying positions, she knew; the women who took them weren't allowed to do any "real" work. Their jobs were considered service for the Lord.

At the nursery, they stopped and looked inside. The room was fitted with Dutch doors, so the kids couldn't escape. One little boy was smacking the bottom of a pail with his hand, laughing with glee at the popping sound it made. Another boy was sprawled on the floor, rolling around with his thumb in his mouth. A girl with long blond hair and a chocolate-stain mustache reached down to pet his head.

"Good doggie," she said, and the boy barked happily in response.

"Mama." A baby girl in a bright pink romper looked up at her, eyes big and dark through her springy little ringlets. Sammie smiled, and the girl put up her hands, chubby fingers clenching and unclenching, wanting to be picked up. The woman beside her reached down to grab her and deposited her in Sammie's arms.

Oh fuck, Sammie thought. But the baby didn't cry. Just put her arms around Sammie's neck, as if she expected to be taken home. She smelled sweet, like apple juice and Cheerios. Sammie wanted to put her nose down into the little girl's neck and breathe it all in.

"They're so cute when they're like that, all clingy and happy to see Mom. Not like that one over there." The woman pointed toward one of the diaper stations, where an overmatched daycare worker was struggling to get a young boy back into his pants. Every time he kicked, the pants leg would fly off. Sammie remembered when Samson was that way—full of energy, impossible to pin down. They might be better off letting this kid run around pantsless, she thought, like a real-life Winnie the Pooh.

The baby girl nuzzled into her chest and Sammie had a brief moment of wonder: *What if she just took this one with her?* She was owed a daughter, wasn't she? And Monika would love this one. She could show up at home with a replacement, a good child to make up for all those years with Samson, when everything had been so hard. She imagined what he'd be like with this child, so small and innocent, and felt her insides curdle. She wasn't sure he could be trusted to take care of a plant.

"Oh, she loves Mama," the woman cooed, smiling. She had on adult braces, with little yellow bands around the brackets. Strange choice, Sammie thought. Like she'd bitten into a corncob.

"Is she like this with your husband?"

There it was, an entire imaginary life spread out before her: a husband who worked a nine-to-five selling life insurance and came home at the end of his hard day to a loving family. Sammie, who'd made dinner—some kind of meat loaf or chicken dish from her family recipe box—and their little girl, pink and pretty, playing quietly in the living room. Maybe she'd even drawn her father a picture at school. They'd go to church on Sundays, her daughter in tiny princess dresses. Ruffles and white on Easter. Big family meals with her parents, who still spoke to her.

"She's even better with my wife," Sammie replied. The woman reared back like she'd been slapped. "They're so cute together. Adorable, really."

"Oh," she said. "That's . . . nice."

"She looks just like my wife. I gave birth to her, though. You know how it is with lesbian pregnancies. That old joke about the U-Haul, except now it's a turkey baster!"

"Oh," the woman repeated, like a broken doll. "Oh."

Sammie was having fun. "Gonna take this little cutie with us to the portrait studio next week. All three of us huddled together for our yearly family photo. The new America!"

The woman kept swallowing, as if trying to keep down whatever reply she really wanted to make. That was the thing with those church women: they could be very nasty, but so much of it was passive-aggressive. When someone put the conflict right in their faces, they acted like it was an unknown animal, something they had no idea how to approach.

I could eat you for dinner, Sammie thought, smiling widely.

The little boy inside wriggled free of his captor and ran away laughing, naked from the waist down. The woman she'd scared with her lesbianism excused herself, opening the little half door to get inside, leaving Sammie there holding her not-daughter.

"You could be mine," Sammie whispered. "I could take you home. Or, better yet, take you away entirely. Where would you like to live? France?"

The little girl was sucking her thumb. She looked tired, Sammie thought. Her nose was dripping as well, and Sammie realized: *She's not tired, she's sick.* A cold at least, maybe the flu. It had been going around all summer. Sammie set her back down on the other side of the door and left before anyone could ask her more questions.

On the drive home, she took the back roads and swung past the playground where that man had tried to abduct her son all those years ago. The place looked mostly the same: the swings and the slide, mulch piled up from kids dumping it on each other, mothers parked on benches with their overstuffed diaper bags. She slowed down and considered turning in, but in the end she just drove on. She'd thought about that day so often that it felt like a dream, wondered how her life would have changed if he'd succeeded. If she'd just let him take her son.

Debbie loved working in the church office. It was a great way to meet people, and she considered herself a real people person. That was one of her spiritual gifts, she knew, and she was always so glad when she could use it to benefit others. She spent most days helping Pastor Steve put his sermon together and helping him answer all the email. His wife ran the children's choir. She was beautiful, inside and out. That was another thing she loved, being around all those babies in the nursery. Debbie's own little girl had gone to heaven after only a few short weeks on earth. It had made her so sad, but that was more than ten years ago, and she knew she'd see Mary again someday with Jesus. That was a balm on her bruised heart. She gathered her things and put the empty Tupperware from her egg-salad sandwich in her purse. She waved goodbye to Dina, the nursery worker, and then thought about the woman who'd stopped in that day. She'd been dressed so sloppily. Mismatched brown shoes with a black dress. Even her hair was flyaway. Debbie had been so embarrassed. She hadn't meant to say husband *to the woman—she knew not everyone had a husband, some people were different—and the look of hurt in the woman's eyes had made Debbie feel horrible. She'd wanted to apologize, to give her sincere regrets at the misunderstanding, but by the time she'd finished helping out, the woman had gone. Dina hadn't recognized her. Hadn't known who she was. Probably a troubled soul in need of a small kindness, Debbie decided. She'd missed her opportunity to witness and lend a hand. Debbie hoped she'd come back again and give her another chance.*

17

If there was ever a time when Sammie felt at home in her own house these days, it was weekday afternoons. Those quiet hours when she had a chance to clean, to catch up on work, to snoop around the house for clues about her family's life.

Samson was at the bowling alley for a shift and Monika was at the office, so Sammie decided to take the day to straighten up, to look for ways to understand this life they'd Frankensteined together.

She knew it wasn't good to go through her son's things, and for the most part she left him alone. But there were days, lately, when she was startled to see him sitting at the breakfast table and noticed how tall he'd gotten. When she saw the shadow of a mustache over his lip, saw his arm muscles ripple as he reached for the juice. She'd stand there, dazed, and wonder who this man was taking up space in her kitchen. And she found herself wanting to know him better, before it was too late. For so long she had read his unresponsiveness as anger, but lately she wondered if he felt more like she did. Anxious and sad.

It's not as if she had a ton of other things taking up her time. When Samson was young, there'd been so much on her plate, she felt like she was being swallowed up by his life. But now there was so much less to do. There was her job, which she could do in her sleep: a few hours a day on the computer, answering emails, knocking off a few small copyediting jobs. She got paid enough that it felt worthwhile, but not enough to pay a mortgage or even a decent rent—not enough to change her life. There was an online book group, which she'd joined on a whim one night after too much wine. The book group was fun, even if it was a little messy; nobody ever read the whole book, and most of the conversation revolved around what they were drinking.

Should be called wine group, she thought.

She always assumed that she'd get back into something once Samson was grown: a new career, going back to school, some kind of immersive hobby, like an instrument or voice lessons—even knitting, like some of those PTA moms did. But she wasn't friends with any of those mothers. They were all so heterosexual, and none of them seemed interested in getting to know Sammie beyond the occasional interaction with her son. Samson made her just barely acceptable, but not acceptable enough to spend time with as a friend.

She replied to one last email, completed her time sheet, and sat back in her desk chair. In-box zero. It wasn't even noon and she was done for the day.

Birds were screaming outside, and there was the sound of a garbage truck rolling down the street. Sammie did not want to be in the house, but where could she go? She didn't even want to be in her own body. She got up and walked over to the window, the one she kept saying she was going to cover with some new curtains. Instead she'd just left up those same shitty mini-blinds for years, and they were cracked from the late-afternoon sun that hit the corner of the house like a laser beam every day at 4:00 P.M. She heard the splash of neighbors diving into their pool.

Monika had always wanted to get one for the yard, but Sammie put her foot down. *Do you know how many kids drown in pools in Florida?* she'd said.

"Fuck, I wish we'd gotten a pool," Sammie muttered.

She took a seltzer outside with a book to read on the back patio. It was sweltering, so she shoved up her linen shorts until they were bunched under her ass and rolled up the sleeves on her T-shirt. *Fuck it*, she thought, and then she took the shirt off altogether. Why not tan her tits? It was her own backyard, and no one was home. Why not enjoy the sun for once?

Birds, maybe the ones she'd heard screaming upstairs, swooped after one another across the yard. Cardinals. Vibrant pops of color amid the greenery. She wondered what it meant to see a cardinal. Did it have any special meaning? She typed it into her phone and lifted up her sunglasses to read. *A spirit is trying to make contact with you* was the very first Google result, so she set down her phone. There was nobody dead she'd trust to give her advice. Both sets of grandparents were very conservative; she'd only ever really known one of her grandmothers, a woman who gave her mother a run for her money when it came to disapproving stares.

"Get lost," she told the dead bird-relatives, and leaned back in her chair.

She picked up her book, a bestseller about a woman who was having sex with what might have been a werewolf. It was a long-ago white elephant gift from one of Monika's coworkers, which had sat on the shelf collecting dust for years before she repurposed it as a coaster for nightstand glasses, and more than once as a prop for her phone so she could watch porn hands-free. Sammie sat with the book shading her face and felt sweat drip down the back of her neck. She read every other sentence, occasionally swatting at herself: a mosquito, another drip of sweat, a leaf spiraling down from an oak. There was a lizard creeping around her cold drink, the glass rings of condensation on the table beside her.

When was the last time she'd gotten enjoyment out of anything? She had always thought of the future as if it were a blinking neon sign: a miraculous EXIT glowing red at the end of a long hallway. She imagined that if she kept walking toward it, that if she put in the time, she might finally reach the future. But now the neon felt like a mirage, the illusion of the dehydrated in the desert when they need something to believe in.

She pulled her shirt back on and wandered upstairs. She figured she'd get up and get moving, maybe clean up the house a little. Organize her life. Get rid of old junk they never used, throw out moldy leftovers from the fridge, toss out some ratty old furniture.

I'll take a quick shower first, she thought. Sammie decided to use the one in Monika's bathroom, because it was nicer. She rarely went into Monika's room. It wasn't a rule or anything, more like an unspoken understanding between them: that is your space, this is my space. Once in a while, if she was doing laundry and felt like being nice, she'd grab Monika's sheets or some of her bath towels—but less often lately, since these days Sammie was always getting in trouble for washing things the wrong way. She'd shrunk something in the dryer, or left a red shirt in the whites, turning a pillowcase pink. Sammie couldn't see the pink, but Monika swore there was a tinge of it. *What does that even mean?* Sammie would ask, and Monika would tell her she needed to get her eyes checked, and Sammie would wonder what kind of glasses could possibly help her see colors.

She opened the door to Monika's room and stood there in her underwear, holding on to her sweaty shorts and shirt. Monika's room smelled different from the rest of the house. One reason was the plug-in air freshener she used—the same white-linen scent that she'd loved for years, that she'd one day splurged on and bought in bulk out of fear that it might someday be discontinued. But there was another smell there, one that lurked beneath that chemical "freshness." It was a yeasty aroma, something like unwashed skin. The scent of a scalp underneath a pile of hair.

It was Monika, Sammie realized. Unlike the rest of the house, which smelled like all three of them, this room contained only her wife.

The room was smaller than Sammie's, but not by much. Sammie had kept the master, but this bedroom also had its own bathroom, with a giant walk-in shower in lieu of a bathtub. When they'd first moved in, she and Monika had fucked in it all the time. Sometimes lesbians complained about shower sex, said it wasn't practical—that feeling of water running all over her, dripping into her eyes and down her throat—but Sammie loved it. What was ever practical about good sex?

She dropped her dirty clothes on the rug next to Monika's bed and went into the bathroom. Monika's toiletries were scattered across the countertop: the hair pomade she liked, which smelled like Granny Smith apples. The men's cologne she favored, its glass bottle shaped like a sailing ship. Her paddle brush with its wooden handle slicked smooth from years of use. There were other things, too, things Sammie didn't recognize: Some expensive-looking brand of shampoo, probably from a salon. A pale pink razor hanging from one of those wineglass holders that suctioned onto the tile. Beside it hung a men's razor, the kind Monika favored. So the pink one was something . . . unexpected.

She got down on her knees on the blue IKEA bathmat and opened Monika's bathroom cabinets. Lavender bath salts, though Monika hardly ever used the tub. (She claimed it made her feel like a boiled chicken in a stockpot.) Cocoa butter lotion. (Monika was allergic to cocoa butter, was always saying that a sunburn would be better than an all-over body rash.) A black makeup towel, the kind they gave out at hotels.

Monika didn't wear makeup.

Sammie turned on the shower and stepped in. She washed her hair with that expensive shampoo and conditioner, then pulled out that pink razor and shaved her legs and armpits, wondering who else had drawn its blades along their limbs. When she got out, she wrapped herself in one of Monika's towels and then went straight into the bedroom. She didn't bother pretending to clean, just opened the drawers in Monika's vanity, unearthing all kinds of powders and face creams and eye shadow palettes. The walk-in closet was stuffed full of Monika's work shirts and suits, but there were also two much smaller dresses hidden between those hangers. One of them was a low-cut, pale ivory lace mini, almost like a slip. Sammie would have had to cut herself in half to fit in that thing. She sniffed at the neck of that dress and picked up a vanilla perfume, an aroma Monika always said she found nauseating.

She sat down on Monika's padded stool and turned on the halogens, a ring of lit gold around the mirror. She opened all the face creams— expensive tubes of stuff with extravagant French names—and slathered the nicest one on her face. She started putting on some of the makeup, but the eye shadow made her look like she'd gotten punched in both eyes.

As she dug around looking for more, she pulled open a drawer and unearthed a stack of bundled letters, covered in bubbly blue handwriting. *How old is this woman?* Sammie thought. *Not woman—girl*, she amended. It was how writing had looked back when she was in middle school. *How old is this girl?*

Megan. A girl named Megan.

Sammie wondered if opening someone else's private letters was as bad as reading their diary, then immediately rejected that thought. They'd made an agreement, she and Monika, that they wouldn't bring another woman into the house while Samson still lived there. Obviously Monika had broken that promise. If she was careless enough to leave evidence lying around, what did it matter if Sammie read them?

The first letter was written on stationery featuring a black kitten playing with a ball of yarn. Megan began the letter addressing Monika as "My Love," which made Sammie want to puke. The rest of it was a series of very schmaltzy paragraphs about missing Monika's hands and thinking about her at night when she was curled up in bed.

It was the next letter, written on that same kitten stationery, that gave Sammie pause. A paralyzing description of a three-night cruise the two of them had apparently taken to the Bahamas.

I look at this ring and all I see is you, Megan wrote, underlining every word.

Sammie turned the envelope over. The letter had been delivered to Monika's office. That made sense, especially since Sammie was usually the one who picked up the mail at the house. How had this woman been able to slip into her home, when Sammie hardly ever left? Maybe they'd snuck in on the nights she'd told Monika that she wouldn't be home, not to wait up, because she was meeting some woman she'd met on the dating app. And that weekend she took Samson and his teammates to the swim meet in Pensacola. The one Monika hadn't been able to make because she was too busy with work. Apparently "work" meant having a very young woman over and fucking her in Sammie's home, eating in their family kitchen, probably wrapping themselves in the Mrs. and Mrs. robes she and Monika had had monogrammed after their wedding.

"What the fuck?" Sammie whispered. She was sitting naked at her ex's vanity, covered in makeup that wasn't hers, reading letters she wasn't supposed to know about—and, *shit, of course*, she was on her period. She was probably dripping blood right onto the cushion where she was sitting. Then she remembered the last time she'd sat on that stool, one evening when they'd showered together and then Monika had stood behind her, brushing the snarls out of her long hair.

Oh, intimacy is a true bitch, isn't it? Sammie thought. She shoved the letters back in the drawer, wishing she'd never seen them. She put the creams and eyeshadow back, too, along with a bottle of lemon-smelling stuff she'd slathered on her arms and legs before realizing it wasn't lotion.

She washed off in the bathroom sink, then walked down the hall to Samson's room. *Might as well go through everything*, she thought.

Her son's room smelled different, too. Not like Monika's, with its fragrances, but . . . weird, that teen-boy funk that reminded her of a petting zoo. Samson's room didn't have any of the decor she'd always associated with teenage boys: No video games or pictures of stupid memes, no images of women in swimsuits perched precariously on the hoods of cars, not a single movie poster. Just plain white walls and shelves filled with the books they'd bought him, which she didn't know if he'd even read. The sole pops of color came from his green plaid bedspread and his swimming duffel, which was upended on the floor. The room was littered with castoffs: an athletic sock on the rug, empty bags of chips and half-empty Gatorade bottles on his dresser, along with a TV he never seemed to watch except to stream YouTube videos of people playing video games he didn't own.

Samson's room smelled like curdled milk, maybe. Something gone sour.

She wished she'd brought one of the plug-in air fresheners from Monika's room, just to get rid of the odor. Sammie picked up all the garbage from the floor and stuffed it in the trash can beneath his desk—empty except for some wadded tissues she didn't care to explore further—and then scooped up the sheets that had fallen off the end of his bed. She fluffed up the pillow, which gave off a puff of dust when she whacked it.

"That can't be healthy," she said, trying to remember when she'd bought him a new one.

His dresser was full of clothes, so many that the drawers were hard to close. As she pulled them open, though, out came pair after pair of pants that were far too short for his lanky frame. Underwear that still featured cartoon characters on them. T-shirts that were stained and full of holes. Samson never asked for stuff. Never said, *Hey, my underwear doesn't fit anymore, they haven't for years* or *By the way, all my socks have ten holes in them, could I get some new ones?* When was the last time she'd bought him new clothes? When was the last time she'd bought *herself* new clothes? All her stuff was faded from washing and continual wear. Most of her things no longer fit right, to the point where her pants caused her active pain to wear, but she never got around to getting herself anything new.

She wondered if this was what depression looked like—when you were so unable to care for yourself that you stopped remembering to take care of your own body, not to mention anyone else's. When you'd become little more than a barely functioning mind: a fuzzy, disintegrating brain floating lonely in a jar of formaldehyde.

"I'll get him some new stuff," she said. She could feel her face flush. "I'll get us both new things." She went downstairs to grab as many Publix bags as she could, then came back up and filled them with the clothes she knew she could toss. She stopped by her room to shrug on a robe, in case Samson came home before she was done. She got out the vacuum and tackled his rug. Scrubbed the toilet in his hall bathroom, which was coated with yellow drips of urine, and then washed out his sink.

After her cleaning frenzy was over, she sat down and looked around his room, wondering what it might tell her about him. This wasn't like digging through Monika's things, which was like subjecting herself to mental torture. It was more of an attempt to know her son a little better without having to embarrass him with questions. To improve their relationship without getting in a big fight over it. At least that's what she told herself.

She didn't expect to find a journal. She'd been an emotional, closeted teen, but she'd never kept one, and Samson's handwriting was a scribbling scrawl. His nightstand was full of typical detritus: bottle caps, ticket stubs, receipts, old tubes of ChapStick, a watch that no longer worked, key rings, paper coasters from various restaurants. Some random old papers from school, all wadded up and gray, as if they'd been unearthed from the bottom of a backpack. The same went for his desk: dried-up old pens with missing caps, pencil stubs with hardened erasers. There were some swim team posters, a couple of pictures of him and his teammates standing beside the pool, arms slung over one another's shoulders, fingers held in the air: *We're number one.* A few medals and ribbons among the paper clips and old birthday cards. *Nothing important*, Sammie thought. *Just a bunch of junk.*

His laptop sat on top of the desk. She realized belatedly that anything personal about her son would be found on his computer. She forgot how old she was sometimes, and the sudden reminders that the world had changed made her brain seize up.

She and Monika had bought him the computer freshman year. *For school*, they'd said, because she'd heard that everyone these days turned in their assignments online. There was even a way to check your child's grades, have them emailed to you, but Sammie had tried that out only once and then gotten frustrated by the convoluted, confusing system and hadn't bothered to look again. Monika had had to handle setting up the log-in for him, making it easy so he'd never forget it. *Just set the passcode as the first line of letters on the keyboard*, she said.

Q-W-E-R-T-Y is what Sammie typed into the box under an icon of Samson swimming, head emerging from the water in his goggles and cap. The log-in screen winked off, replaced by an open browser. It was a porn site. The video itself was paused, but it was very graphic: a close up of a woman with long blond hair and very big eyes giving a man a blow job.

Sammie slammed the laptop shut. What the hell had she been thinking? Searching a teenage boy's computer? What'd she expect to find, a letter describing his thoughts and feelings? Images of puppies cavorting in an open field? A bulleted list of all the reasons he hated her?

For a wild moment she contemplated wiping her fingerprints from the top of the computer with the sleeve of her robe, as if he might deduce through some kind of investigative work that she'd been nosing around on his computer and decide to dust the lid for prints.

She turned off the lights and went out into the hallway. So she'd looked at porn on her kid's computer, she thought. Big deal. It was one of the dumbest things that had happened in her life in a while, and if she'd heard the story from anyone else, she would have laughed about it. So that's what she did. She laughed all the way down the hallway, laughed walking into Monika's room. Laughed as she lay down on her wife's bed, crawled under the covers with her robe still on, and smothered her face into the pillow. Muffled like that, it was hard to tell if she was laughing or crying. That made as much sense as anything else that had happened that day.

She woke up several hours later with the robe tangled around her neck, dreaming that someone was strangling her. The makeup she'd put on earlier had smeared all over the pillowcase. Worried that someone might already be home, she quickly stripped it and put on a fresh one, then took the stained pillowcase into her own room and stuffed it deep inside her hamper. She was going to have to talk to Monika about what she'd seen, but she wanted to do it on her own terms.

How do you ask your wife if she's engaged to another woman? Sammie wondered, and then corrected herself. *How do you ask your ex, to whom you're still married, if she's planning on marrying somebody else?*

She knew Samson was home when she heard the front door slam. No matter how often she talked to him about it, he inevitably slammed the door like he was trying to knock it off its hinges. Sammie poked her head out and asked if he was going to need dinner. He grunted and shuffled into his bedroom, slamming that door, too.

She hoped he wouldn't notice she'd touched the computer.

She got up and rifled through her closet, trying to find something that didn't look like it should be immediately airlifted to Goodwill. There were so few things she owned that looked . . . *fresh*. That was the word she was looking for: not new, as in something she'd just bought, but fresh, as in something that didn't look like she'd worn it eight hundred times. A shirt that didn't need to be put on life support.

Everything she owned was old, and all the fabrics looked weird draped over her body. Pants that were too short, too tight around the waist, faded in strange ways. Jeans from twelve years ago. Boot cut? Did people still wear those? So many pairs of linen shorts. Ratty sneakers and ballet flats, their insides dark and gutted. Shapeless dresses she wore around the house, which sometimes doubled as nightgowns. She stood in front of her closet and swept the clothes back and forth, as if one of the creatures from Narnia would burst out and toss her a blouse.

She finally decided on a pair of too-tight jean shorts and a white button-up that Monika once said made her look like a college professor on sabbatical. Her hair was a lost cause; she just swept the mess up in a loose knot. She bit at her lips to brighten them. Trying to make herself look presentable. If she could manage presentable, then she'd be fine.

She went back downstairs and cleaned the kitchen, then cracked open a beer and went outside to sit on the patio as night swept in and the sun sank below the tree line. She sat down and tried to relax. Made herself do some breathing exercises. The beer made her feel a little better, so she took some pictures of herself in the dying light and sent them to Myra. She didn't bother opening the dating app; that was just another way to feel bad about herself, answering inane questions like *Have you ever read* Little Women? or *What's your favorite pizza topping?* Once, a woman had asked her to name her childhood pet and her mother's maiden name, and she'd almost given out the information before realizing she was being catfished.

Dating is embarrassing, Sammie thought. *Like one of those dreams where you show up for your finals naked.* She wanted to skip all that stuff and get to the part where they already knew everything about each other. Except that she also wanted the newness and strangeness of fucking a complete stranger, someone who had absolutely no expectations. But then she also wanted someone who knew her body well enough to get her off—to know what she liked without her having to tell them, or to fake an orgasm just to get them to stop. She wanted what she'd had with Monika, back in that good space when they first got to know each other: how her wife's breath smelled in the morning after breakfast; the way she had to put the orange juice in front of the milk in the fridge, every single time; the way Monika knew to suck just below her ear in order to get her to come fast.

Myra liked the pictures and responded with one of her own. In the photo she was drinking a glass of wine out on her balcony. Her daughter sat in the background, hunched over the glowing screen of her own phone. Sammie couldn't imagine doing something like that: sending someone she was trying to sleep with photos of herself with Samson. She and Samson hardly ever took pictures together. The few she had were from years ago, taken on family trips after Monika yelled at the two of them to *get together*. They'd both sit stone-faced as Monika snapped shots, muttering, *You're not gonna like these, look at your faces.*

Ants marched along a crack in the patio. Sammie sat and sipped her drink and watched the moon emerge in the sky while the sun was still setting. Birds were flocking in the distance, probably heading to the trees at the nearby lake. Beside her, in the bougainvillea, something crunched along in the dead leaves.

She heard Monika's car beep in the driveway and headed back inside. She was tossing her empty into the recycling bin when Monika walked into the kitchen, her suit jacket slung over her shoulder. The suit was one of Sammie's favorites, charcoal gray with tiny white pinstripes; she was wearing the vest over her button-down with the sleeves cuffed up to her elbows. Black butch oxfords. She looked like a character on some lesbian TV drama—so much so that Sammie almost wanted to make fun of her—but the most infuriating part was that she looked great. After all these years, she was still very attracted to her wife.

"What's for dinner?" Monika asked.

Sammie gripped the countertop to keep herself from bringing up the letters.

"Not sure. Didn't know what was going on tonight." She was proud of herself for managing that. Her voice sounded easy. Bright.

"You have plans?" Monika asked, still not making eye contact.

Sammie wondered how she'd gone so long without picking up on her wife's deception. If anything, Monika was almost religious about looking at another person when she spoke. It was something she'd drilled into Samson since he was young: *Make eye contact with the people you're talking to*, she said, grabbing his chin when he didn't look directly at her when she was speaking. *It shows that you're really listening and that you're not hiding anything.*

"Maybe," Sammie said. She caught her own reflection in the microwave window—not as good as she'd hoped, but then she always expected to see herself ten years ago when she looked in the mirror.

"What about Samson?" Monika asked. There—now she was looking. She stood on the other side of the counter, tapping her fingers on the marble in that anxious way she always did when she was thinking something but didn't know exactly how to say it.

"You look good" is what she finally said, and Sammie forced down a smile.

"I think I'm gonna order him a pizza. You want some?"

"Maybe," Monika parroted back, picking up her phone and scrolling through it. Sammie let her gut resettle again over the lip of her pants. No use sucking it in if nobody was even paying attention. Her body was never really her own, was it? It was always for the benefit of somebody else's gaze. A body was really only ever on loan, Sammie supposed.

She picked up her own phone and went to the Domino's pizza app. She'd been thinking of deleting it for the past year, because she knew she used it too often, but if she ordered enough she'd qualify for a free pizza, so deleting it now felt like tossing an entire pizza in the garbage.

"How about just pepperoni?" she asked.

Monika shrugged. "Have you thought about what I asked?"

Sammie knew what she meant, but decided to play dumb. "About what?"

"You know what I'm talking about. Don't do that, Samandra."

Sammie hated when Monika called her by her full name. It sounded like being yelled at by her mother.

"You mean meeting up? With your . . . person?"

"Yes, that." Monika took out her laptop and opened it on the countertop, even though Sammie had asked her a million times not to do work there, so the kitchen was always for family. Was she even really working? Maybe she was just emailing that woman.

That woman. Maybe she could use this moment as a fact-finding opportunity. "What's her name, by the way?"

"Megan."

"Megan what?"

Monika scrubbed a hand through her hair, face glowing blue from the computer screen. "Just Megan."

"Wow. *Just Megan*," Sammie replied, grinning. "Is that a family name or something? What's her middle name, *In Case*?"

Monika didn't respond. She never thought Sammie was very funny.

"What's she like?" Sammie asked, poking at the information like she would a bruise. "Tall? Smart? Does she have kids? Did she graduate from college? Does she like dogs or cats?"

"She's . . . kind, I guess. Thoughtful. Pretty and sweet." Monika paused a moment, then shrugged. "Just different."

Oh, that stung.

"Where does she live?" Sammie asked. "Is she nearby? Seminole County or Orange?"

"She's kind of between places," Monika replied, avoiding eye contact. "She had some problems with her roommate, so she's moved back in with her mom. Just temporarily."

"Oh." A girlfriend who still lived with her parents. How embarrassing. At least Sammie didn't have to feel bad about herself for *that*.

"We could go out together some weekend soon," Monika said. She still wouldn't make eye contact with Sammie, which meant the whole conversation must really be stressing her out. "Get dinner someplace, the three of us."

The idea of getting dinner with her wife and her wife's girlfriend sounded about as good as someone jabbing toothpicks under her fingernails. She could just imagine the two of them sharing significant looks and making private jokes as Sammie sat across the table alone, wondering if she had food stuck in her teeth. She thought of the years of experience she and Monika had shared, slowly being eclipsed by the new life she'd be creating with this other person. The new relationship they'd form with her son. It made her want to bite something.

Her phone buzzed on the countertop. She looked down, expecting a pizza delivery notification, but it was a text from Myra. *Thinking of you*, it said.

"Yeah, sure. Fine," she said, picking up her phone and scrolling through the day's messages from Myra. They still sent each other sexts, but recently they'd begun just asking each other about their days, their kids, what was new. It was nice to have someone who cared about her. Who wanted to talk to her even when she was grumpy or stressed-out. "But I'm going to bring someone, too."

Monika looked up then. Sammie could see her screen reflected in her glasses. She wasn't working at all. She was on Facebook. "Who?"

"My girlfriend," Sammie said, relishing the startled look that passed over Monika's face. "You'll love her. She's incredible."

Sometimes Aja wished that, instead of becoming a therapist, she'd gone to veterinary school. She could have learned to care for injured birds. Treat iguanas and boa constrictors. Give puppies medicine and hold fluffy kittens in the palm of her hand. The best part of being a vet was that the animals would listen. She could do all the talking for once, unlike her current job, where she just listened to other people all day long. She knew that wasn't fair, and she definitely didn't feel that way all the time. Therapy was something she'd been passionate about for years, and she still felt that most days. It was just when her clients made the same bad choices over and over again that it . . . frustrated her. It had been like that with Sammie Lucas. The woman had started out in couples therapy with her wife. Porcupines, both so prickly. And mad! But then Aja kept seeing Sammie on her own, after they split, and Sammie would not examine her life. Wouldn't sit inside any of her choices and think about how she might change them. The worst part was, Sammie was an appealing person. She was smart and attractive. She was even kind of funny. More than once, Aja found herself talking about her own life in an effort to crack Sammie open: how her girlfriend wouldn't listen to her, how she got aggravated with her parents. Eventually she found herself zoning out as Sammie talked about her problems—always on repeat—and started fantasizing about having sex with her during sessions. That had been a big red flag, and she'd worried herself sick over it. But then Sammie called to say she wouldn't be coming in anymore. It was an incredible relief, as if fate had intervened to catch her before things went horribly wrong. She popped a couple Advil and waited for her two o'clock to show up. Three more hours and she could finally go home. Glass of wine and a book. Curl up on the couch and maybe call her best friend, Marjorie. Talk to somebody else about her problems. Finally.

18

Sammie still chauffeured Samson to therapy every other week. He got rides to and from swim practice from other boys on the team, and he often begged rides home from other bowling alley employees after his shifts, but therapy was different. She worried he wouldn't show up for sessions if left to his own devices. He'd never liked going. So over the years, Sammie had spent a huge swath of her free time sitting in the therapist's lobby waiting on him. Because if she didn't, she knew he'd find a way to sneak out early and kill time in the parking lot until she came back to pick him up.

That was the thing: She wanted her son to be well. To feel good about himself. She wanted to be able to connect with him in a way that didn't feel forced, and she believed that therapy might help with that. Might eventually break something open. So she was willing to wait on him. See if something finally clicked.

He piled into the back seat after swim practice, hair still sopping wet. It was dripping all over her interior. Over the years, he'd dripped so much pool water onto the seats and carpet that he'd bleached out the fabric. She'd tried reminding him to rinse off after practice, but he still showed up reeking of chlorine.

The drive from practice to therapy was longer than the trip from their house, which gave Sammie a chance to talk to him when he couldn't escape. She always waited to spring things on him until they took long car trips, so he had to listen—unless he wanted to stick his fingers in his ears and make pterodactyl noises, the way he'd done during his middle school years.

"How was practice?" It was a dumb question, if only because Samson never answered the kinds of everyday questions parents ask: *How was school?* or *What's new with your friends?*

"Can we get Slurpees?" Samson asked, spotting the 7-Eleven up ahead. She pulled up to a gas pump in the parking lot and dug a couple of fives out of her purse, asking him to get her one, too, along with a seltzer. She got so thirsty in that waiting room; by the time Samson's session was over, she always felt like she was emerging from a food dehydrator.

Her son loped across the lot and walked directly in front of a car. The driver—an elderly woman who could barely see over the steering wheel of her Chrysler—braked suddenly and honked, clearly more scared than mad. Samson didn't stop, though. He just flipped the bird at the car and headed into the convenience store.

Mortified, Sammie hid her nose in her bag, as if she were hunting around for her wallet, so she wouldn't have to see the appalled look on the driver's face. She wondered if people thought she'd taught him to do those kinds of things. That maybe he'd seen her do them and he was imitating her. Had he seen her flipping off other drivers? Not unlikely.

The 7-Eleven parking lot smelled like car exhaust and rotting food from the dumpster that sat catty-corner to the store. As she slid her credit card into the reader, she watched one of the employees come out and chuck a box of old bananas into that dumpster. A couple of crows lifted and resettled on the lip, jostling against each other and uttering short, urgent little squawks as they fought over a stale muffin. Sammie could see lines of heat curling up off the pavement. The freshest asphalt, near the gas pumps, resembled burnt bread.

Years ago, her mother had told her a story about hot Florida pavement. When she was young, she'd taken an egg from the kitchen to see if she could fry it on the sidewalk outside their home. She sat there for hours in the sweltering heat, watching the yellow goo ooze across the pavement, and all that happened was that the egg got covered in ants and she got a wicked sunburn on her neck and shoulders. When she got home, her mother spanked her with a wooden kitchen spoon for wasting an egg.

I bet you could fry an omelet in this parking lot, Sammie thought. *Global warming is real.*

As she finished pumping her gas, she watched a tall line of palms sway behind the storefront, their fronds flapping frantically in the breeze, as if trying to grab the attention of passing cars. It was broiling out, but Sammie didn't mind. She preferred all that sun and the blue, burning sky to the clouds that would come later, banking themselves before the daily thunderstorm hit. A car slowly squeezed past her own, its tire running up over the curb, and that's when she heard the yelling behind her.

She turned around and saw Samson standing in front of the store holding two large Slurpee cups. A woman was reaching through the doorway, shouting at him, grabbing his arm. Sammie capped the gas tank and ran over to them.

"Don't touch him," she said, but the woman wouldn't let go. She had on a green employee shirt tucked into a pair of oversize Dockers. Her crew cut was threaded with gray, and she kept shoving her wire-rimmed glasses up her nose with the hand that wasn't clutching her son's sleeve.

"He stole those." Her voice was deep and gruff, as if she needed to clear her throat. "He didn't pay."

"Of course he paid," Sammie said, but then she wondered if he actually had. "Didn't you, Samson?"

"Yes," he replied, and the woman just shook him again, hard enough that his head rocked back.

Sammie was filled with rage. "Don't fucking touch my kid," Sammie said, grabbing the woman's arm. She had to stop herself from shaking the woman like she'd just shaken her son. Anger coursed through her like an energy drink; in her rage she felt like she could lift a car.

"He still needs to pay for those." The woman wiped her hands on her khakis. Sammie saw that her pants were stained. Coffee, maybe. It was midafternoon; the woman had probably been on her shift all day. Sammie felt herself deflate. She told Samson to get in the car.

"Let me just pay for it, whatever it is," Sammie said, watching her son climb into the back seat. He sat there with the door cracked, legs hanging out the side. She followed the woman inside and stood at the counter as she rang her up. DONNA, her name tag read. Sammie had given Samson all the cash from her purse, so she gave the woman her credit card, adding on a pack of gum and a scratch-off ticket so the bill would be more than five dollars.

"Listen, he does this all the time."

"What?" Sammie looked at Donna, who was making a very serious face. She was afraid she already knew what the woman was about to say.

"He comes in here all the time and steals stuff. Next time I'm not being so nice. I'm calling the cops."

"How do you even know it's him?" Sammie asked, and wished she could just have one normal day. Of course her kid had to do this. Of course he'd steal stupid, worthless stuff, even though he had money to pay for it. Of course she'd stand there defending him, because that's what she always did. Of course.

"Listen, I'm not an idiot. I know who he is, and I know what he's been doing." Donna handed her the receipt. She didn't look mad. If anything, the look in her eyes was one of pity.

She sees how I am as a mother, and she feels sorry for me, Sammie thought. *This gay woman is looking at me like I've fucked it up for all of us.* But then she thought, *I bet she doesn't even have a kid. What the hell does she know about it?*

"I'd like to pay the whole amount, everything you think he's taken." Sammie put her wallet back down on the counter next to the lottery ticket. On the front was a picture of a duck holding a shotgun, with a slogan in the corner reading QUACK YOU! She wished she hadn't bought it.

"That's not necessary," Donna said. She was already waving in the next customer in line, a man in a flannel shirt holding a sweating gallon of whole milk. "Just talk to your kid."

"I always talk to my kid," Sammie replied, indignant, as she took her things and left.

The parking lot was even more stifling than before. The breeze had stalled out, leaving her feeling like the breath had been sucked from her lungs. She was damp under her arms, along her hairline, sweating through the crotch of her pants. She climbed into the front seat and barked at Samson to put on his seat belt and close the door.

"What's with you?" Samson asked. He was slouched over, taking pulls from his Slurpee, which looked like it contained every flavor from the machine. She wanted to reach back between the seats and smack him. Instead she picked up the Slurpee he'd gotten her and took a long, angry sip. It was horribly sour, not a flavor she'd ever pick for herself. Her face puckered as she set down the drink, rolling over the curb next to her as she pulled back onto the road.

"What's with *me*? You're funny." She looked at the seat next to her, then at the floor. Nothing. "Where's my seltzer?"

"I forgot."

"Huh. I guess if it's not about you, it's not worth remembering."

She realized she was speeding through the neighborhood and forced herself to take her foot off the gas. They were driving along the cut-through she liked to take to avoid the afternoon highway traffic jams. This street was famous locally for having the best Christmas displays every year. Drippy strings of white lights hanging off palm trees. Humongous inflatable Santas and their reindeer perched perilously on rooftops. A window nativity display that featured an animatronic baby Jesus. Every year, people in shorts and T-shirts cavorted through the neighborhood drinking hot chocolate and mulled cider out of Styrofoam cups. Their little family used to drive through on Christmas Eve, gathered in Monika's car with all the windows rolled down. Bing Crosby would sing about making "the yuletide gay," and the two of them would laugh while Samson rolled his eyes in the back seat. It was one of her favorite things they did as a family.

The grass always looked overgrown this time of year, no matter how often people mowed. There were weeds sprouting along the cracks in the sidewalks, overtaking the people's yards. In the harsh light of day, those cheery holiday houses looked in serious need of summer paint jobs. They passed an annual favorite of hers, a home with white icicle lights in the windows and a human-size snow globe that held a snowman, a Christmas tree, and sprinkled fake snow. In the front yard, a balding man in his bathrobe picked up a wet newspaper from the path of his sprinkler. It was almost 3:00 P.M.

"Why would you steal? Do you understand how dumb that is?"

"I didn't steal anything."

"Why would that woman make it up?"

"Because she's a fucking bitch."

Sammie took another sip of her Slurpee even though she hated it, just so she wouldn't start yelling right away. That never worked.

"She is, though. You saw her."

"Why do you lie about everything?" Sammie asked. "Life would be so much easier if you would just . . ." She didn't know how to finish the thought. He'd heard it from her a million times, and he wouldn't listen, today or any day. She drank more of the Slurpee. She was liking it a little more now, she thought; maybe her tongue had just numbed to the terrible, biting flavor. A body could get used to anything, she decided. All it needed was time.

"Your mom and I are going out on a date," she said, taking another long pull from the straw. Immediate brain freeze. She put down the cup and pushed a hand against her forehead, as if the pressure alone could stop the pain.

"So?"

"With other people," Sammie continued. "Like a double date."

No response. She looked at him again in the rearview mirror; his face was pressed directly against the glass, as if to avoid looking at her. She was already afraid she was approaching this the wrong way. "It's not any big thing," she continued, speaking as carefully as if she were talking through a mouthful of broken glass. "Your mom is seeing somebody, and I'm seeing somebody, and they both seem nice, so we thought it would be good for us all to meet. Get to know each other a little better. That's all."

"Why are you both so weird?" Samson mumbled. "Everything you do is weird. And confusing. You don't make sense."

Her son pressed his head so hard against the glass that she worried he'd give himself whiplash if she stopped the car too quickly. They were back on the main drag now, and the world outside passed by in a blur of green and blue and gray: trees, palms, restaurants, banks. Here was the cow pasture next to one of the charter schools where all the hard-core Christian families sent their kids to protect them from learning anything too sacrilegious. An Arby's next to an exotic-plant nursery. A topless bar, its pink neon lights reflecting off the blue wall of a pool repair shop.

"If it goes well, then maybe you'll meet the two of them at some point."

"I doubt it."

"It'll be fine. Okay?"

"I wish you guys would just be normal," Samson said. He still wasn't looking at her, just staring out the window, his shoulders so hunched he looked like he was drawing into himself.

"This is gonna be a good thing, really," Sammie replied. "I promise."

He made a noise that could have been assent or dissent, there was no way to tell without seeing his face. But she'd said what she needed to say, and now she could take him to therapy, where he could talk it over with someone who was qualified to deal with his reaction to it. Someone more qualified than Sammie, at least.

When she pulled into the parking lot of the therapist's office, he got out without saying a word. This time, instead of going inside, she decided to wait in the car. He was old enough now to do this without her, she thought. Overhead a plane flew by, heading for destinations unknown.

Sammie knew people always described their orgasms as cresting waves. Invoked the beauty of a starburst, or fireworks all in a row: *bang, bang, bang.* But for her, coming felt more like finally sitting down for a good meal after starving for weeks. The movement of it—spasms like a jaw clenching and unclenching. Like her pussy wanted to swallow everything and ask for seconds.

She fisted a hand in Myra's hair and rode out that first big one. If Myra kept swirling her tongue like that, she might come again. Then it would be like having leftovers. Just thinking about it that way led to her next orgasm. She yelled a word that almost sounded like *fuck*, and tightened her grip until she knew there'd be strands of Myra's hair twined between her fingers when she let go. She almost came a third time, but she was spent, it was done, and when she finally let go and Myra sat up, smiling, she saw blood ringing the other woman's mouth.

"Well," Sammie said. "Whoops." And then she started laughing.

"What's funny, baby?" Myra wiped at her face with the back of her hand. Then she looked down at the smears. "Oh, fuck."

Then they were both laughing, rolling around on the bed together. Sammie's cunt kept clenching every few seconds, and it still felt orgasm good. It was nice to enjoy another person in bed. Sex during her period always felt the best: messy, sure, but there was already so much blood pooling down there that she was horny for days. And it wasn't like she could have a one-night stand with a person from the dating app and bleed all over them. She hadn't had good period sex since Monika, and that had been years ago, so this was something . . . nice.

After all that rolling around together, she wound up sprawled on top of Myra near the edge of the mattress. She grabbed the glass of water she'd brought in earlier and gulped it down in three swallows. They were at Myra's apartment. Myra's daughter was with her ex-wife, so there wasn't anyone to walk in on them while they fucked. That was nice. Sammie couldn't remember the last time she hadn't had to worry about a kid walking in on her during sex.

"You feel good?"

Sammie nodded.

Myra combed her fingers through Sammie's hair. "You should let me cut this for you."

"You want to cut my hair?"

"I could do it. Trim the split ends." She mimed a cutting motion with her fingers, and Sammie told her she knew something else she could scissor. Then they were both laughing again. And then they were kissing, and then the kissing turned into more fucking. It was hard to get out of bed once they got into it, Sammie thought. When you're hungry, it's hard to make yourself think of anything else but being hungry.

"I should get going," Sammie said, finally rolling away. "I'm probably bleeding all over your sheets."

"I don't care about that." Myra put her arms over her head and stretched. She had very soft, dimpled skin. There were stretch marks on her belly and breasts and thighs that Sammie thought looked like swirls made in frosting. She wanted to run her tongue over them some more. Instead she got up and forced herself to put on her underwear.

"You'll probably care once it soaks through and stains the mattress. Do you have any tampons?" Sammie asked, and Myra said there should be some in the cabinet under the sink in the hall bathroom.

The luxury of walking down a hallway naked, Sammie thought. Knowing that your house was all your own.

She opened up the cabinet and dug through, upsetting several rolls of toilet paper, a bag of Epsom salts, and enough boxes of Crest whitening toothpaste to keep their teeth bright through the apocalypse. Finally, a box of tampons. Regular. "Is this all you have?"

Myra came padding down the hallway. She'd put on a pair of plaid boxers and an old Florida State T-shirt with cutoff sleeves.

"I think I might have some other ones in my purse. Those are my daughter's."

"Oh," Sammie replied. "Don't worry about it, this should be fine until I get home."

She pulled down her underwear to her knees and inserted the tampon while Myra dug around in the medicine cabinet looking for something. Sammie saw mint-flavored floss, a couple of prescription bottles, Flintstones vitamins, and calamine lotion.

"Here. Sit down."

"What?"

Myra was holding a pair of scissors. "Sit. I'll trim your hair before you go."

Sammie laughed. "I thought you were joking."

"It'll take like two seconds."

"This is ridiculous," Sammie replied, but she put down the toilet seat and sat down anyway. Her knees knocked against the tub, and the air-conditioning kicked on overhead, blowing directly onto her bare skin. Her nipples crinkled and all the hair rose on her legs and arms. She felt the small hairs around her nipples rise up and thought, *I should probably pluck those when I get home.* There's nothing like someone else's harsh fluorescent bathroom light to really get you thinking about your body.

Myra brushed her hair, so gently it felt like she was barely being touched at all.

"You can be rougher than that," Sammie said, and Myra shushed her.

She hadn't gotten a haircut at a real place for a while. She used to go all the time before Samson was born. She was a regular at the salon near her apartment. Loved the smells, listening to the women talk. Loved the feeling of someone washing her hair, leaning over her, scratching their nails against her scalp. The care that came with someone being so close to her, pampering her. But after Samson—more precisely, after things went sour with Monika—it had all felt way too intimate for Sammie. Too vulnerable.

With Myra, though, her tumble into intimacy had been surprisingly swift. Even after months of texting, they hadn't seen each other that often until Sammie finally asked her to go to dinner with Monika and her girlfriend. When Myra said yes, it was as though something changed in Sammie. It was that U-Haul feeling she hadn't had in a very long time—that urge to merge. Even Sammie wasn't sure why that made such a difference. She wondered if it was because she felt terrified at the prospect of being alone, of having to do something all by herself. In the end, though, it seemed simpler than that: It was that being with Myra was so easy, so uncomplicated. Whatever Sammie suggested, she was open to it. *She said yes.* It was a heady feeling, having another person like her that much. Monika had been like that, once upon a time. Sammie was surprised to think it could happen again.

"It's so long," Myra said, and Sammie hummed in agreement. Her hair *was* long. It fell halfway down her back in a waterfall of frizz. It had *always* been long, never short.

"You could cut more off, if you want," Sammie said. "I know it's pretty damaged."

"How much?"

"As much as you want." Sammie closed her eyes. "Whatever you think would look best."

She sat there as Myra cut and shaped, feeling the gentle sweep of the woman's fingers against her neck. It could be nice, the two of them together. Agreeing on everything. Helping each other. Doing things to make each other's lives easier. She wondered what Samson would think of Myra and her big, loud laugh. The way she mispronounced the word *library* even though she went there at least once a week. Wondered what it would be like for Myra to take him to school. Go on trips. Help her purchase birthday gifts and groceries. Pick her son up from school.

Samson would think she was weird, she thought. *He'd hate her.*

The gentle sound of the scissors cutting through her hair made Sammie feel relaxed and sleepy. "Almost finished," Myra said, and then she was sweeping the strands from Sammie's bare shoulders, dusting all the trimmings onto a towel she'd spread out on the floor.

"All done?"

"There," Myra said. "It's a little different from what you're used to, but it's good."

Sammie got up off the toilet and kept her eyes closed, waiting until Myra positioned her in front of the mirror. Wanting to be surprised. Then she opened them. Myra had clipped her hair to just above her shoulders. Her new hair framed her face like a set of curtains, swinging as she turned her head slowly from left to right. Her face looked small and pale. Her eyes were huge. It was a stranger's face. Monika wouldn't recognize her. Even Samson might not, for that matter.

"Do you like it?" Myra asked, cupping her hand around Sammie's bare neck. She smiled and leaned down to kiss her ear.

Sammie burst into tears.

Donna was in the home stretch of an eight-hour shift and more than anything she wanted to crack open a beer and watch the basketball game. In her boxer shorts. No fucking shoes. She flexed her cramped toes in her sneakers, which had claimed to be orthopedic when she'd bought them, and wondered if her bruised soles could manage standing another forty minutes. A guy came up while she was making more coffee and told her that the Slurpee machine was broken. When she went to look, she saw some of the kids who'd been in earlier had jammed a bunch of straws up the nozzles of the blue raspberry and the wild cherry. Sticky puddles gathered on the floor. Tracks all around the aisles. She went to get the mop. The kids who came into the store drove her crazy. They had money. They had free time. None of them had to work part-time jobs, it seemed, though Donna'd had to do that the whole way through high school. The kid earlier who'd stolen the Slurpees made her so mad she thought she could happily kill him. She'd told his mom that he stole all the time, because it seemed like he had, because all those fucking privileged little assholes looked the same. Even if he hadn't stolen from her before, she was sure he'd done it to somebody sometime. They all did. And, no, she didn't feel bad about the look on that woman's face. Let her go home and tell her rich fucking husband that their kid was a klepto. Serves them right.

19

They decided to meet at the restaurant because they were coming from different places, but all that really meant was that they had to take four separate cars. For a moment Sammie prayed she'd be the last to arrive, just so she wouldn't have to make any awkward small talk—but then she thought about what it would be like if Monika and Myra both got there before she did, and she quickly found herself on the verge of a panic attack.

For a moment, she considered getting there twenty minutes early. Then she imagined having to sit alone with Monika's new girlfriend (*fiancée*, she corrected in her head, *with her wife's new fiancée*) and she thought she might throw up. After half an hour of hyperventilating in the shower, she came up with a workable plan: she'd go early, find a spot at the bar, and wait. She'd been there before with Monika, and she knew she could watch the door from the bar without much chance of being noticed herself. This would also give her the chance to down a glass of white wine before having to speak with anyone. Medicinal assistance, she reassured herself, for what was sure to be a stressful night.

A pile of clothes was spread out on her bed. Several shirts draped over a chair in the corner. Shoes scattered all over the floor. She'd gone online and ordered outfits from a few different places: floral dresses, brightly patterned capris (were those still a thing, did anyone under the age of fifty-five still wear capri pants?), tights and skirts and ruffly blouses. There was even a blue velvet blazer slung over her nightstand, though she absolutely would not wear that—after trying it on and standing in front of her mirror she realized she looked like a waiter in a Vegas-themed restaurant.

And she'd bought new underwear and bras, finally, as well as some things for Samson, though she hadn't given those to him yet. For some reason handing over a random package of Hanes felt unsavory. When was the right time to do it? Over breakfast? *Here, son, thought you could use these*, and chuck a stack of athletic socks across the table? Why did it feel so goddamn hard to have a normal conversation with her kid?

She tugged a black dress over her head and then stood in front of the mirror with two different shoes on her feet. She kicked back one of her legs, like a flamingo, then shifted to the other, trying to see which looked better. The clothes all felt as foreign to her body as Halloween costumes. For some wild reason, she'd thought it would be easier to choose an outfit once she had lots of new things to choose from. Instead it made everything a million times harder. When she asked Myra what she was going to wear, she'd texted back *Clothes* and a cry-face laughing emoji, and Sammie had gotten so irrationally angry at the dad joke that she clicked out of the message app altogether.

Finally, tired of changing, she left on the black dress and kept on the pair of shoes with the lower heel, already worried she might trip in the middle of the restaurant. It wasn't even that fancy a place, but she didn't want to show up looking worse than Monika's new person.

Remember when you were that new person? Remember when Monika spent all her time trying to tell you how good you looked? She called you her arm candy, remember that? How she showed you off at parties and dinners and work events? Think about how young and pretty this one must be.

Whenever she really got hard on herself, it was always her mother's voice that piped up in her head. Her mother, who never wore anything new and hardly even put on makeup and never owned a hair dryer. It wasn't just Sammie who grew up in an extremely conservative household. Her mother had, too. She'd loved the best she could, Sammie thought. Made sure she had everything she needed. It was just that she did it in a way that didn't feel good. Doling out affection in the context of strict evangelical faith meant constantly withholding tenderness if Sammie didn't perform right. That was the thing about parents: they fucked you up royally even when they were trying their best. Long after you were old enough to know better, you still sat and thought about them, allowed all the different ways they hurt you continue to shape how you felt about yourself.

A gigantic roach chose that moment to crawl out from underneath her bed. Sammie screamed, chucking her shoe at it. It missed entirely, bouncing off the side of the mattress, and the roach scuttled forth unbothered, then stalled and seemed to stare at her before scooting directly under a white linen sundress she'd left puddled at the foot of her bed.

Lizards she could deal with. Snakes, sure. Grasshoppers, mosquitoes, beetles? No problem. Even spiders didn't bother her, though she knew they freaked Monika out. Once, her wife had seen one in the car and almost drove them off the side of the highway. It took hours to calm her down.

But roaches? That was something different. As a child of Central

Florida, Sammie should have been used to them, but there was something about roaches that made her want to climb onto the nearest piece of furniture. Which is what she did, immediately, as soon as that humongous roach crawled under her dress.

Perched atop a wooden chest full of sweaters she never wore, Sammie hollered for her son, who was still in his bedroom getting ready for his shift at the bowling alley. He'd complained that Sammie hadn't washed his work pants, but Sammie told him she didn't wash anything that wasn't in the laundry basket downstairs, and he said she should know his pants needed washing, he wore them every week, and she said how was she supposed to know they needed to be washed if he didn't bring them to her, and then he said did she want people to think he smelled like a bowling alley, and she said it probably wouldn't matter if he smelled like a bowling alley because he was wearing them to a goddamn bowling alley, and then he slammed his door in her face.

The roach hadn't moved yet, but she knew that as soon as she climbed down from the chest it would run straight for her bare feet. That was the thing about roaches, they were totally unafraid. They were always perched for direct assault, like one of those ratty little terriers that seemed to think they were Dobermans.

If she was forced to think about it, she could probably admit that her hatred of cockroaches stemmed from a time in childhood when her father was out of town on a business trip and her mother, scared of bugs of any variety, had refused to kill a very large roach in the dining room. Instead of smacking it, she tried to poison it with an ancient can of Raid. As the roach lay there in its death throes, Sammie stood watching, fascinated by its gyrations. She was only four, not even in school yet, and bored most of the time. (Her mother never wanted to play with her and often took naps in the middle of the day.) She watched that roach squirming around, and then it seemed to quiet. She'd turned to tell her mother it was finally dead, but that's when she'd felt the scrabbling on her arm—a tickling, feathery feeling—and when she looked down the roach was crawling on her bare skin, heading up toward her shoulder, toward her face.

She didn't remember what happened after that, if her mother had swatted it away from her and actually crushed it, or if Sammie had just stood there screaming until it scrambled away. What Sammie did know was that she never wanted to be around roaches again. Which made living in Florida a big problem, because they were everywhere. They outnumbered the humans.

Sammie yelled for her son, louder this time. She thought she heard him coming down the hall, prayed that he might actually listen, since she sounded like she was fending off a murderer.

Monika used to kill all the roaches. She'd gladly gotten up in the middle of the night to swat one off the ceiling or from the bottom of the bathtub. She'd even picked Sammie up a few times when one had run across the ground in front of them. Let Sammie leap right into her arms, acted like she weighed nothing at all. Carried her like a bride, straight out of *An Officer and a Gentleman*. And maybe she hadn't weighed as much then as she did now, but the point was, her wife had taken her issues seriously. Back then, anyway.

But then they'd hired an exterminator to come out regularly, and they set out traps, and it hadn't mattered anymore. They weren't together in that way, and there was no need to calm someone's fears when you weren't even worried about their sadness.

A knock on her bedroom door. Finally. "It's unlocked," she yelled, looking down to see if her screaming had disturbed the roach. No movement so far.

Muffled talking. The door didn't open.

"Just come in, I'm not naked or anything."

He was saying something to her, but she couldn't make it out.

"I can't hear anything you're saying," she shouted, exasperated. "*Open the door!*"

He finally did, but just a crack. "You told me never to come in your room if the door was closed," Samson said. He was already in his work clothes. A long yellowish-orange drip had spilled down one of the legs. He was going to look slovenly at work, and Brandon would yell at Samson, and then he would wonder what kind of mother Sammie was that she let her child leave the house in such dirty clothes.

"I asked you to come in. I told you it was okay."

"I'm just trying to do what you tell me," Samson replied. "It's hard to keep things straight with you. You never know what you want."

"There's a roach, under that dress. The white one. I need you to kill it."

Samson stayed in the doorway, staring at her. "I don't see a roach."

"That's because it's under the dress. Like I said."

"Why can't you kill it?" Even though he wasn't smiling, she could tell he was enjoying the situation. Watching her freak out, terrified of a bug. For a minute she felt so mad that she almost climbed down to kill it herself. But then it occurred to her that it might be able to fly. Sometimes they did that, especially the big ones. No, she wasn't getting down unless she absolutely had to.

Samson leaned into the doorframe a little more. His bowling alley polo was dirty, too, she could see. A crusty stain near the neck that looked like he'd dripped yogurt on himself at one point, though she knew they didn't serve yogurt at the bowling alley. Ten feet away from her and she could still smell the concession counter on him: that old, embedded cigarette stink combined with fried foods. His hair was long, curled down over his collar. It looked dirty, too. Matted, like he'd been wearing a hat all day.

"You know I don't like them."

"I don't like them, either," he countered. "Nobody likes roaches. They're fucking gross."

"Don't talk that way," she said, but she talked that way all the time, and honestly she really didn't care when he did, as long as it wasn't around Monika. Her wife always got upset and called it "garbage mouth," even though she swore more than Sammie and Samson combined.

"Maybe I'm scared of them, too." He looked at her very seriously and raised his voice into a baby drawl. "I'm afwaid of a wittle bug."

"Can't you just help me without making it a struggle every goddamn time?" Her head was killing her. She still needed to finish getting ready. Put on the new makeup she'd just bought to replace the old crap she'd had for years. When she told the lady at the department store she'd been wearing mascara from ten years ago, she looked at her like she was crazy. *It's a miracle you didn't give yourself pink eye. Or blind yourself.*

Her phone pinged on the bedside table and they both looked over at it. "I need to finish getting ready, Samson," she said. "Please."

She tucked her hair behind her ears. It was a sensation she was trying to get used to, that short hair swinging around her face, getting stuck in her ChapStick. The cut didn't make her look younger. If anything, it made her look older. That's what Sammie thought, anyway. Myra loved it. Kept asking her to send pictures. Monika hadn't said anything about it—out loud, anyway—but she'd made a face before schooling her expression into bland nothingness. Monika had always loved her long hair, even when she hadn't seemed to love Sammie all that much. When Samson saw her, all he said was "You look worse" before wiping his dirty hands on the couch and turning back to watch TV. Instead of yelling at him she'd gone upstairs, climbed into her closet so no one could hear her, and cried.

Now Samson finally stepped all the way into the room and flipped up the sundress. There was the roach, bigger than she remembered. A tank of a bug, so big and old that its shiny outer coating had dulled to a dusty matte. Its wings started to flap. It was going to fly.

"Kill it!" she yelled, waiting for him to stomp it with his foot.

Instead he reached down and picked it up. With his hand. There he stood, holding the massive roach between his thumb and pointer finger, examining it from every angle.

Sammie wasn't able to form words, so she just screamed. He held it up over his face, staring at it while it squirmed.

"Huh," he said, raising and lowering it. The wings had spread when he'd picked it up, like a macabre kind of butterfly. "She looks pregnant. Lotta babies in there. A big fat roach egg, just waiting to hatch."

She was hyperventilating. Sammie crouched there, arms crossed over her chest, fingers crawling up until they covered her mouth, watching her son play with the giant roach. Suddenly her mind flashed on another memory, one she hadn't thought of for years: As a baby, Samson had found a dead roach on the kitchen floor while she'd been cooking dinner. Sammie was stirring the spaghetti sauce. It was a mushroom sauce, and she didn't even like mushrooms, but she put them in because they were Monika's favorite. She'd been watching her son out of the corner of her eye as he crawled around the floor, but then she remembered that she'd promised to make garlic bread, and she got distracted. There was a dead roach under the counter, a crispy old one she hadn't gotten around to sweeping up yet—and a minute later, when she turned around to check on him, the dead bug was gone and her son was looking at her, a roach-eating grin on his face.

If I pretend the roach was never there, it never happened, she told herself, and then she went back to stirring the sauce. All at once she was flooded with an anger that seemed to flow into everything. She hated mushrooms. She hated this mushroom sauce, and her wife for making her make it. She hated roaches, and her dirty floor—and, my God, as she watched her one-year-old clamber around, drooling onto the tile and the clean front of his red corduroy overalls, she realized she hated him, too. She hated her baby and she hated her wife, but most of all, she really hated Sammie. Then Monika came home from work and kissed her, all excited about the mushroom sauce, and she picked up their son from the floor and kissed him right on the lips.

What you got in there, buddy? she'd asked him in the goofy voice she used when he was a baby, the same sweet, dumb voice she used with Sammie when they first started dating, and then she plucked a roach leg from his tongue.

Now, in her bedroom, it was the kitchen floor all over again. Motherhood was essentially time travel, Sammie thought. Just reliving the same experiences over and over again. Especially the bad ones.

"Please," she said, watching him, watching her son watch the roach. Worried he'd put it in his mouth. Worried about what she'd do if she saw him put it in there. Throw up. Yell some more. Tell him something she couldn't take back. "Please don't."

"Don't what?" Samson asked. He walked over to her, and she put up her hands, unsure if she was defending herself from the roach or from her son.

"Stop," she said, fingers curling into fists. "I said don't."

He smiled at her then—a rare sight, but not a nice one. It was the kind of look she gave to people when she saw them being outrageously stupid. The kind of smile that was really a big *fuck you*.

"Do you know how many of these you've had me kill over the years?" he said. "Since I was in first grade. Maybe earlier and I just don't remember. Killing these things for you. And they're nothing. They're insignificant." He crushed it then. It was sudden, like snapping his fingers. The bug's guts oozed out, a sickly yellow bile. "You hate them so much and you won't do anything about it. You could kill them and you don't. Instead you do nothing. You never *do* anything."

He let go. The roach landed on the ground near a pair of new pants she'd probably never wear. Its body was nearly severed in two. Samson wiped his fingers on his dirty work pants and left the room.

Sammie stood there on the chest awhile longer. Then she grabbed the sundress and dropped it over the body of the roach so she wouldn't have to look at it anymore.

The parking lot was half empty when Sammie arrived—the restaurant had only just opened—but she still circled the lot a few times, checking for Monika's car. She didn't see it, or Myra's, so she pulled into a spot near the edge of the lot, close to the exit, so she could make a quick escape at the end of the night.

She assessed her makeup in the visor mirror. It looked . . . okay. Not great, but honestly, she hadn't known what she was doing. It had been a while since she'd worn some of that stuff. She'd tried watching some tutorials online about how to apply eyeliner, but even the simple ones had assumed she'd understand the basic principles of applying makeup. She followed the woman's instructions as best she could, but instead of winged eyeliner, she'd ended up with a long dark smudge over her eye, a curlicued mistake.

She put on more lipstick (a red called "Crime of Passion" she'd bought at Walgreens) and smacked her lips around a bit, rubbing them together like she'd seen other women do. Wasn't she femme? She was always attracted to butch women, like Monika, and when she was younger she'd loved wearing skirts and dresses and putting her hair up. So why was she so bad at making herself look pretty? It was embarrassing; she felt like a failure at being gay. Hadn't been able to be heterosexual. Couldn't do gay right. Wasn't a good mother. What exactly was she good at?

She didn't blot her lips, lest she wind up with minuscule shards of lint on her lips. Instead she fluffed up her hair—she'd curled the ends, hoping she'd look like Renée Zellweger in *Chicago*, though she worried the result was more like a deranged Shirley Temple—and climbed out of the car, slipping her purse over her shoulder.

It was the first time that summer she didn't feel smothered by the humidity. It was a beautiful balmy night, one she'd much rather have spent on her patio than on this horrifying group date. She wondered what Myra would wear and if they would look good together. At the last minute, before leaving the house, she'd taken off her black dress and put on the white linen one, then tried some too-small black pants with legs so pegged she felt like a pirate, and then put the black dress back on again. Now she wished she'd worn something else entirely.

Sammie told the bored-looking young blonde behind the hostess stand that she was there to meet a party but that she'd wait for them at the bar. She sat down and ordered a mojito, then pulled out her phone and scrolled through her texts from Myra.

Excited to see you tonight, she'd written.

Was she excited to see Myra? It was a good question. The problem was . . . she wasn't sure. It didn't feel bad with Myra. It just felt different. She didn't have those weird butterfly-sick-I-wanna-vomit feelings she'd always had with Monika. That was the actual problem, the shark circling under the surface of this new relationship: Sammie compared everything to the feelings she'd had with her ex-wife, and that made it so no one could possibly compare.

It was a nice night to be out on a date, Sammie thought. The music was soft and low. The lighting was the kind of soft, pink strobing that made everyone's skin look lit up by candle flame.

A hand appeared at the small of her back. She sat up quickly, ready to smack it away.

"Chill out," Monika said, laughing. "You're so uptight."

Sammie laughed, too, but only because it seemed like a better response than freaking out. "You scared me," she said, which was the truth, but really she'd felt transported back to the days when they came there together and Monika had done that kind of thing to her—sneaking an arm around her waist, or settling a hand at the base of her spine and leaving it there. How strange to know a person so intimately and then have them be gone from you, already attached to another body that wasn't yours.

"You're early." There were no more seats, so Monika leaned over the bar to get the bartender's attention. "I knew you'd be early."

"I'm always early," Sammie replied, which was true.

Monika ordered herself a martini, after waffling on the old-fashioned (*You know they don't make them right here*, Sammie whispered, and Monika agreed), and then they both drank in silence. For a moment it felt good, which was weird enough that they both tried to recalibrate.

"So, when does Megan get here?" Sammie said, sucking so hard at her drink that an ice cube attached itself to the bottom of the straw.

"Oh, she's already here." Monika pointed at the hostess stand. There was no one there except the same bored blonde who'd greeted her, but now she seemed much more eager. She waved over at the two of them enthusiastically.

"Wait. Megan is the hostess?"

"Yeah," Monika said. "That's her."

"Hmm," Sammie said, staring at the girl with her unlined face and her long legs all shiny with lotion. "How's it feel?"

"How does what feel?"

Sammie laughed and put her hand on Monika's arm, watching Megan's face, which squinched up to show how not-cool she was with it. "How does it feel to be dating someone closer to Samson's age than your own?"

"Don't be like that." Monika downed the rest of her drink. "Let's be civil."

"Sure," Sammie replied. Then she ordered another mojito and checked her phone. No text from Myra yet, but that could mean anything. Probably still on her way. Sammie had no idea if Myra was an early bird like she was or perpetually late like Monika. That was the fun of getting to know a new love interest, wasn't it? Discovering the little details along the way. She finished her drink and paid out the tab with Monika's credit card. They walked over to the hostess stand together.

"Sammie, Megan. Megan, Sammie." Monika gestured between the two of them, as if this were some kind of PTA meeting where all that mattered was the new person's observed role: Parent to so-and-so. Bringer of gluten-free cupcakes.

"Hey." Megan smiled tightly. "How's it going?"

"Fine." Sammie offered the exact same smile in return.

"Great," Monika said. She didn't smile at all.

After several tense moments, Sammie asked Megan how long she'd been working at the restaurant. "Two years," Megan replied, and then smiled again, this time with teeth, and looked at Monika. "We met here."

"That's nice," Sammie said. She personally thought it was kind of tacky that Monika would pick up a woman—a very *young* woman—at her place of business. But then Monika had a way of getting away with things that would get anyone else in trouble.

Sammie didn't bother hiding her disdain. Monika rolled her eyes. Megan stood fiddling with a pen. Sammie wanted to snatch it from her and throw it across the restaurant, but it was chained to the stand.

"Sorry I'm late! Traffic was awful."

Sammie turned around and there was Myra coming through the entryway, waving. She looked good, Sammie thought. Handsome. Myra jostled past a couple with a toddler, who was trying to pull leaves off a giant fern, and came to join them at the hostess stand. Myra kissed Sammie's cheek carefully, avoiding her lipstick, then introduced herself to Monika, shaking her hand. The two of them were wearing nearly identical blazers and black pants. They even had the same haircut, except that Myra's was a little scruffier and less curly, maybe a shade or two lighter. They both wore glasses that looked like they'd come straight from Instagram.

Monika introduced Megan and then Megan smiled hugely at Myra, which aggravated Sammie. Too many *M* names; she was sure she was going to call Megan something awful, like Missy or Mandy or Mariah. Myra mentioned the traffic again, and Megan laughed inexplicably. Even Monika grimaced at the exchange.

Oh, this is gonna be fun, Sammie thought, and then Megan led them out onto the patio.

It was beautiful next to the lake. The sun was beginning to set, and light glanced off the water, glinting gold and silver in the wake of a nearby pontoon boat. It was the kind of lazy Florida evening when it might be nice to sit out on a dock and palm a sweaty drink, holding hands with someone. Spend a lazy hour watching the birds fly out over the cattails, the anhingas drying their wings on the shore, slick-wet from diving for their dinner.

Instead the four of them walked to a table overlooking the water, so uncomfortable that they couldn't even appreciate the breeze circling the deck.

Samson would love this, she thought. *Watching how awkward we all are.* She wondered what it would be like to have the kind of relationship with your son where she could sit down and trade stories about what terrible evenings you'd both had. The kind that could turn into a real adult friendship.

Gilmore Girls *was a lie*, she thought.

Megan and Monika sat down on the side of the table that faced the condos along the lakefront. Sammie scooched into her seat, and Myra sat next to her, facing out toward the open water. A trio of ducks paddled lazily toward them, skirting the nearby reeds.

"It's nice of them to let you have dinner while you're in the middle of a shift," Sammie said, unfolding her napkin and spreading it over her lap.

"You work here?" Myra asked. Megan said she wasn't actually on shift, she'd just agreed to watch the hostess stand for one of her friends for a few minutes while she waited for everyone to get there.

"Oh," Sammie said, and just like that, they'd run out of things to talk about.

A waiter came over to take their drink orders. Sammie sat silently, taking everything in. Megan wore a short red dress, low-cut, and her hair was the kind of blond mop that people only had in shampoo commercials. Sammie bet she had to use those extra-thick elastic bands to put up her hair. She also had one of those necklaces that certain girls always wore—*girls*, that's right, not women—that was delicate and gold and held a pendant that spelled out her name in blingy gold script.

I bet Monika bought it for her, Sammie thought, which made her angry all over again, because Monika had never bought her a single piece of jewelry. She'd even had to pick out her own engagement ring because Monika said she wouldn't know what would look best on Sammie's hand. When she chose an opal, Monika was surprised. *I never would have chosen that for you*, she'd said. When Sammie asked what she would have chosen, Monika had just shrugged and said, *I dunno, maybe a diamond?*

Sammie looked at Megan's hand and, yes, there was the ring, sitting on her perfectly manicured finger. And it wasn't a diamond—it was a very large opal. Bigger than Sammie's.

"I like your ring," Sammie said, pointing at it with her pinky. She had already finished half her wine.

"Thanks," Megan said. "It's really special to me."

"I bet," Sammie replied, and when Megan looked confused, Sammie just smiled and stared at Monika, who was focusing intently on the bread basket.

"The bread here is really good," she said.

Myra said she loved dark bread, and Monika said it was especially good with the butter, which had little traces of local honey.

"They make it with orange blossoms," Megan added.

Myra nodded and said she'd heard that local honey could cure allergies. Monika said that she'd heard that, too, but wasn't sure if it was true.

Myra reached over and took Sammie's hand, which was bunched into a fist in her lap.

"Could I have another glass of wine?" Sammie asked the server, and Monika said make it a bottle.

Sammie felt grateful, then mad at herself for feeling that way.

Myra was telling a story about a school trip her daughter had taken to St. Augustine in the spring.

"What grade is she in?" Monika asked, and when Myra told her, she said, "Oh, my son's a sophomore in high school."

"Our son," Sammie corrected. "And he's not a sophomore. He's going to be a junior this fall. His sophomore year is over, remember?"

"I know that. But he's still technically a sophomore. That's the last grade he finished."

Megan cut in to say how much she'd loved high school, that she'd been in the color guard her junior year. Sammie picked up her wineglass to stop herself from asking how long ago that was. Myra said she'd been in marching band; Monika had, too, playing the saxophone. Sammie finished her drink and signaled to the waiter for a refill, even though they were already waiting on a bottle.

They ordered food when the server came back with the bottle of wine, and Sammie told him he should bring another when this one ran low. Megan said she probably wouldn't be having too much to drink, anyway, so Sammie could have her share. Monika put her arm around the back of Megan's chair, and the woman leaned into Monika, nuzzling into her like a kitten.

That's what Megan reminded her of, Sammie realized: a helpless little kitten. She looked like one of those very young women who'd been straight all her life until she met Monika. Her wife had an affinity for finding "straight" women and serving as their introduction to queer life. Sammie sometimes wondered if she was just looking for women who wouldn't know any better.

"You feel okay?" Myra put her hand on Sammie's thigh. Sammie wanted to scream, but instead she patted Myra's hand and told her she felt terrific, which was a lie.

"Two glasses of wine," she said. "I should eat something."

"Here," Myra said, cutting open one of the small dark loaves and slathering butter across the warm, soft middle.

"Doesn't Sammie's hair look good?" she said.

"You don't have to do that," Sammie whispered.

Monika nodded. "It does look good," she said. "Just . . . different."

"Different?"

"Yeah, I'm just not used to it."

Sammie frowned. "What's there to get used to?"

Out came the server with their food.

Thank God, Sammie thought, using her clam pasta to distract herself from the women sitting across from her.

"So how long have you two been dating?" Myra asked. Sammie was so tense it felt like her shoulders were lodged up around her ears. She felt Myra put her arm around her back and tried to relax into it.

"About eight months," Megan said. Monika picked up her free hand and kissed the back of it.

"That's sweet," Myra said, and Sammie restrained herself from rolling her eyes. The trio of ducks that had been out near the boats in the middle of the water had paddled over to the edge of the patio. Megan cooed at them, then took some bread and started dropping hunks of it into the water. They quacked and splashed, ducking under to try and snap them up before the fish could get them.

"Bread is actually bad for ducks," Sammie said, taking a bite of pasta. "It's not good nutrition for them."

"How long have you two been dating?" Monika asked, handing Megan another piece of bread for the ducks.

"Three months and two weeks," Myra said.

She'd been keeping track? Sammie was shocked. Was she counting from the time they made out by the parking garage downtown? Was that their first date? Or was it the first time they made small talk in the dating app?

How horrible, Sammie thought.

"It's too bad Samson couldn't make it," Megan said, dusting off her hands. Crumbs rained down on the ducks' heads.

"He had work," Sammie said, but what she thought was, *I'd rather set myself on fire than let you talk to my kid.*

"I know, I just feel like I should get to know him a little better. Before we live together," Megan said.

Sammie's brain dissolved into fuzzy white static. "What?"

Monika wouldn't look at Sammie. She was staring down at her plate—she'd picked the short ribs, even though she'd always hated eating anything that messy in public—and Sammie thought, *This is what it feels like to go crazy, I am gonna lose it.*

The ducks had given up on Megan and had drifted over to the table next to them. An elderly couple was sharing a single plate and passing bites of steak back and forth to each other. One of them threw down a cube of meat to the ducks.

Ducks can't eat beef, can they? she wondered idly.

"I mean, I broke my lease with my shitty roommate anyway," Megan went on. "And now I won't have to live with my mom anymore."

"Right," Sammie replied. "How convenient for you."

She couldn't believe Monika had done this. Solved the problem of her girlfriend's living situation by moving her directly into Sammie's home. Monika was still looking down, fiddling with her napkin.

"It just makes the most sense. I can move right into the house, right away. Easiest for everyone."

"Congratulations," Myra said, and held her wineglass up like she might give a toast.

Sammie squeezed her own glass so hard that it shattered in her palm.

Megan loved holding Monika's hand. There was something so beautiful about her girlfriend's fingers. Fiancée, she corrected herself, so giddy she wanted to bounce in her seat. She forced herself to calm down and took a sip of water. She watched Monika handle the knife. Butter the bread. Fold those perfect fingers neatly inside a napkin. Megan had never felt like this before. Not with her last girlfriend, Sarah, and definitely not with her first and only boyfriend, James. Monika was sweet and thoughtful. She always sent Megan flowers, even had them delivered to work. And Megan thought the dinner with her ex-wife was going really well! It was a relief to finally meet this other woman, a huge part of Monika's life, and feel completely relaxed about the whole thing. She liked Sammie, who seemed really smart, if a little quiet, and she very much liked Myra, who was like a big teddy bear. It was so nice to think about having a built-in family. Megan's parents had divorced when she was only two, and she didn't have any siblings. Her parents lived on opposite sides of the country and she had moved down to Florida, alone, just a few years ago, after that awful breakup with Sarah. She'd been brokenhearted. So lonely. But now here she was, happily engaged to a beautiful woman who loved her. A woman with a kid! Megan loved kids, and Samson sounded terrific. And she had friends from the restaurant, but now she could have these people, too. Sammie and Myra. Samson. A whole new life. She looked at Monika and smiled. Huge, happy grin. Everything was perfect.

20

It wasn't a bad enough cut to go to the hospital, Sammie kept saying, but Myra insisted on taking her to urgent care if she wouldn't go to the emergency room. They waited on padded chairs behind an elderly woman in a pink plastic raincoat nursing a fractured arm and a young mother with a boy who was hacking and wheezing his way through a garden-variety cold. The kid was touching everything in sight—magazines, doorknobs, windowpanes—even though his mother kept telling him to sit down.

Sammie was still tipsy—nearly full-on drunk, if she was being honest—and the fluorescent lights overhead were giving her a migraine. She rested her head on Myra's shoulder and pretended she was drifting off to sleep, just to keep Myra from asking her anything about what had happened at the restaurant.

By the time the harried woman in a white lab coat had taken a look at her hand, the cut was already sealing shut. The woman gave it a cursory cleaning and then wrote her a prescription for a painkiller and some kind of antibiotic, in case it got infected by the wine or anything else that might have seeped inside.

"You can't drink with either of these prescriptions," the woman advised, obviously smelling the booze on Sammie's breath. "No mixing painkillers with alcohol, especially."

"I won't," Sammie replied, though she wanted nothing more than to go home and lose herself in a follow-up bottle of wine. Maybe even tequila, she thought. It had been a minute since she'd really gone to town on tequila—not since the first night of her honeymoon, in fact, when she and Monika had done shots with everyone at the bar: the couple at the next table, strangers on dates, even the bartender. She'd puked for hours afterward, and Monika had been there to smooth her hair back from her forehead, bring her seltzer, get her the only hangover remedy that ever really worked: a big pack of plain M&Ms, which she fed to her one by one until Sammie felt better again. Then they had dinner out on their balcony and watched the sunset. *My life is a movie*, Sammie remembered thinking, *this is the most romantic anything will ever get*, and maybe she was right.

"Let me take you home," Myra said, walking her out to the parking lot. She'd driven Sammie to urgent care, leaving her car back at the restaurant. "Or you can stay at my place."

Mostly Sammie wanted to get her car, but she absolutely didn't want Myra thinking she needed to take care of her. She didn't want to stay at Myra's place, didn't want to talk about anything that had happened. "Home, please. I just want to go to bed."

Myra took her back to the house, following Sammie's directions.

"This is nice," Myra said as she pulled into the long, curved driveway.

Sammie looked up at the house, where she'd built a life with her family, and thought, *Yes, absolutely, this is nice. Maybe the nicest anything will ever be for me.* The porch lights were flickering and warm.

The azalea bushes that lined the windows were in full bloom, sprays of pink and white hovering like ghosts in the moonlight. The dark shutters gave the house a sleepy look. It was a comfortable house. Her house.

"I think we should talk," Myra said, and Sammie closed her eyes and wished herself anywhere else. Teleported out of the car, flying through the air, landing anywhere—Ireland, Australia, even Phoenix, Arizona. She'd never been to Phoenix, but she'd had a friend in elementary school who visited her grandmother there on winter holidays. It seemed nice. Warm and dry. She'd never seen a cactus in real life. Were they even real? Weird, spiny little freaks.

"About what?" Sammie finally asked.

Myra said she wasn't exactly sure, but it seemed like something was wrong.

"Yeah, I cut my hand on a wineglass."

"That's not what I mean. You and your ex-wife . . . it was very uncomfortable."

"We're always very uncomfortable."

Myra sighed. Sammie wanted to sigh, too, but managed to hold it in.

"I'm just saying, I understand. The weirdness. It's just—you two were together a long time, right?"

"I guess."

"You guess? You were. So it must be strange to see her with a new person she's serious about."

"Yes." Sammie agreed. It was—completely surreal. Like being dropped into a bizarre dream. "It was."

"But the way you acted . . . I guess I'm wondering if maybe you still have feelings for her."

"I don't," Sammie said. Which was true enough, because she didn't have feelings for Monika as she was now—the Monika who'd come to the restaurant for a date with her girlfriend. She had feelings for the

Monika who married her. The one who was sweet and thoughtful, who'd taken care of her for so long. Who'd raised a son with her. Where was *that* person?

"I think you do. Maybe you still need time to figure things out for yourself. Be alone and understand what's going on in your own brain."

"Oh, great. So now—after I've already had to go to urgent care because I sliced up my hand like a piece of roast beef, after I ruined dinner for everyone—now you're going to break up with me, too? Right here, sitting in my own driveway?"

"That's not what I'm saying."

Sammie laughed. She felt on the verge of something, she wasn't quite sure what. Her body was all worked up from the injury. Her ex-wife was engaged to a woman practically her son's age. Soon, she realized, she'd be without a home—literally homeless. And now the woman she'd let cut all her hair off in a bathroom was going to break up with her.

She took a breath. Composed herself a little. "I was just . . . surprised. I didn't know about any of the things that were brought up tonight, and it was all pretty startling. We have a kid together. I don't know what all of this is going to look like, and it scares me."

Myra put her hand on Sammie's shoulder and squeezed. "I know that. I get it."

"Then please just be patient about this. Give me this one."

When Myra didn't respond, Sammie pulled out the big guns.

"I'm just worried about my son."

"Okay," Myra said, pulling her in for a hug. "Okay, yes."

"Thank you," she said, and declined when Myra offered to stay there with her for a little while. She stood at the front door, on her welcome mat that read HOME TO STAY, and dug into her purse with her one good hand, searching for her keys. Myra waited until she was all the way inside before Sammie saw her headlights backing out of the driveway.

Monika wasn't home. No lights on in the entryway, none on any-where in the house. Sammie went into the kitchen, poured herself a big glass of water, and took some of her medication. Her hand didn't hurt that badly, though tomorrow morning it probably would throb and pulse, and she'd feel maybe everything a little too much.

She took her water out onto the back porch and waited for her pain-killer to kick in. She didn't want to think about what happened at the restaurant, but she knew it wouldn't matter if she did or not—it was all going to happen regardless. Because Monika had decided something, and when Monika decided a thing it meant that thing was going to happen.

The cicadas were shrieking high in the trees. A large bird, probably an owl, swooped down low and made a pass across the bushes, search-ing for prey. The sky was still clear of clouds, and for once Sammie could see the stars, gleaming in the night like tiny rips in velvet. She lit a citronella candle and sprayed herself with some OFF! to keep the mos-quitoes away. She looked over at the house behind them, where the woman had lived with her dogs—that woman she'd felt compelled to spy on, wondering about her life. Maybe wanting her life, the ease of it. A life built around things that Sammie wanted. Not Monika. Not Samson.

Because that was the thing: What had been decided was that Megan was moving in to the house. They would be married at some point, but that wasn't the issue. The issue was that Megan was moving in to Sam-mie's house, and that meant that Sammie could no longer live in it.

No one had actually voiced that part aloud, but it sat there regard-less, the thing that made all of it so awful. Because it meant leaving the place that was hers, but it also meant leaving the only life she'd really known. Then there was Samson. It meant her son would have this new person in his life. Someone young and beautiful—Sammie could admit that to herself. Even if the girl did have rabbity teeth that made her top lip poke out. Even if one of her ears stuck out a little sharply from the side of her head. Maybe that's why she kept her hair long, to cover it? Sammie touched one of her own ears and thought they were nicely proportioned. The woman had a weak chin, too. A Picasso face, Sammie decided. No, she wasn't all that pretty.

She realized her painkillers were kicking in. Her mind wouldn't stick to a single topic, kept slipping from one to the next—a feeling like she was on the verge of sleep, where she couldn't tell what was a dream and what was real life. *I wasn't supposed to take them yet*, she thought, remembering the drinks she'd had. Not supposed to take them with alcohol. Her stomach that night was essentially a box of wine.

She drank some more water and let herself drift. The pain in her palm was starting to blossom, working its way up her arm until everything radiated heat. Samson had busted his head open once. She watched the memory in her mind, eyes closed, like a tiny TV screen playing behind her lids. Three-year-old Samson, galloping around the living room on a tennis racket. Monika's racket, though she didn't play anymore, but she refused to get rid of any of the equipment. Samson riding around on that racket like it was a pony, wearing only a diaper and one of Sammie's college T-shirts, even though he was getting too old for diapers by that point, and Sammie hated changing him so much that she nearly cried every time. Round and round he galloped, Monika cheering him on, until he tripped and fell face-first into the corner of the coffee table, the glass one that Monika loved and Sammie hated, ultramodern and hideous. His forehead burst open, and blood sprayed everywhere: on the carpet, on the glass, on the shirt. It streamed down his face, ran into his eyes, ran everywhere.

That's when he started screaming. Not yelling at the impact of the fall, it seemed, but at the unsettling sting of his own blood welling up under his lashes. Sammie picked him up and cradled him, pressing her own shirt against the wound while Monika ran to call 911. When she looked at her baby's broken face that day, Sammie realized for the first time that she was incapable of handling any of it. Then she'd burst into tears, too. Shocked by the fact that a person she could love so fiercely could draw such agony out of her as well.

He'd gotten five stitches in his forehead, and once the wound closed up and healed and he got sun on his face and tanned, it was barely visible. Just one of the many scars they'd gifted him. She rubbed her fingers against her own wrist, feeling for the one he'd given her, but it had faded, too. His bite mark had never been as visible as the ones she'd put on him, that marked him as her own. They were Sammie's gift to Samson, a mark of their connection. Because she was the one who had given birth to him, hadn't she? She was the one he really belonged to, after all.

The bird made another pass across the yard, swooping down this time to take something live from the ground—a rat, maybe, or a mouse. A live thing that screamed when it was grabbed. Sammie watched the bird lift off, heavy with its meal, and the shrieks silenced almost immediately.

She woke to more screaming.

Not yelling. That she knew intimately. How it made a throat sound like it was trying to cough life into an argument. Theirs was a household that yelled often: when someone forgot to lock the front door at night, when someone left the oven on after cooking a frozen pizza, when someone didn't clean right, cook right, speak right, act right.

Yelling, Sammie was used to. This wasn't yelling. It was screaming.

She stood up wobbly from the patio chair, grabbing the table when her knees buckled. Her glass of water overturned, spilling off the side and down her legs.

"Fuck," she whispered, voice thick, and pressed her hand against the table for support.

She hadn't meant to fall asleep. Didn't think it was possible—not with all the thoughts roiling around in her head about her wife and her son and where she would live and what was going to happen next—but the medication she'd popped had taken care of that. She wasn't sure what time it was. Late, it seemed, though it could have been any hour. The stars were still out, though they appeared smeary to her sleep-smudged eyes. She looked through the window at the neighbor's house and saw the lights were on.

Sammie smacked her face to wake herself up. She was really out of it. Still under her heavy blanket of wine and painkillers. Her injured hand mercifully felt numb, though she thought that might not be a good thing.

"Probably not," she said, and realized she was voicing her thoughts aloud.

Why had she woken up? The screaming, which was back after a brief intermission. Even at their worst, she'd never heard Monika make a sound like that. It couldn't have been Samson, too high-pitched. It sounded like a cat being strangled.

She was so thirsty, she wished she hadn't spilled her water. When she stood up, the world swayed in front of her, like she was standing on the prow of a ship. She worried she might throw up.

"Oh, I did throw up," Sammie said, then puked again off the side of the deck into the bougainvillea. When she picked her head up again, a thorn scraped her face, hard enough to draw blood.

She felt a little clearer then, if not exactly better, and wiped at her mouth with the back of her hand. She carried the empty cup over to the sliding glass door. When she slid it open, the noise overwhelmed her.

Samson and Monika were standing at the entrance to the kitchen. All the lights were on now, blinding Sammie, who felt as if she were walking through a dream. Her plastic baggies from the urgent care were flung out on the counter where she'd dropped them. The painkiller bottle was turned on its side, and some of the pills had spilled out.

"What," she said, putting a hand to her throat. "What?"

Neither of them paid her any attention. She wasn't even sure they'd noticed her. Monika was gesturing wildly, as if she were directing an orchestra. Samson was pushing his head back against the doorframe every time Monika said something, rolling his entire skull as if rolling his eyes just wasn't enough. Every time Samson did it, Monika's voice got louder, until she was screaming again.

Sammie tossed her glass down into the sink and it burst into a million pieces.

"Second broken glass of the night," she said. "Probably very bad luck. Or is that just with mirrors?"

Monika and Samson both stared at her. Good, she had their attention.

"Yes, you have our attention," Monika said.

Wait, Sammie thought, *am I still voicing my thoughts aloud?*

"Yes, you're still talking."

Her wife's face was bright red. It looked like she'd been crying, which was unlike her.

"I'm your ex-wife," Monika said, wiping at her face with her sleeve.

No, she wasn't, Sammie thought, they hadn't gotten divorced yet.

"It'll get done."

Sammie picked up the largest pieces of glass very carefully with her good hand. *Better get that done soon*, she thought, *you're already engaged to someone else.*

Monika shut her eyes, hard, and breathed in and out through her mouth. Her fists were balled up just like Samson's. Maybe they had more in common than Sammie thought.

"We're not anything alike," Samson said. He was still wearing his bowling alley uniform—the outfit she'd neglected to wash for him just a few hours earlier. Had all of that been today? Standing on the chest while he killed the roach? Sitting at dinner with her ex-wife's fiancée? It felt longer. Samson's clothes were even dirtier now, though. They were covered in stains. A lot of bright yellow.

"Your son," said Monika. Somehow she managed to stress both *your* and *son*, which Sammie found impressive.

"My son," Sammie replied, pointing at the stains. "Got in a food fight?"

"Your son," Monika repeated, "got in a food fight, yes, but he also spit directly in a girl's face."

"The same one from before?"

"The very goddamn same."

"Well . . . that's not good," Sammie said.

No shit, Monika said with a look.

"It's not that big a deal," Samson said, and Monika turned to face him again.

"You got fired. They had to call the police."

"I didn't go to jail or anything."

"You didn't *go to jail* or anything?" Monika laughed, but it came out loud and forced, a bark that hurt Sammie's ears. "It doesn't matter. I stuck up for you last time. We both did. Your boss is a friend of ours. You embarrassed us."

"I didn't embarrass Mom. I embarrassed you." Samson was kicking at the doorframe with the heel of his sneaker, leaving dirty scuffs on the white woodwork. Normally Sammie would have been upset at this, probably yelled at him for it, but now everything felt smudged and hazy, like someone was kicking her brain with the sole of a sneaker. *Let him kick*, she thought, and then Monika told her not to encourage him.

"Encourage me? When has anyone *ever* encouraged me?" Samson said, kicking his foot harder than ever. "No one gives a fuck in this house."

"That's not true," Monika argued, even as Sammie was nodding along with Samson.

"See? Even Mom knows it's true." Samson stopped kicking and started pacing.

Sammie couldn't remember the last time she'd seen her son this animated. He was so in his own head most of the time. So separate from her.

"What the fuck does that even mean?" Samson asked, and Monika told him to shut his mouth.

"Don't talk to him like that," Sammie said, and moved carefully around the island to reach the cupboard. She pulled down a glass and poured herself some more water. She was so very thirsty.

"You're so *drunk*," Monika countered. "You're always so drunk."

"Well, you're not wrong," Sammie said.

"You know this is your fault." Monika pointed at her, and Sammie tried to focus on that finger, which was wobbling in and out of focus.

"My fault? How?"

"You're the reason he's like this."

"Like what?" Samson asked. "A normal person? Not two freaks pretending to play house?"

Sammie took a huge gulp of her water. Some of it splashed down her chin. She swiped at it and missed most of it. Her shirt was drenched. "Wow, he's got us pegged."

"Stop it. We need to be on the same side."

Sammie tried to sit down on one of the kitchen stools, but her aim was bad and she slid off the edge, directly onto the floor. It hurt. The zing started in her tailbone, a bolt of electricity stinging up along her spine until it left her mouth as a prolonged yelp.

No one came to help her up, so Sammie struggled to her knees, trying to keep her bandaged hand out of the puddles. She set the glass on the floor and tried to remember not to kick it over. "Glass, don't kick," she said.

"God, you're pathetic." Monika was looking at her like she wanted to punch her in the face.

Good, Sammie thought, and didn't care if she'd said it aloud.

"You're the one who's dating someone Samson's age," Sammie countered. "Oh, wait. Not dating, remember? Engaged."

Monika scrubbed a hand through her hair and it stuck up wildly on her head, poking out over her ears like an owl. "Why would you mention that in front of him?"

"Are you joking? You're the one who's kicking me out of the house and bringing in some toddler you're planning to marry. Someone he doesn't even know."

Suddenly, Sammie felt tired—more tired than she'd ever felt in her life. More tired than when she left home for the first time after telling her parents she was gay. More tired than she'd felt after giving birth, lying in that hospital bed, wondering if her body would ever work right again. She hadn't even been able to pee alone. A nurse had to help her, tell her to "imagine squeezing a water balloon" between her legs. Now she wet herself a little if she sneezed too hard.

"We'll figure it out," Monika said, but she wasn't looking at either of them, not Sammie or Samson, so it was obviously a lie. She said as much to Monika, who immediately started screaming again.

Sammie, for once, felt in control of her emotions. This time, it was Monika whose face was red, whose eyes were leaking tears. And she was swearing, not just at Sammie but at both of them. Sammie understood it was the mixture of painkillers and alcohol that allowed her some perspective. She found herself comfortably above everything. As if she were up on the ceiling, looking down on the whole mess below.

Monika noticed the bottle on the counter. She picked it up and shook it, spilling the rest. "You took painkillers with alcohol? Are you fucking insane?" Pills plinked off the counter and flew all over the floor.

"You're a psychopath," Samson said to Monika. He crouched down and helped Sammie pick up the pills, which warmed her heart.

He's helping me.

"Yeah I'm helping you. Mom's being crazy."

Monika took a deep breath. "I'm not being *crazy*!" The last word came in a piercing shriek, so loud that Sammie clapped her good hand over one of her ears.

"You sound crazy to me," Sammie said. Yelling that you weren't crazy made a person seem crazy, in her opinion.

"I want you out of here by the end of the month," Monika said. "Do you hear me? By the end. Of the *month*."

"You can't do that," Sammie spat back. "These are my things. My kid. This is my house, too."

"Your house? You don't own shit, Samandra." Monika paced, crushing some of the pills with her heel. "I'm the one with an actual job. I pay the mortgage. You don't even have any credit. You use all my cards. You spend *my* money."

"I have a job," Sammie said, which was true.

"That is not a job, it's a hobby."

Monika watched her try to put a single pill into the bottle with her good hand. "Who. Gives. A. Fuck." She punctuated each word by stomping down on one of Sammie's pills.

Sammie felt like she was watching a bad Lifetime original of her life. Who would play her? She'd hope for somebody like Julia Roberts, but she'd probably end up with Mayim Bialik. She could imagine it all playing out: Starting out in the church, a closeted baby gay. Conservative parents who refused to understand her. Whirlwind romance and marriage to Monika, the two of them kissing on a beach as the sun set, liquid fire over the ocean. Then real life sets in. Play up the lost-baby angle, maybe. *But she was my daughter, don't you understand? I lost her; I lost my only daughter.*

"If you mention that baby one more time, I swear to Christ I will lose it."

Sammie was holding a pill she couldn't manage to get back in the bottle, so she set it on the counter. "I can talk about the baby whenever I want. Just because you don't care doesn't mean I don't still have pain over it."

Monika scraped her fingernails down her face, digging red welts into her cheeks. It was disturbing, Sammie thought. Her wife looked like that painting *The Scream*. Samson must have thought so, too, because he stopped attempting to pick up the pills and scooted back until he was nearly sitting on Sammie's feet.

"There was no baby. How many times do I have to tell you this? There was only Samson."

"Of course there was a baby," Sammie replied. "Just because she wasn't born alive doesn't mean she wasn't real."

"There was no baby, Samandra." Monika clapped her hands together, a sound sharp as a shot. "You were spotting during the middle of your pregnancy. Then you came up with the twin idea and were so adamant about it, so goddamn hysterical, the doctor worried you were going to have a breakdown. We just let you believe it."

Sammie saw a hole open up on the floor in front of her, a big, dark sinkhole, and realized she was on the cusp of blacking out. "I can't believe you'd say that."

"I'm just sick of it," Monika said, but she looked shaken. Her cheeks were still red from where she'd scraped at them. "I just want to be honest."

"Honest!" Sammie laughed at that, or thought she was going to laugh, until she realized that the seal-bark noise she was making was a precursor to crying. Not normal crying, either. The bad kind of crying where she was going to have a panic attack.

"I should have said it more nicely," Monika said, but Sammie pushed past her, out of the room. Headed for the stairs.

If I can just get to my room, I can go to sleep, she thought. *If I can just climb into bed, I can pretend this is all a nightmare. Something that didn't happen. Pretend this person I once loved more than myself wouldn't hurt me so badly.*

"This isn't my fault!" Monika said, trailing after her.

Sammie bounded up the stairs, but Monika was coming up fast behind her. "You can't handle real honesty. You make us all live in limbo because you can't deal with change."

"I need sleep," Sammie said. She was going into shock. The pain medication and the wine, her hand, now this, her wife telling her something that couldn't possibly be true. Could it?

"You're not a child, Sammie. I shouldn't have to treat you like one." Monika grabbed her arm, held her there. They were halfway up the staircase. Sammie was a few steps above Monika, closer to the top of the landing. She swayed on her feet, dizzy. Her body still hurt from her accident, but now so did her insides.

"Let go of me," she said, and Monika told her no.

Samson was standing at the bottom of the stairs, looking up at both of them. His mouth was open, like he wanted to say something, but then he just closed it again. He looked scared, Sammie thought. He looked like a little kid.

"We have to talk about this." Monika shook her. When Sammie struggled to pull away, Monika shook her again, harder. Her breath was heavy in Sammie's face. It smelled like dinner, that garlicky, uncomfortable dinner with Megan. It was making Sammie sick. She worried she was going to puke again.

Samson was starting up the stairs, yelling at the two of them. Telling them to stop it.

"Look at me when I'm talking to you!" Monika shook her one last time, hard enough that Sammie's teeth cracked together and her vision went dark.

I have to get away, Sammie thought, terrified, and then she yanked her arm as hard as she could, pushing Monika off at the same time, and her arm was suddenly free.

There was a sound, a falling away. Sammie closed her eyes, taking a few deep, calming breaths, and leaned against the banister for support. When she looked down, past her son, there was Monika at the bottom of the stairs. Crumpled in a heap. Leg bent beneath her.

It had happened so quickly. One minute her wife was there, shaking her, and then she was gone. Samson ran up the stairs and took her arm, the one her wife had grasped so tight. Too tightly. Her wife, her son. Wife and son.

Samson's eyes were all pupil. Those eyes that looked so much like hers. He was touching her gently, just barely supporting her. His face. The indentation in his chin that looked just like her own father's chin. The small curl of hair that flipped over his collar.

"Your hair is getting so long," she whispered, and he flinched away.

Monika groaned from the floor. Moved around for a moment, then settled and whimpered.

"Go wait in your room," Sammie said, and watched her son walk up the stairs. Head bowed. Legs long, arms swinging. A man. A boy. Hers. Her body. Her human. Samson. Part of her. She rubbed her wrist. Thumbed the scar and felt the flick of it slip through her veins. She wasn't sure if ghosts were real, but she believed in magic. Wasn't motherhood a sleight of hand?

"Sammie," Monika moaned. She was waving her arms across the floor, making shapes. A Florida starfish. The leg that wasn't bent behind her was kicking, contracting in lazy little pumps, like it was trying to move on its own. That was a leg she'd held on to, licked, embraced. It was a leg that had wrapped around her when they fucked, that kicked the front door shut that one time they'd come home, running to get out of the rain, kissing each other's wet faces.

"Help me," Monika said. She looked up at Sammie, eyes big and liquid. Scared. "Please. Sammie. I'm hurt."

I'm hurt, Sammie thought.

Fall

The man took her son's hand and walked casually toward the playground exit.

ground exit.

That's what she remembered, anyway.

MISSING CHILD FOUND AFTER ALLEGED "JOYRIDE"

A missing Seminole County child has turned up after a frantic two-day search. Six-year-old Damon Bradshaw was last spotted walking home from the dog park in his neighborhood with the family's golden retriever. After two days of searching, parents reported that the child rang the doorbell of his own home. According to police, the child claims a man in a "big truck" allowed him to use the truck's radio, but they refused to answer further questions.

BODY OF SEVEN-YEAR-OLD RECOVERED IN LAKE MARY RESERVOIR

The body of a seven-year-old was pulled from a nearby reservoir in Orange County early yesterday morning after a jogger noticed an "odd smell" coming from the reeds. The body has been identified as missing seven-year-old Kissimmee resident Hunter Timmons. Blake and Nora Timmons, of Osceola County, have been searching for their son for over a year. He was last seen leaving his elementary school. Reports state that he climbed into the truck of an unknown driver, a man described as "approximately forty years old, scruffy dark beard, white baseball cap, sunglasses."

OSCEOLA COUNTY MAN ARRESTED AFTER
ATTEMPTED CHILD ABDUCTION

A 44-year-old Kissimmee man has been arrested for attempted child abduction today in Seminole County. Charges were filed against John Taylor Soblevski after a six-year-old Altamonte Springs boy was discovered in his truck in a Denny's parking lot. A patron of the restaurant spotted the boy sitting alone in the cab crying and notified the police. The boy had been declared missing by his parents three days earlier.

JOHN TAYLOR SOBLEVSKI OF OSCEOLA COUNTY
TO SERVE EIGHT YEARS

John Taylor Soblevski was found guilty of child abduction and child rape in the case of a six-year-old Altamonte Springs boy earlier this year. Soblevski, who pled not guilty to all charges, was found guilty by a jury after only two days of deliberation. Soblevski's attorney has stated that they plan to appeal the conviction.

CONVICTED SEXUAL OFFENDER
KILLED IN RIOT

John Taylor Soblevski, convicted in the child abduction and rape of a six-year-old Altamonte Springs boy last year, was killed in a prison riot after fights broke out during a supervised yard session. Several other inmates were treated for stab wounds and minor injuries. Soblevski was the only casualty. He was 45 years old.

From: Samandra Lucas (samandra.lucas@gmail.com)

To: Samson Thomas Carlisle (carlisle_samson@my.fau.edu)

Subj: holiday break + money

Samson,

This isn't a letter about either of those things mentioned in the subject line—I just wanted to make sure you opened the email, and I know if it's not about vacation or food I never hear from you. (You WILL be getting a separate email about break from me later, because I won't be home this year—Myra scheduled us a two-week Carnival cruise as a Christmas gift, so we're going to need to figure out plans for you.) I know you're "busy"—hopefully some of that "busy" actually involves school? (Just kidding.) (But seriously.)

I attached a document to this that I'd like you to read. It's about that thing that happened when you were little. You know, at the playground? When that man tried to take you. I know we've never really talked about that. And you were so little. I mean, not little-little, not a baby or anything, but pretty young.

I guess what I'm saying is, I want you to take a look at the document because I want you to know that I wasn't the only one who experienced it. That I wasn't crazy.

And I know what I'm about to say isn't the point, I know that, but I can't help asking because I've always wondered about it. It's just something I've never understood and it's always, always bothered me. Here's the thing: You *wanted* to get in the truck with that man. I mean, I get it. You were little, and it was a big shiny truck, and you *loved* trucks, so of course you'd want to see it.

The thing I can't get over, though, is how you were able to run away from me in the first place. Why would you leave me to follow a stranger? To get away from me? Was I that bad a mother?

Anyway. Hope school is going well. Your grades from last semester were good (shockingly good, I almost couldn't believe it, you never really seemed to be that into school, so I have to say I'm *very* pleasantly surprised). Lots of stuff going on over here. Myra and I just repainted the kitchen—now it's light blue instead of that ugly yellow I always hated—and we're going to get a new dishwasher sometime soon. A nice one, not like that one with the white plastic front.

Would love to hear from you (more often, hint hint). Let me know what you think.

Lots of love,
Mom

From: Samandra Lucas (samandra.lucas@gmail.com)
To: Samson Thomas Carlisle (carlisle_samson@my.fau.edu)
Subj: re: holiday break + money

Samson, I obviously did not mean to upset you. I'm not sure what you mean by my "weird memory," but I think it's rude to put it like that. All I said was that I wanted to understand you.

So let's break it down. You say you remember the man and the truck, but you didn't want to go with him? Samson, I had to physically restrain you. And I know you said I hurt you when I did that, when I pulled you away, but is that what really mattered in that moment? That I stretched your shirt collar a little bit? That I *yelled* at you? You were being *abducted*, Samson.

And those other things you bring up. Like that bite in the car? I don't think we remember that the same way, Samson. It was so long ago. You were always blowing things out of proportion when you were a kid—that's why you were in therapy.

And what you said about your mom and the stairs? That's just not what happened. You're an adult now, Samson, whether you like it or not. You can't just toy with people's lives this way. You know I didn't hurt your mom that day. That was a bad night for all of us, and I think you're taking what was a very stressful event and twisting it into something it wasn't.

I'm sure this is the last thing your mom would want to deal with, so don't bring her into it, okay? I don't need anybody chewing me out right now. That reminds me, did you ever get a check for your books? You should have gotten it by now, but I never know if that actually happens unless I ask.

So let's just agree to let all this go, all right? We'll just drop it. Like it never happened.

Okay? Let me know about break. Maybe we can do the holiday lights at Disney.

Love,
Mom

Acknowledgments

I am immensely grateful to all the people, places, things, dogs, BOGO wines, six-packs of beer, Publix subs, and convenience stores that allowed me to bring this book to life. A huge thank you to all the beautiful humans at Riverhead for believing in a novel that started as a scrawny preteen shadow of a story: Cal Morgan, wonderful editor and great friend, as well as Ashley Garland, May-Zhee Lim, Jynne Dilling Martin, Ashley Sutton, Nora Alice Demick, Catalina Trigo, and the rest of the gang. Thank you to my agent, Serene Hakim, and Pande Literary for continually taking chances on me and letting me be my worst goofball self. Huge thanks to everyone at Black Mountain Institute in Las Vegas and the Shearing Fellowship for allowing me the time, space, and infinite love to work on this novel. Sara Ortiz, thank you for letting us use your pool and always making sure we were hydrated with Topo Chico when I would have had a margarita instead. Lisa Ko, fellow-FELLOW, thank you for sharing space with me and for the Zoom Karaoke. Wine bottles make the best microphones! Nicholas Russell, incredible writer and wonderful human: thank you for looking after Lola so many times and for talking endlessly with me about Tom Cruise and Stephen King. Thank you to everyone at the Writer's Block, Las Vegas, and Books & Books, Miami; you are my dear friends. Thank you to Willie Fitzgerald, the Roast Beef to my Ray, who has always been my reader and will always be my buddy. Thank you to Vivian Lee, true literary superstar, who has sent me more postcards and letters and support than I can count. So many friends and writers who've let me talk their ear off about writing and have provided me with so much selfless, wonderful love: Tommy Pico, Elissa Washuta, Sarah Rose Etter, Morgan Parker, T Kira Madden, Laura van den Berg, Danielle Evans, Caroline Casey, Esme Weijun Wang, Tara Atkinson, Frances Dinger, so many more. To Jami Attenberg, who has been a lighthouse in my life. You are more than a friend, you're an illumination; all my best writing talks happen with you. To all my loves at Tin House Books and Tony Perez. To Karen Russell, who is the world's best writer. To all my loves in Orlando, my forever home. Greg Golden, thank you for the fruit leather and for Holly Golden. Maria Jones, friend to the end, best beach buddy, no one I'd rather drunk text at 3 A.M. James, Alicia, Kristopher, Jairo. Margo. Emily. Cathleen Bota, heart pal, you always know . . . everything? . . . before I even have to say it. To my 7-Eleven and my cashiers: I miss you terribly. Chips aren't the same without you. Thank you to Jessica Bryce Young and *Orlando Weekly*. Thank you to everyone who follows me on Twitter and still seems to like me, even when I compare ravioli to mattresses. All my love to Mattie, who is funnier and better looking than me. And to Kayla, who has cooked me endless beautiful meals and let me be myself. Thanks for letting me slide into your DMs. I love you, and I am really goddamn lucky.

Next round of drinks is on me, everybody.